I0630142

VEGAS ODDS

THE VEGAS TRILOGY
BOOK 3

DALLAS BARNES

ROUGH
EDGES
PRESS

ALSO BY DALLAS BARNES

Rough Edges Press
An Imprint of Wolfpack Publishing
1707 E. Diana Street
Tampa, FL 33610

www.roughedgespress.com

Paperback ISBN 978-1-68549-725-5
Ebook ISBN 978-1-68549-724-8
LCCN 2025931604

AUTHOR'S NOTE

Although based on the writer's experience as Director of Security & Surveillance in Resort & Casino operations, the characters, locations, and events herein are the product of the writer's imagination and used fictitiously.

Any resemblance to real persons, living or dead, is purely coincidental. All references to Resort & Casino operations, locations, protocols, and procedures are fictional presentations in an effort to protect the integrity of actual operations, the safety of staff, support personnel, and those who make Las Vegas real, our guests.

This book is dedicated to the men & women you don't see. Serving behind the scenes in Resort & Casino operations, they protect the lives, the property and the safety of guests and employees as well as the integrity of gaming. Their qualifications and standards are set by a State Gaming Commission.

The security challenges are not an easy task in an environment where emotions, money, alcohol, and nudity seem the norm. Many times, the money is mixed with blood. It takes more than luck to protect **Vegas Odds***.*

THE CHARACTERS

Luke Mitchel—Director of Security Silver Palace Resort & Casino
Greg Larson—General Manager Silver Palace
Charlotte Johnson—Director of Rooms Cosmo Resort & Casino
Tom Roberts—Card Room Manager
Gayle Turner—Surveillance—OIC
Jackie Fallon—Executive Assistant
Mario Lopez—Security Supervisor Day Watch
KC King—Security Supervisor AM Watch
Anakoni Stone—Security Supervisor PM Watch
Candice Harmon—Surveillance PM Watch Supervisor
The Strip—Las Vegas, Nevada

VEGAS ODDS

ONE

COVER YOUR EARS...

THE UNSHAVEN MAN was in his late thirties. He had colored tattoos of dragons on both sides of his neck. Dressed casually in jeans and a hoody, he stood in line, briefcase in hand, at the Silver Palace's cash cage on the Vegas Strip. He watched as those ahead of him spoke with the young cashiers sitting behind heavy protective glass. The line moved quickly, and the man was soon in front of thirty-one-year-old Tracy Young, who had been on duty less than two hours.

An attractive brunette, Tracy, offered the man a smile. "How can I help you, sir?"

The Dragon Neck set his briefcase on a service counter outside the protective glass. He held a garage door opener in his right hand. He glanced around nervously before speaking to Tracy through the service opening at the base of the heavy glass.

"Yeah," the Dragon Neck said over the voices, slot chimes, and music from the casino, "See this briefcase?" He patted the briefcase with one hand as he held up the garage door opener in the other.

"Yes." Tracy smiled innocently.

"Well, good." The Dragon Neck smiled, holding the garage door opener even higher. "Because it's a fucking bomb. I push this button and you're all going to hell with one big boom. You got that?"

A young couple from Cleveland, married for only seven hours, standing behind the man, heard his threats. They turned and hurried away. An unaware, graying senior at the window of a second cashier continued his cash out.

"Here's what you're gonna do." The Dragon Neck leaned closer to the glass, glaring at Tracy. "You're gonna push cash out here until I say stop."

Tracy's heart raced as she moved a foot over a robbery alarm on the floor. She depressed it without the Dragon Neck seeing.

"You keep your hands where I can see 'em. You got that. Now get busy, bitch."

Tracy's hands gathered cash from the open drawer in front of her. Her smile was gone. A cash ops supervisor, a middle-aged woman, sat at a desk in front of a computer on a raised platform near the center of the windowed cash cage. A warning light flashed on her computer screen. Her eyes went to Tracy and the Dragon Neck on the other side of the glass. The message on the computer told her what her eyes confirmed. Tracy was being robbed. She pushed a second silent alarm.

Luke Mitchel, the forty-two-year-old director of security for the Silver Palace, was at his desk three floors above, working on an internal email on a synopsis of the evening's events. His computer gave an electronic beep. The screen blinked, and a PTZ, Pan-Tilt & Zoom image of the Dragon Neck standing outside the window of the cash cage appeared. Luke saw the briefcase, the man's hand holding something in the air, cash being pushed to him by Tracy. Luke grabbed a radio on his desk.

"All units, Code Alpha. Gate Keeper Ten, robbery in progress. Cash Cage. Cover the exits. Uniforms stay clear of the cage. Possible bomb involved."

Saying the words chilled Luke. A bomb in the casino! What could be worse? Was this guy crazy? He had to be.

"Copy Ten. We got the alarm," a filtered Hawaiian accent answered on the radio.

Luke pushed from his desk and moved for the door. His radio spoke again.

"Suspect on camera," a calm female voice advised. It was Gayle Turner, the OIC in surveillance. "Cash cage supervisor says the suspect may have a bomb."

Luke was quickly out the door. Waiting on a back-of-the-house elevator wasn't an option. He took the stairs, scrambling down the steps on the run, nearly colliding with a housekeeper on her way up. The woman cried in shock as Luke bolted by.

The casino in the Silver Palace was busy when Luke emerged from a door at the rear of the room. Rows of slots filled the air with electronic chimes. The card tables were busy. Laughter and voices filled the air. Drink servers carrying trays in short skirts maneuvered through the maze. All seemed normal. Luke resisted his urge to run to the cash cage.

The Dragon Neck stuffed bills into the pockets of his pants, inside his hoodie, and beneath his belt. Some fell to his feet. Luke, dressed in a sports jacket over a black tee shirt drew little attention as he neared the man.

"Stay back," the Dragon Neck warned as Luke got closer, thinking he was just another customer. Luke paused and looked at the briefcase sitting on the counter of the cash cage window. The man continued stuffing bills with the garage door opener in hand. He gave Luke a threatening look. "I said stay back."

"What's in the briefcase?" Luke questioned, not knowing what else to say.

"A bomb," the Dragon Neck answered. "Now, get the fuck away."

The man wasn't rational. Rational or not, the brief-case could still hide a bomb. Luke had served in under-cover narcotics with the LAPD. He knew a doper when he saw one and the man in front of him fit the profile. He decided to push. "I think you're lying."

"Get out of my way or the bomb goes off," the Dragon neck warned, lifting the briefcase from the window's shelf. Tracy Young's cash drawer was empty. She pushed up and ran from the window.

"That means you'll die too," Luke countered, hoping his tone was firm. "The fact you want money tells me you have plans."

The Dragon Neck burned a look at Luke as he moved the briefcase to his chest. "Oh, so that's it, not only are you a fucking know it all, you want some of my money."

"It's not your money," Luke answered, pulling back the bottom of his jacket to reveal his badge and the 9MM Glock holstered on his belt. Now, put the briefcase on the floor."

"Fuck you," the man growled, gripping the briefcase even tighter against his chest. "I'm leaving, or we all die."

"Leaving?" Luke smirked. His confidence after assessing the man was growing. The tattoos, the irra-tional threats, the color of the man's face, his rapid speech. Luke knew the man was high. "You got a car in guest parking? We've closed the iron gates. You're not going anywhere. It's over, dude. I'm betting the only thing in that briefcase is bullshit."

The Dragon Neck hesitated. A wad of bills slipped from beneath his hoody to flutter to the floor. He drew in a breath, then threw the briefcase hard at Luke and ran. He didn't get far before two uniformed security officers tackled him, forcing him face down on the floor. Pulling his arms behind his back, they snapped on handcuffs.

Luke picked up the briefcase he had defected with an arm. He clicked it open to reveal a woman's purse, a cell phone, makeup, and several prescription bottles. Sergeant Anakoni Stone, a burly thirty-six-year-old Hawaiian, the PM security watch commander, joined Luke, patting him on the shoulder. "Nice work, Chief."

Luke closed the briefcase and offered it to the sergeant. His hands were trembling. "Get him out of sight," he said with a dry mouth. "Then get statements from the crew in the cage. I'll reach out to Metro. He's going to jail." Luke was giving orders to hide his anxiety. He knew he had to sound out of breath.

"How did you know it wasn't a bomb?" Stone questioned, closing the briefcase.

"I didn't," Luke confessed.

Sergeant Stone had the uniformed officers quickly hustle the handcuffed man out of sight. Luke held a thumbs up to the cluster of five women standing far back in the cash cage. Luke walked to the service opening in the thick glass. "Nice work, ladies. The sergeant will be back to get statements."

The cluster of cashiers raised their thumbs in response to Luke's, followed by a round of their hardy applause. Luke returned their smiles and hurried away. The Dragon Neck and his bomb had, for the most part, gone unnoticed. Luke allowed himself a sigh as he headed for the back of the house. He envied the crowd in the casino. They were having fun, laughing, drinking, filling the air with shouts from a win at roulette. Few, if any, knew of the threat at the cash cage. Luke was envious of them.

Luke left the handcuffed dragon-necked man in the custody of his crew, telling them he was going to surveillance to have them prepare a CD for the metro police, but Luke didn't go there. Instead, he went to the nearest back-of-the-house men's room, where he slammed open the metal door, gagged over the toilet bowl and threw up. He flushed the toilet and wiped at his face, spitting in the water to clear his throat. He braced himself on the metal walls and drew in a deep breath. He felt better. He took another breath and stepped out of the stall to find a man standing at a urinal. A tool belt the man wore told Luke he was from the engineering department. Their eyes met. Luke considered speaking, but there were no words. The man stepped closer to the urinal, unzipped. Luke and moved for the door.

Luke made his way to the surveillance unit on the third floor. He was worried about the man. How long had he been there? What did he hear? What would he say? Luke finally reached surveillance. There, he found Gayle Turner, the attractive thirty-four-old busty director of the surveillance unit at her desk in the shaded blue, white light from the monitors on her desk. Three were sequenced, playing a variety of images from the front of the house, the cash cage, slots, and the card room. A tall, thick glass wall separated Gayle's desk from the main surveillance deck, where sixteen wide CCTV monitors covered the walls with live video images. Most were sequenced, switching from one camera to another.

The constant hum from the screens, computers, and radios filled the room with a low-frequency rumble. Five surveillance agents, two male and three women, in casual streetwear, sat watching the images coming from two thousand seven hundred and thirty-three discretely placed cameras. Candice Harmon, an attractive thirty-six-year-old blonde, Vegas-looking woman, the female watch supervisor, Gayle Turner's subordinate assistant, sat at a desk on the far right of the surveillance deck.

Luke noticed an image of his entrance appeared on a screen in front of Candice on the other side of the glass wall. She turned and offered a wave to Luke. They knew one another well. Luke answered her wave with a nod as he sat down beside Gayle. "You know what I need."

"Got it ready," Gayle answered, punching a CD from a VCR on her desk. She offered the disk to Luke. "The Dragon Neck, briefcase in hand, came in from guest parking. He was driving a green Toyota. It's still out there. Space forty-three. He was alone, twenty-two minutes before appearing at the cash cage. He wandered around slots. Played a couple bucks with no wins. Solicited a drink from a server. You'll see him dig in a pocket, push something in his mouth."

"Drugs," Luke suggested.

Gale nodded agreement. "Then he went to the cage. You know the rest."

Luke took the CD and slipped it into an inside pocket of his jacket. "This one's for Metro PD. Stone has him downstairs in security. I'll have him search the car. Order impound if Metro agrees."

"We'll cover it," Gayle assured.

Luke pushed out of his chair. "Send me and the GM a link to the video."

"Will do," Gayle answered.

"Be careful out there in the world," a female voice said over an intercom speaker. Luke looked toward the voice. Candice offered a smile from the other side of the glass wall. Luke returned the smile and stepped out.

Reaching his office, Luke sat at his desk and breathed before calling Anakoni Stone, his PM watch commander. The sergeant answered on the second ring. "This guy won't shut up," Anakoni complained. "He's higher than the Strat Tower."

"He drove a green Toyota in," Luke explained. "It's in space forty-three. Guest parking."

"Yeah, we found the keys in his pocket. Along with six tabs of oxy, a California driver's license with an address in Beaumont and the nine thousand six hundred and thirty-eight dollars he got from the cash cage."

"I'll call Metro. You search the car. Give me a heads-up if you find anything."

"Will do. I've got Jan down in the cage getting statements from the ladies. When she's got them, I'll email you copies."

"I'm betting the briefcase with the woman's wallet and cell is stolen," Luke suggested.

"Bingo," Stone answered. "*Lefty* already copped to stealing it at Circus Circus."

"Give them a call. Tell them what you've got."

"Will do. I know a couple guys over there."

"This guy's name is really *Lefty*?" Luke questioned.

"Nah, his real name is Lawrence Klinger. He goes by Lefty because he's, you know, left-handed. He says he just got out of County in LA. Did eight months for grand theft at a Walgreens."

"Walgreens? What have they got to steal."

"Lefty says ladies' makeup. Oxy dealers like that shit."

Luke's next call was to the Las Vegas metropolitan police. He called their non-emergency number and spoke with a detective. Lawrence Klinger would go to jail in Clark County for several major felonies, including robbery, grand theft, and bomb threats. Luke spent two hours writing the reports. Lefty's car, stolen in Redlands, California, was impounded. He was turned over to Metro for transport to jail.

Traffic on the Strip was light when Luke finally drove away from the Silver Palace. The night was dark, but the lights of the Strip erased the shadows with their colorful digital lighting, trucks with their illuminated signs inviting a Massage & More. The sidewalks were busy with guests, working girls, near vacant buses, and the occasional beggar. Eventually, the color of the Strip gave way to the night, and Luke, like the darkness around him, found the return of a reality he hid in at the Silver Palace was returning. Death had found its way into his life again. Barbara Nichols, a woman he loved, a woman who knew his hopes, his fears, and his dreams, was gone. She had died in a collision with a truck. Vegas, the city of chance, had turned its back on him. The Silver Palace provided a place to hide but now, the Strip and the Palace were behind him, and he was driving to a home Barabara was never to see. A place they had hoped to share, a place now filled with nothing but emptiness.

The crowd at the Silver Palace didn't care. Most still dreamed of winning. Among those filled with alcohol and hope was sixty-one-year-old Norm Davis from Fort Wayne, Indiana.

Davis and his wife were staying at the Silver Palace for a four-day convention of Hardware Managers. Norm wasn't a rich man, but he owned a hardware store on North Wells Street. Norm's wife, Cleo, was at his shoulder praying as he put the last of his silver dollars into a Megabucks slot machine.

Norm sipped his Spicy Moscow Mule Vodka as he watched the images on the slot's video screen. He was shocked when the screen froze, and a siren sounded with lights flashing in front of him. The slot manager and a scantily clad server were quickly to Norm's side. He stared at the flashing screen. The slot manager studied the screen and then patted Norm on the back.

"Congratulations, sir." The manager smiled. "You've just won eighteen million dollars."

Cleo, hearing the slot manager's words, staggered and nearly fainted. The server in high heels caught her.

Three floors above the new millionaire from Fort Wayne, a light blinked beneath a video screen in the surveillance complex where four agents of the PM Watch monitored the two thousand seven hundred and thirty-three cameras displaying big screen images of every move in the resort. The blinking light was beneath a PTZ, Pan-Tilt & Zoom Camera, focusing on Norm, his shocked wife, and a growing crowd of curious. Candice Harmon, the surveillance supervisor, was quickly to the two men watching the winner in slots.

"What's the payout?" Candice questioned, looking at the images from the casino floor.

The crowd around the shocked Norm Davis was growing, pushing, shoving, cell phone cameras were held high.

"Looks like eighteen million," one of the agents answered. "Slot manager will confirm it in a minute."

"Got it," Candice advised. "I'll reach out to security. Get more uniforms out there. Stay on it until slots opens the machine to record the payout. Money this big means we pass it up the line."

———

Sixteen miles away in the neighboring city of Henderson, Luke Mitchel had just collapsed in a recliner in the living room of his condo. He had been there long enough to take off his holstered 9MM Glock and toss it to the couch. Stephen Colbert was drawing laughs on a TV Luke turned on just to have someone in the room with him. It had been a long day at the Palace. There was a fight between two pastry chefs over a cake recipe. One was left with a bloody nose, then there was the loud-mouthed drunk who slapped a female dealer at Twenty-One. The prick turned out to be a cop from Oakland. Courtesy of Metro PD, he was in jail. Luke called the on-duty commander in Oakland just to give them a heads-up on their man. It hadn't gone well. Then, an attractive escort stole a high roller's wallet after their frolic in one of the penthouses, and finally, Lefty Klinger with the dragon tattoos on his neck, lying about having a bomb in a briefcase. Luke's thoughts went to the toilet where he threw up. The engineer at the urinal. It had been a long day.

More than tired, Luke was weary. Somehow, the weariness brought memories of the excitement he felt when first hired at the Silver Palace. His path was unique. First, war as a Marine in Afghanistan, where he met death, up close and personal. Fellow Marines, combat companions, died, some piece by piece. Luke took their haunting memories with him when he became a cop in Los Angeles. It was there, with the LAPD, that once more, death became reality. His police partner was

shot and killed. The ripple effect cost Luke more than
the loss of a partner. Remorse, regret and then divorce
followed, costing him both a wife and infant daughter.

Everything Luke Mitchel valued seemed to die. Even
his career. He left the LAPD after eight years and tried
hiding in the Arizona desert. It was there, ironically, in
the desert heat, that he found himself once again
carrying a gun. This time at the Wild River Casino.

Built by the Mojaves, the resort was big, modern, and
popular. There, with an alcoholic mentor from Vegas,
Luke learned the nuance of cheating as well as insight
into casino security. It was much like being a cop, he
carried a badge and a gun, but it was different, in that
gambling, for many, was compulsive and filled with risk.
Risk that was deeply personal. Everyone, at one time or
another felt lucky, felt the compulsion to gamble. Luke
learned odds were much more than emotions. They
were a stark reality.

Chance seemed the allure, but luck was an elusive
factor. Was luck real or just another four-letter word?
Luke was to find his mentor dead with a bottle of liquor
in hand. He ran away again. This time to Vegas. There,
Luke got lost in the crowd. There, no one cared what
time it was. There, you could get drunk, get lucky, get
laid and no one cared. In Vegas, the days were hot, and
the nights were filled with light and laughter. Luke hid
among all of it. He was like a butterfly circling the flame
of a candle. That was until he found a naked woman
about to jump to her death from a balcony at the Silver
Palace where he was staying. Luke saved the woman's
life, but he was now haunted by a feeling that saving her
may have started him down a path to a growing darkness. A darkness filled with pain and loss.

Saving the woman led to Luke's fame and identity.

Proving Vegas was truly the epicenter of chance, the GM of the Silver Palace hired Luke as its director of security. Vegas fit like a fine, smooth glove. Luke flourished in his newfound role. The multi-billion dollar Silver Palace was growing into one of the big dogs on the Vegas Strip and deep in its heart, keeping the forces of darkness away, was the new director of security, Luke Mitchel. A match made in Heaven. Until Hell burst onto the scene.

The Mojaves, in addition to giving meaning to Luke's life, had also given him Barbara Nichols. She was a bartender at the Mojaves' Wild River Casino when Luke met her. She soon became Luke's newfound love. In addition to Barbara's beauty was her wit and charm. Without either admitting it, Barbara and Luke knew they had found love. Their love hung on an edge after Luke took his job in Vegas, but Barbara saved it by agreeing to join him.

Again, fate got in the way. Barbara died when a truck hit her car head-on the day she drove to Vegas to join him. Luke Mitchel's world turned dark. After Barbara's death, Luke tried again to lose himself on the Strip, but his heart, the glove that had fit so neatly, had been torn away. Luke found the real face of Vegas. It truly was a city built on chance, and only some of it was good.

Luke's cell phone vibrating in circles on the glass cocktail table in front of his recliner brought him back to the moment. He reached and picked up the phone, glancing at the caller ID. It was a number he knew well. Surveillance at the Silver Palace. Luke knew the caller was likely Candice Harmon. Luke's feelings for Candice were a mix of admiration for performance and suppressed lust for her femininity. An unspoken mutual attraction had found its way into their relationship. It ended abruptly the day Barbara died. Luke and Candice had kissed only hours before Barbara's death. Now, their kiss was an unspoken haunting memory. Luke knew a relationship with a subordinate was thin ice, but it happened. When managed discretely, kept from the workplace, it seldom resulted in issues, but the death of a loved one and their kiss became much more than a revelation of desire, it was now a towering obstacle between them.

"This is Luke," he said into his cell phone.

"Luke, it's Candice," her voice answered. "We just had a major win in slots. An eighteen million dollar payout."

Luke knew what the call meant. He drew in a deep breath. "I'll be in. Get a CD of the last six hours on the machine as well as the win. Where's the winner."

Candice pulled up a PTZ image on her computer. "Still on the floor in slots. He's all smiles. Surrounded by a crowd. Security has two uniforms with him. One of them is Stone. He said the winner is an in-house guest. Looks like his wife at his shoulder."

Luke pushed a foot into one of his shoes. "In-house. That's good. Have Anakoni escort him to his room. Post someone there. His popularity is going to go up fast. Have the in-house operator hold his incoming calls until I arrive. I'll pay him a visit as soon as I get in."

"Got it," Candice assured.

Luke gathered his holstered 9MM pistol and badge from the couch and strapped them on.

———

Norm Davis and his wife had been in a two-bed suite on the eleventh floor. They were escorted to a new spacious two-room suite on the fifty-second floor after a Gust Relations Officer learned of the win.

"Housekeeping will bring everything up, the guest relations officer assured, there will be no charge for the upgrade."

The move had its practical dimensions. Norm Davis was being isolated from ill-intentioned visits and calls from those seeing or hearing of his big win. It also provided him and his wife an assurance the Silver Palace cared for its winners. Cleo immediately went to a telephone to call family and friends in Fort Wayne to share the exciting news. Norm opened a bottle of champagne, arriving on ice, courtesy of the casino manager. It was all a subtle clue the Silver Palace wanted its money back.

Luke Mitchel pulled into employee parking at the Silver Palace forty-two minutes after Candice's call. His speed on the interstate linking Henderson, Nevada with the Vegas Strip went undetected by the Nevada Highway Patrol. He called Candice as he scrambled from his Corvette to learn where he could find the winner. Six minutes later, he was at the door of guest room fifty-two-oh-six, where he found two uniformed security officers and a server pushing a loaded cart arriving at the same moment. The cart's aroma left no questions.

One held a steak for Norm and fresh lobster for Cleo, along with yet another bottle of champagne. Norm, drink in hand, opened the door in response to the server's knock.

"Norm," Luke said, extending a hand. "I'm Luke Mitchel. The director of security here at the Silver Palace. I'd like to offer my congratulations."

Norm offered a big smile and shook Luke's hand. "Come on in. They said you'd be by."

"My apology for arriving at the same time as dinner." Luke balked at entering. The server pushed by him into the room.

"Nonsense," Norm answered. "I run a hardware store. I like talking while I eat. Come on in."

The server unfolded the cart into a dining table covered with fine linen as he set up the dinners. He opened and poured champagne, pulled chairs close, lit a candle, bowed and excused himself.

Luke sat on a couch as Norm and Cleo sat at their new table. It was obvious they were awed by the dinners.

"We went to a show and forgot all about dinner," Norm explained as he reached across the table for his wife's hand. They closed their eyes and bowed their heads. "Lord," Norm said. "Thank you for this our daily bread and the great big win. We'll do our best to spend it wisely. Amen."

Luke watched in silence.

"So, what do you need from me, Luke?" Norm questioned, raising his head to cut into his aromatic steak.

"Driver's license and a social security card if you have them?" Luke answered.

"Gut 'em both," Norm answered as a fork delivered a cut of crisp meat.

"Norm, offer the man a drink," Cleo suggested, pausing over her lobster.

"No, please," Luke said, raising a hand. "Enjoy your dinners. Norm, we are obligated to notify the IRS, the State of Nevada, as well as the State Gaming Commission of your win, but how and when you choose to pay taxes or withholdings is entirely your business. We do recommend you provide us bank account information so the money can be transferred to your account. A bank transfer provides security and assures all a proper transfer has occurred. Our Cash Operations Officer, Jessica Dillion, will reach out in the morning for all the information. She'll need signatures for your authorization."

"You get that, Mother," Norm said to Cleo. "Her name's Jessica."

"Jessia. I'll remember," Cleo assured.

"We want you to be comfortable with your winnings," Luke continued. "We'll provide security while you're our guests but what you've won is no secret. A lot of people will be after your newfound wealth. Unfortunately, there will be scams and threats. Be careful who you talk to, especially on the telephone. Don't give information to anyone you don't know or trust. The fact you're in business back home assures you're savvy. Nevertheless, you need to be careful,"

Luke pushed to his feet, pulled a business card from an inside jacket pocket and laid it on a table. "That's my business card. You need anything or have any questions, call me. I'll keep an officer outside your door until you check out. Like me, he or she, is out there to serve you. Don't be shy. Now, I'm going to leave so you can celebrate what's left of your evening."

Norm began pushing out of his chair.

"Please, don't get up." Luke stepped closure to again offer a hand. After they shook he offered a hand to Cleo. She smiled and reached to it.

"Good night, folks." Luke smiled. "It's been a pleasure meeting you." He moved for the door.

TWO
THE EYE OF THE TIGER

LUKE NEEDED images of the slot win. It was back to surveillance again. He was surprised who he found sitting beside Candice Harmon at the surveillance supervisor's desk. Greg Larson, the fifty-six-year-old general manager of the Silver Palace, dressed in suit and tie, looking much like a mature male model, offered a smile when Luke entered.

"Card room manager called with a heads-up on the big win," the GM explained. "Eighteen million is enough to keep me awake so I thought I'd come in, have a look." He guested at the images Candice had on the computer screens on her desk.

"And what has she shown you?" Luke questioned with a glance at Candice.

"She started with the bomber at the cash cage," the GM answered. "You know, the one I didn't get a call on."

"He didn't really have a bomb," Luke defended.

"Which you didn't know until he threw his briefcase at you." The GM added, "Nice piece of work, Luke.

Really took balls." Realizing what he said, Larson looked to Candice. "I'm sorry, Miss."

"No need." Candice smiled. "I agree." Then, looking to Luke, she added, "I showed the GM what you requested." She used her professional tone with the GM sitting beside her. "We reached back six hours on the machine. It was a Megabucks slot, number one-sixty-eight, on row three."

"Eleven unidentified players preceded the big win with six minor payouts." Candice glanced at notes she had penciled on her desk. "One for seventy-five, two for three hundred, two more for fifty, another for eight hundred, then the big one." She paused and looked from her notes to the two men. "Slot manager was on site. He verified the win on screen. Unlocking it, he found all the circuitry aligned. Stills were taken. The machine was set for a ninety-five percent RTP, return-to-player. Intake drop count balanced with the payouts, excluding the big win."

Luke and the GM exchanged a look when Candice finished. They were impressed.

"And this girl is just a shift supervisor in surveillance." The GM smiled at Luke.

"No," Luke suggested. "She's more than a supervisor. She's the PM surveillance watch commander."

The GM pushed out of his chair. "Well, nice work. Pass my appreciation on to your troops." He looked to Candice. "And you, young lady, thanks for the show. It was a dammed good one." Larson returned his attention to Luke. "Come on, Mr. Director. Let's go for a walk."

Luke looked to Candice. "Burn me a CD with all this and call Nevada Gaming. Put the time and the contacts name in your log."

"Got it," Candice assured.

The GM and Luke shared a back-of-the-house elevator with two Hispanic housekeepers on their way to the casino level. The two women chattered casually in Spanish during the ride. Neither seemed to recognize the men.

"We're going to the Eye of the Tiger," Greg Lawson said, leading Luke off the elevator and across the kitchen, where preparations were underway for breakfast orders for in-house guests numbering in the thousands. Luke glanced at his watch as they pushed through the doors leading from the kitchen into the busy card room. It was ten minutes after two. He was tired and walking with a man who had been asleep before his call over the win. Not only was Luke tired, he was intimidated. He was trying to keep up with a well-groomed man wearing a twenty-five-hundred-dollar suit while he wore a black tee shirt under a sports jacket. He was also in need of a shave.

The GM may not have been recognized in the back of the house by two housekeepers, but his presence did not go unnoticed, leading Luke across the card room. Luke was aware of the time, but the faces at the tables didn't seem to care. Chimes from slots mixed with the laughter and voices in the card room. Two Twenty-One dealers, a busty, long-legged server in heels and a roulette dealer all offered smiles and nods to the GM.

The Eye of the Tiger was the Silver Palace's premier watering hole. It was a spacious bar and lounge favored by most visiting the Strip. The Tiger's reputation had been built on a drink called, not surprisingly, The *Tail of the Tiger*. It was a mix of exotic liquors allegedly from a chain of islands in the South Pacific. The lounge was quiet. A few guests sat at a long, curved cushioned bar. Several couples relaxed in the light from shaded candles on tables spread across the spacious lounge. Larson led the way to a table in a quiet corner. An attractive, scantily clad waitress followed the two men. She approached as they sat down.

"Gentlemen, it would be my pleasure to bring you drinks."

"We'll both have the Tail of the Tiger," the GM said as he sat, pushing back into the curve of a comfortable chair. Luke nodded a smile of appreciation. The waitress bowed and moved away.

When the girl was gone, Greg Lawson leaned his elbows onto the table and studied Luke. "I haven't seen much of you lately. How are you?"

Luke pushed back in his chair, considering the GM's question. He knew what he was being asked. The two knew each other well. Larson had once saved Luke's life by shooting a man intent on killing him. Thanks to social media the story was to become a Vegas legend, especially on the Strip. Few recognized either man in person, but the images and story lived on. An accused thief had knocked Luke to the floor in the GM's office after hitting him in the head with a vase. The man grabbed Luke's gun and was about to shoot him when the GM pulled a gun of his own and shot the man. The story added allure to the Silver Palace. In Vegas, who attracted what and how was the stuff of legends.

Luke decided candor was the best path in answering Larson. "The Eye of the Tiger fits," Luke said, reaching deep for an answer. "Here, I don't have to think about her. Out in the world. It's different out there, it hurts."

Larson nodded agreement. "It's feelings like that that

makes this town. Come to Vegas and you can forget about anything," he suggested candidly. "I lied about tonight. I wasn't sleeping, I was drinking. Sitting in the darkness when the phone rang. I've got an ex-wife, an ex-lover and an ex-daughter. She's in rehab, arrested for prostitution. Like you don't know that. My Ex and I are having dinner with Tammy tonight. Wanna guess how that will go."

Luke thought about the GM's words. They were a confession, and he recognized that. The Silver Palace had ten thousand employees, but there weren't many the GM could talk to. Luke knew Larson trusted him. It was mutual. He smelled alcohol on the GM when they shared the elevator. The waitress returned with their drinks. She set them on the table and smiled. "Enjoy." And moved away quietly.

The GM picked up his drink and raised it. "To memories. Sometimes that's all there is."

Luke raised his drink and clinked it carefully against Larson's. "Agreed." He sampled his. The alcohol warmed his mouth and then his throat. "Damn, the Tigers Tail is sharp."

The GM took a heavy swallow of his. "I heard Charlotte offered you a job at the Cosmo. You considering it?"

"You're out of luck. I'm staying."

"Well, damn." Larson smiled, wiping condensation from the glass. "If you left, I thought I'd move Candice, what's her name, into your spot."

"Yeah, she's better looking than me," Luke said, taking another drink.

"You know it's looks that make this town." Larson's elbows found their way to the tabletop. He studied his drink for a moment, then looked to Luke. "Something else that counts is the odds. Odds of winning in our casino is around forty-seven percent. Every game is different. Poker, Blackjack, Craps."

"I've heard that," Luke suggested, tasting more of his drink. "Damn, this is wild."

"It should be for eighty-two bucks a pop," Larson defended. "You know the cliché, *Vegas was built by losers.* Resorts World cost four point three billion to build. The Fontaine Bleau, three-point-seven billion, and ours, nearly five billion. Where do you think all the money came from?"

"I'm not into numbers, boss. I chase guys with bombs," Luke answered, thinking of his encounter with the man in the restroom.

The attractive waitress returned with a tray and two more Tail of the Tiger drinks. "Courtesy of the bartender." She smiled, setting the drinks on the table. "He recognized both of you. Sorry, gentlemen, I'm a creature of the night."

"Nothing wrong with that," Luke suggested, admiring the girl.

The waitress granted Luke a smile in return.

Larson downed the remainder of his drink. "Regards to the bartender." He smiled. The girl bowed and moved away. The GM took several swallows from his fresh drink and continued, "Earnings last year came in at seven billion plus. That's an eighteen percent increase. Some of it may have come from the couple from Dayton, they were in Vegas to celebrate their twentieth, or maybe it was those two guys from Trenton who had a system for Twenty-One. Remember them? You nailed both of them."

The mention of the two made Luke smile.

"Then there was the just-married couple from

Orlando who lost all theirs at roulette. They called Mom for tickets home on Southwest."

"Is this guilt or what?" Luke questioned. He pushed his drink aside. He was wary of both the alcohol and the hour.

"Everyone coming to Vegas, loses," Larson continued. "So why do they come back? And most do!" Larson pointed a finger at Luke. "They come back because maybe next time they might win. Maybe next time, their luck will change."

"And maybe it won't," Luke defended.

"The average number of visitors we welcome every day, counting walk-ins and guests, is about seventy thousand. The house take is near forty-four million a day."

"That's serious money," Luke suggested, shaking the ice in his drink. "Are these really eighty-eight bucks? He knew Larson was hiding his anxiety in the numbers. Luke looked for bad guys. Larson counted money. Their worlds were different, but Luke knew Vegas needed both of them.

"I've done the math," Larson went on. "Our average daily is forty-four million with a two percent loss, that comes out to about eighty-eight thousand every day."

"Every day?" Luke said. He wasn't following the numbers, but he knew they were important to Larson.

"And our payout percentage has spiked two points." Larson smiled confidently.

Luke leaned into the table. "Spiking points or not. I have to go home, shave, maybe get a couple hours sleep. You have a room here?"

"I've always got a room here." Larson slumped back in his chair, drink in hand. "You want one? I'll call the front desk."

"No, thanks. I need clean socks." Luke pushed out of

his chair, granting Larson a smile. "Good night, boss, don't get your hopes up. I'll be back tomorrow."

"Don't let anybody throw a briefcase at you on your way out," Larson said, watching Luke walk away.

He noticed Luke wave to the bartender and the server. Nice touch, he decided, thinking about where he would go next. The idea of going to his always available, spacious empty suite on the sixty-third floor wasn't appealing. The Silver Palace had five more bars. None as inviting as the Cave of the Tiger, but they all had alcohol. He decided on Harry's Garage. Drinks were cheaper there, which meant he wouldn't be drinking alone. He promised himself two more drinks, and then he would head for his room.

———

FIFTY-ONE FLOORS above the Cave of the Tiger, in room fifty-two-oh-six, Norm and Cleo Davis were awake, even with daylight beginning to show outside the panorama of their floor-to-ceiling window. Norm had found a Silver Palace letterhead and a pen. Sitting on the couch in the living room of their three-room suite, they worked on the challenge of what to do with eighteen million dollars. They had two children. A twenty-seven-year-old married boy who had a three-year-old, their first grandchild, and a twenty-three-year-old single daughter, still at home. They decided to give each child two million. Leaving fourteen million. Norm worked on the taxes they might owe and came up with twenty-four percent. After the allowance for the two kids and taxes, he figured they would still have about eight million.

"How about this...I won the money. So, it's five

million for me." Norm added to the notes he made. "And then the other three million, well, that's all yours."

"Three million dollars," Cleo gasped with a hand to her chest, "Just me?"

"So, agreed." Norm smiled. "Spend it any way we want."

"Norm, you already have all the hunting rifles a man could want," Cleo cautioned.

SLEEPLESSNESS SEEMED LESS than out of the ordinary in the Valley of the Sun. Naomi Larson, the forty-eight-year-old estranged wife of Greg Larson, the GM of the Silver Palace, sat in a patio recliner wrapped in a bathrobe, petting the ears of the Rottweilers beside her. The dog, like the twenty-nine-million dollar home she once shared with her husband, was in the Lakes District, miles above the towers on the Strip, pushing into the distant haze of morning light.

The five-bedroom house no longer seemed like a home. Her husband and her eighteen-year-old daughter, Tammy, were both gone. A court would soon decide the future of the property as well as the division of the monies in the bitterly disputed divorce. Greg Larson, for reasons she could only guess, had forsaken her for a Black woman who, at the time, was the HR director at the Silver Palace. Naomi knew she was five years younger than Charlotte Johnson. She knew most of the directors and managers at the Silver Palace. Luke Mitchel, the director of security, had proven pivotal when Tammy was arrested. As the GM's wife, she attended many of the resorts social events and retreats where she met most of her husband's team.

Charlotte Johnson was attractive, but Naomi knew she could still turn heads, too. She had met Greg at the Rio where she was director of talent, and he was rooms director. Twenty-two years of marriage were lost when he secretly betrayed her after lying about why he needed a condo downtown. It was made worse when Greg's unfaithfulness was discovered by their then seventeen-year-old daughter, Tammy.

Their lives began unraveling like a towel from a cheap hotel. The teenage Tammy, after bringing home the news she had found her father in bed with a Black woman in his downtown condo, became distant as the battle over truth, monies, and love began. The gap between parents and child was to grow wider as weeks turned to months, with attorneys demanding not only money, but time. Time, like distrust, bitterness and anger, became a canyon none could cross.

Tammy Larson, having lived the good life filled with Mom and Dad as well as privilege, found neither showed much interest in her emerging maturity. Thus, the young woman filled the vacuum first with drugs from friends, then with those stolen from her mother, and finally buying them on the street with money pushed at her by both her uncaring mother and her absent father. When Greg Larson and Naomi failed to provide Tammy with the time and attention she needed, they tried filling the gaps with money. Tammy quickly worked her way from stolen prescriptions to meth.

Addiction was costly. Tammy's meth quickly overcame the giveaways provided by her unsuspecting parents. They were busy with attorneys, court dates and hate, while Tammy became an attractive head-turning eighteen-year-old. In Vegas, the beauty of youth and femininity was a highly sought-after commodity. No one had to tell Tammy Larson that. Her Father managed the Silver Palace on the Vegas Strip where beauty was wrapped in business. Tammy saw it, and decided if they could, she would.

High on meth on her eighteenth birthday and desperate for money, Tammy Larson took to the night-time-crowded Fremont Street in downtown Las Vegas as a whore. Whoring in Las Vegas was not for the faint of heart. Tammy was arrested for prostitution by an under-cover agent from the metropolitan police when her first date turned out to be a cop.

Tammy's arrest and the discovery of her addiction became a grim wake-up call for her warring parents. Her arrest and release on bail was followed by two alarming meth ODs that nearly cost Tammy her life.

The once divorcing, arguing, separated, hate-filled, estranged husband and wife, without their attorney's help, advice, guidance, or costly words, found a common ground to share while helping a daughter worth far more than an affair in a downtown condo, a mansion in the hills or agreement on how to divide millions.

Tammy was in rehab at a Christian facility, Out of the Shadows, in nearby Boulder. Naomi's housekeeper had recommended it. There was no space in the love Greg Lawson and Naomi shared for their daughter. The knives they carried had been laid aside. Today, Naomi and her estranged husband, Greg, would be sharing an evening meal with Tammy at the rehab ranch in Boulder. It would be the first time the three had been together in thirteen months. The thought of the gathering, which was now only twelve hours away, was what was robbing Naomi of her sleep. She was filled with anxiety and fear that Tammy would no longer need or want her love. Her anxiety was compounded by the fact the time shared with Tammy would be shared with her estranged husband, a man who had turned twenty-two years of marriage into betrayal. A man she once loved, a man whose words and deeds could not be trusted. There was to be a mother, a father and a daughter gathering for a quiet dinner, but the husband and wife Naomi remembered would not be there. They were now just a bitter fading memory.

THREE
DON'T BRING ME ROSES...

THIRTY-THREE MILES from where Naomi Larson sat on the patio of her home in Las Vegas, eighteen-year-old Tammy Larson, wearing latex gloves, worked in a shaded greenhouse with two other recovering addicts, cultivating the soil around rows of budding pepper plants. The overnight low in Boulder at the Out of the Shadows Rehab Ranch was seventy-eight degrees. The morning sun was now up and so was the growing temperature.

Tammy was sweating, something she rarely did when high on meth. She was now into her third week of sobriety. The first two were difficult. No, they were an outright bitch, but now, she was sleeping, eating, talking, listening. She felt almost human. Ironic, Tammy decided as she picked at the soil around the green stem of a plant. She felt good, well almost, not because of what she took, but because of what she hadn't taken. Maybe sobriety really worked. Maybe there was a God. Josh Logan, top dog at the ranch, had encouraged asking whoever was important in their life what they believed. Was it a career, loved ones, money. Tammy had taken the challenge to heart. She asked herself who was most important in her life. The answer was simple. Her mother and dad, but Josh Logan was right. She had no idea what they believed. Was it love? How could that be? Was it money? They had far more of that than they needed. It was painful for the young meth addict digging around the base of pepper plants, but she didn't really know what her parents believed.

The Strip in Las Vegas didn't have many pepper plants although it did share in the morning sunlight, but sunlight didn't compliment the Strip's array of digital glitter and color. Mornings on the Strip meant the world was turning a little bit slower. It was sleep late if you won, check out if you lost. The card rooms were their quietest. Big restaurants were dark. Housekeepers were gathering for the coming vacancies, and thoughts were turning to the coming night. What shows to see, what games to play, where to have dinner. It was often said light chased away darkness. Las Vegas turned that around. In Vegas, when the sunlight faded, nighttime brought on not only darkness, it brought on a new day, but for now, in the early light, the city yawed, put on fresh socks and filled the offices that made the Vegas clock tick. Among them was Greg Larson. After a brief, fleeting sleep, he was having coffee and a sweet roll in the employee dining room at a table where he sat with two room service employees, an attractive Black Jack dealer and a Black female security officer. They talked about the price of gasoline, taxes on tips and the big win in slots.

The GM finally pushed to his feet and smiled at the group. "Good coffee. Thanks for sharing, guys. Hope you all have a great day." Larson patted the Black Jack dealer on the shoulder and walked away. He felt good leaving the group. He was glad he had joined them.

What Larson didn't hear was what was said after he was gone. The Black Jack dealer was the first to make a comment. "Housekeeper cleans his office, every morning," the woman said, toying skillfully with a ten-dollar token. "She tells me the GM's assistant brings him Starbucks and a roll, every morning."

"So, why's he down here with us?" the older of the two servers questioned.

"He come comes down here to spend time with what makes the Silver Palace shine," the younger server offered, gesturing with open hands to those at the table. "Us."

They laughed. When the laughter faded, the Black female security officer suggested, "Might be, he's got no one to talk to upstairs."

Nods of agreement followed.

———

COFFEE WAS ALSO an issue in Guest Suite 5206 at the Silver Palace but resolved when the new multi-millionaire slot jackpot winner, Norm Davis, found a cold bottle of Starbucks in the suite's refrigerator. Room service wasn't an option because after his wife made excited calls to friends and family back in Fort Wayne announcing their win, followed by two hour talk between husband and wife on how the money would be divided, left her exhausted. She was asleep in the king-size bed in one of the suite's two bedrooms. Norm quietly pushed on his shoes, intent on setting out to turn a lifelong fantasy into reality.

Dianna Jackson, the uniformed twenty-nine-year-old

Black woman, and veteran of four years with the Silver Palace security team who had earlier sat with the GM in employee dining, was now stationed outside the double doors of the Davis suite. She was surprised when Norm Davis opened the door and stepped out raising a finger to his lips, signaling her to be quiet as he closed the door.

"My wife's sleeping," Norm said, reaching for the surprised Dianna's hand. Holding her right hand, he pushed something into her palm, folding her fingers over it.

"If she comes out," Norm added. "Tell her I'll be back in a little while." Norm shook Dianna's closed hand and moved for the nearby elevator.

Dianna opened her palm as Norm stepped onto an arriving elevator. She looked, finding five folded one-hundred-dollar bills. "Wait," the shocked Dianna called, following after Norm. "I can't take this. Thank you, but we're prohibited from accepting gratuities."

"Really." Norm smiled, holding the door of the elevator. "Okay, then it's not a gratuity. It's a gift." He allowed the elevator doors to close.

IN THE CITY of Nearby Henderson, Nevada, Luke Mitchel was preparing to leave his condo by strapping on a holstered 9MM pistol and the gold security director badge worn on his belt. His few hours at home after a nineteen-hour day were fleeting and elusive. Thinking about it, Luke decided it was a combination of grief and shock.

The quietness of his condo haunted him, and the encounter with the engineer in the restroom at the Silver Palace troubled him. What would the man say? Who would he tell? Luke was worried he might be labeled a coward.

"Screw them all," Luke said aloud as he pushed an arm into the sleeve of his jacket. The words, spoke to no one, brought a smile to Luke's face. Where did his anger come from? It wasn't the engineer in the restroom that created the problem. It was the man with the briefcase at the cash cage. "Well, they can all go to hell," Luke added, grabbing his car keys from a kitchen counter.

———

AFTER LEAVING EMPLOYEE DINING, Greg Larson walked across the busy kitchen, making it a point to smile and speak to every chef, prime, assistant, and helper. Their white uniforms and gloves were surprisingly clean. The air was filled with the aroma of sweet rolls and scrambled eggs. He left the kitchen and walked across the card room to the cash cage. He made it a point to offer a subtle wave to the card room manager, a graying man in suit and tie on his perch atop the podium in the center of the room. He waved again to the ladies behind the thick glass of the cash cage. A different crew was now on duty, but they returned his wave.

Jackie Fallon, the shapely, smartly dressed, thirty-two-year-old year executive assistant to the GM, was at her desk outside the general manager's open office, telephone in hand, when Greg Larson entered.

"Casey," Jackie said into the telephone as she glanced at Larson. "He just walked in. Hold on." Jackie moved the telephone to her breasts. "It's Sue Grayson. Cash cage supervisor. She says it's important."

Larson nodded and walked into his office. The lights had been turned on. A Starbucks cup and a sweet roll sat on the top of the desk. Larson picked up the cup as he rounded his wide desk to sink down into a high-backed executive recliner. Settled he gathered up the telephone from the multiply line receiver on his desk. "This is Larson."

"Sir, I just had a call from Citibank in New York," the cash cage supervisor said in a matter-of-fact tone. "They would like to wire us thirty-five million dollars for a discrete TBA guest."

The GM understood the supervisors' code. He knew who the TBA guest would be. A Rag Head, an Arad. Jamal Hassan, the twenty-nine-year-old son of Akeen Hassan, the eighty-two-year-old Petroleum Minister of the Abu Dhabi National Oil Company and one of the richest men in the world. The kid was a PIA for the Silver Palace, but he always left millions behind.

"Transfer is approved," Larson said into the phone. "Send me the numbers and the account code when you get it and put cash ops in the loop," he ordered as he made notes on his desk. Jamal wouldn't be far behind his father's money, and that was an issue. An issue because the kid would want the Eagle's Nest. The Eagle's Nest was the Silver Palace's three-story penthouse overlooking its near-completed Desert Sky pool seventy-three floors above the Strip. The problem was the Nest was occupied. Occupied by their current headliner, Lady Luck. They had a long and difficult time getting her and she was no cheap date. Luck was bringing in millions, but she didn't own any oil wells. Akeen Hassan did, and if his son wanted the Eagle's Nest, Luck had to go. Larson would pass the buck onto his rooms director.

Larson was looking at numbers from the day just passed when Jackie leaned from behind her desk to the open door of his office. "Sir, the minister is on line three."

Larson reached and gathered the telephone again. "As-salaam-alaikum," he said, which meant *peace be upon you*. He had long ago mastered the challenge of dealing with language. It was a traditional greeting among Muslims.

"Wa 'alaikum as-salaam." Which essentially meant, *and also with you*."

A harsh, dry old voice answered. "Gregory, how are you."

"I'm well, Minister, how can I serve you?" Larson straightened in his chair.

"It is Jamal," the minister answered. "My youngest. He's been working in Iran. He's not enjoying it. I thought I might reward him when he comes home."

"We are always at your service," Larson said. "How can we help."

"You have an airplane. Could you come get Jamal? It would make him feel good. Important."

"Our airplane is not cheap, Minister."

The minister chuckled. "And nor am I. I understand it is comfortable. Jamal deserves comfort. Would you please make sure he's made comfortable. And the last time you sent a woman. Guest relations, I believe."

"Yes, just to ensure all went well."

"I see," the minister continued. "We would appreciate a man this time. Sometimes customs become an issue."

"Of course," Larson agreed. "I have just the man. When would you like your son picked up?"

"He's coming home in a day or so. Can you send your plane? I would be very appreciative."

It had been almost a year since Jamal Hassan and the eighteen people he brought in had been to the Silver

Palace for their three-day stay. Jamal had lost nearly twenty-two million dollars at Sportsbook, slots and Hold 'Em. Another eleven million dollars was collected for Spa Services, extra rooms, the Eagle's Nest and shopping. Three days after Jamal checked out, Greg Larson received his Montblanc Time Walker Men's wristwatch via FedEx. It appraised at $35,954.00.

Greg Larson knew exactly who he wanted to send on the plane to Dubai.

"Jackie," Greg Larson called from behind his desk. "Find Luke Mitchel. Tell him I need to see him."

————

NORM DAVIS CLIMBED INTO A CAB. There were many waiting in front of the Silver Palace. Norm had looked at most. He chose the one with a driver wearing a turban. His choice became obvious when he spoke to the driver. "I'm looking for a new car. A sports car, but not a Dodge Charger. Maybe not even American. I want it hot, bad, big and expensive. Can you take me to a dealer?"

The turban smiled and nodded agreement. "I know such a place."

"Take me there," Norm said, slapping the driver on the shoulder with several hundred-dollar bills.

The cab with Norm relaxing in the back seat snaked its way through the challenging maze of traffic on the Strip. Norm studied those on the sidewalks. Kids holding hands, smiling, hurrying to get somewhere. Women in uniforms carrying bags. Casual dress mixed with high heels and makeup. Norm smiled at them. He silently wished them well. They were in the right place, now if they could just get the time right. Norm had. He was smiling. He felt like a winner.

The Turban turned the cab onto East Sahara, where there was less traffic. He drove three blocks and pulled to the curb in front of a sign announcing *Exotic Sports Cars of the Desert-Buy or Rent.* Norm straightened in the back seat and looked. His eyes searched the rows of shining, colorful Mercedes, Rolls Royces, Bentleys and Maseratis.

"Yes, sir. This is it," Norm agreed.

———

GAYLE TURNER, the supervisor of surveillance, was at her desk watching images on her desktop computer. She saw a car pulling into sheltered employee parking. She recognized the red Corvette. It was Luke Mitchel's car. Gayle watched until Luke climbed out of his car before she picked up her telephone and dialed.

Luke felt the vibration of the cell phone clipped to his belt. He pulled it out as he walked. "Good morning, Gayle. What's up?"

"Jackie Fallon called. She said the GM is looking for you. Did you break something last night?"

Luke knew he was being watched. "No, he probably just wants advice on how to manage the Palace today."

"Yeah, my thoughts exactly," Gayle agreed as she reached for a radio setting on her desk. "All units, Gate Keeper Ten is on property."

Luke walked to the back of the house to the elevators. He shared a lift with a server pushing a loaded cart. He could smell the scent of bacon and potatoes. He wondered if eggs had a smell but decided not to ask. Two housekeepers got on at the elevator's next stop. One was young, shapely and attractive. Luke stood behind the woman. She had a scent, too. It came from her hair, Luke guessed. The elevator finally reached what was called the admin floor. Luke pushed by the young housekeeper to get off.

"Excuse me, please."

Their eyes met briefly. She smiled. Her eyes were dark. Hispanic Luke guessed. No, Filipino. He got off, promising himself he would find out who she was. No, he reasoned, she was too young. Thirty at the most. It was too soon, Luke warned himself.

———

AT THE EXOTIC *Sports Cars of the Desert*, Norm Davis was living the dream. He sat behind the wheel of a Rolls Royce, he dove a Bently and a Maserati and then he found the Silver Mercedes Benz SL AMG SL3. Sitting behind the wheel, he allowed the new car scent to race his heart. "This is the one," he said to Candy, the thirty-year-old saleswoman dressed in short shorts and cowboy boots. "What's the ticket on it?"

"I think she comes in around two-fifty," Candy answered, leaning in the open door as Norm sat behind the wheel of the car, dreaming of driving slowly down Calhoun Street in Fort Wayne allowing all to see.

"Will you take a check?" he questioned.

"Only if I can cash it before you drive away." Candy smiled.

"Let's go write her up," Norm answered, running a hand over the smooth dash.

———

"SIR," Jacki Fallon called into the GM's open door as Luke stepped in from the hallway. "Luke Mitchel is here."

"Morning, Jackie," Luke said, pausing.

"Send him in," Larson called from his open office.

Luke added a nod to Jackie and moved for the open door to the general manager's office.

"Close the door, Luke," Larson said from behind his desk. "You get any sleep?"

"Couple hours in the recliner," Luke answered, closing the door. "It helped." He sat down in one of the two chairs facing the GM's desk.

Larson leaned his elbows onto his desktop. "Got a call from Dubai. Oil Minister there wants to treat his son with a surprise trip. He wants us to pick up the kid in our plane and bring him over for three days. He already wired us a big chunk of change to cover expenses."

Luke relaxed in his chair and laced his fingers together. "If I remember right, we're talking about Jamal?"

Larson pushed back in his chair. "Jamal it is, and he'll want the Eagle's Nest."

"But Lady Luck's in the nest," Luke reminded him.

"Only until you tell her she has to move," Larson said soberly.

Luke straightened in his chair. "Don't tease me, boss. This belongs to your rooms director. Jill what's her name."

"Jill doesn't have the horsepower. You do. Jamal's father is important. I have to call the State Department every time the kid comes over here."

"So, tell Luck that?" Luke argued.

"I can't be the bad guy. I'm the one that put her up there. I don't want her pissed and not come back."

"You're serious. You want me to tell her."

"I'm serious. Talk to her aide. Lynne Strong. She takes care of all Luck's business."

"And what do I tell Lynne what's her name? Other than we want the Nest."

"You'll think of something."

"When's Jamal arriving?"

"You have to go get him."

Luke knew the GM's tone was serious. "I have to go get him? He's in Dubai."

"We have a jet. It's comfortable and fast." Larson pushed forward in his chair to lean on his desk, adding to his sober tone. "They're Arabs, Luke. Their customs are different. They don't want women in charge. Just men. You're it, dude."

Luke leaned toward the GM's desk. "So I tell Lady Luck she's downgraded, she has to move. And then I fly to Dubai and pick up Jamal."

"Flight crew will be ready for you tomorrow," Larson answered.

"And I do all this in two days. The Luck thing alone is tough. Who do I talk to?"

"Start with Lynne Strong. She's her Lady Luck's right hand."

Luke pushed to his feet. "The last time I was in the Middle East, I was wearing a helmet."

"Wardrobe is your choice," Larson answered. "And listen, I know this is challenging, but I need it done and done right. It's the math. Vegas runs on odds. This time, they favor Jamal."

"That helps," Luke granted.

"Maybe you should get what I've got on the other side of that door."

"Jackie?" Luke questioned.

"Jackie's got lots to do where she's at. I'm suggesting you get an assistant."

"An assistant. Where do I find the money for that?" a surprised Luke asked.

"You make things happen, I'll find the money."

———

NORM DAVIS WROTE a check for two hundred and forty-nine thousand, nine hundred and sixty-eight dollars. Candy called his bank and then the Silver Palace before she had the Mercedes SL filled with gas. Assured Norm Davis's check was good, Candy smiled and dropped the keys in his open hand. "Keep it under a hundred for the first couple weeks. Change the oil in a month," she urged.

"May God bless you." Norm smiled, heading for his waiting silver Mercedes.

"He just did," Candy answered.

———

LUKE WENT to his office a worried man. The first thing he did was Google the flight time from Vegas to Dubai. The answer was grim. Eighteen hours plus one way.

Round trip would mean thirty-six hours of flight. Factor in crew rest, passenger interface, and it became almost three days. The GM was right. He needed help. Surveillance had detected what they thought was cheating between a dealer and a player in Twenty-One. Gayle Turner was watching the situation. The player had been identified as a guest from Ceasar's Palace. They were turning both the player and the dealer inside out while monitoring action at the table. A decision would have to be made soon. The player had pocketed twenty-six thousand in one night. Was it luck, odds or cheating?

Gayle would have to find an answer. The dealer was scheduled on a table again tonight. Luke's thoughts turned to the GM's suggestion that he needed help. The thought took him back to Larson's comment and reaction when he met Candice Harmon in surveillance. She was a plus. The GM liked her. Luke knew Candice would make a good assistant. His office was big enough for another desk. Sounded simple, he was confident the GM would like his choice, but promoting Candice over Gayle Turner could create a situation between the two women. It was further complicated by the fact Luke and Candice had kissed. Had she told anyone? Would having her in his office complicate their relationship even further? He had to find a balance. He liked the idea, decided on it, because he needed help, but he was uncertain how to make it happen. The security logs and reports were awaiting his review. He deliberately pulled them up on his computer, hoping they would allow him time to think of the challenges. Among them, Lady Luck was first in line.

———

NORM DAVIS WAS in his new, shiny, expensive silver Mercedes SL and lost somewhere on Las Vegas's East Charleston Avenue, but he didn't care. He was all smiles, blowing the horn and waving to those on the sidewalk. He could feel the car's power, not only feel it, but it invigorated him. He gripped the steering wheel as if it might somehow escape his hold. He was eager to show the car to Cleo.

He spoke to the car's navigator. "Take me to the Silver Palace," Norm ordered with delight.

"Taking you to the Silver Palace Resort in Las Vegas,

Nevada," a soft feminine voice answered Norm confidently. "Your drive time is twenty-eight minutes. Turn right at the next intersection."

Norm decided to soften Cleo's surprise with his new car and the money he spent by buying flowers. He got the idea after seeing a vendor on a corner waving colorful arrangements at passing cars. The flower vendor was on the wrong side of the street, but Norm decided it was important. He pulled to the curb, turned on the Mercedes flashers, pushed the car into park, and climbed out. He had to wait for a break in passing traffic, but it finally came, and Norm made a dash across the street. He looked at a variety of bouquets the eager Hispanic vendor had spread on the sidewalk. Norm studied them all before choosing an arrangement of roses and lilies mixed with ferns.

"Des one is one hundred and twenty," the vendor said with an accent.

Norm dug in a pocket and came out with a wad of hundred-dollar bills. He pulled two from the bunch and smiled at the vendor. "Keep the change." Norm smiled and turned to the passing traffic. It was heavy. He looked for the silver Mercedes. His mouth fell open as his eyes searched the curb on the far side of the street. The Mercedes was gone. Bouquet in hand, Norm ignored the traffic, walking into the street. Tires screeched as cars braked and swerved to miss him. Horns followed. Norm ignored it all as cars flashed by. More brakes and horns sounded. Norm reached the curb where he had parked. He stared, eyes wide, mouth open. Shock gripped him. The Mercedes was gone.

———

LUKE GAVE up reviewing the logs and reports. The clock was running. He had to do something. He punched in the roster on his computer and searched for Candice's telephone number. There were two. One a residence and a cell.

Luke chose the cell and dialed. He took a deep breath to steady himself, hoping he would find the words. He was haunted by the feeling he chose Candice because of her body, because of their kiss. How would Barbara feel? Had enough time passed. He didn't allow the thought. This was business. His heart raced as he listened to the phone ring.

Candice's voice put an end to his thoughts. "Hello, Luke, and yes, I'm sorry I forgot the CD for the GM."

"That's not why I'm calling."

"Gayle covered for me, right?"

"Candice, we need to talk. I need you to come in?"

"So, I really stepped in it, right?"

Luke was annoyed. He tightened his grip on the telephone. "How long before you get here?"

"Mid-morning. Forty minutes."

"I'll be waiting," Luke said, ending the call abruptly. He had no sooner hung up when the telephone rang again. He gathered the receiver. "This is Luke."

"Luke, it's Norm Davis. You said if I ever needed anything to give you a call."

"Yes, Norm. How can I help?"

"Well, I'm out here on East Charleston and Del Amo. I need a ride."

"That's a busy street, Norm. Just wave at a passing cab. They'll stop."

"That's a problem, Luke, because I don't have any money on me. I just spent my last two hundred on some flowers. Someone stole my car."

"Someone stole your car?" Luke was surprised.

"A brand-new Mercedes SL. Just bought it. I let it run while I got out to get flowers. Stolen in broad daylight. I didn't see a thing. The man selling flowers let me use his cell. I don't have a dime on me, Luke."

"Okay, Norm. East Charleston and Del Amo. I'll find you. Stay where I can see you."

"I'll be the guy with a bouquet of roses."

Luke had no idea where East Charleston and Del Amo was, but his car navigation system found it. A map appeared, and a calm female voice provided verbal commands. Traffic was heavy. Luke was annoyed. He wasn't accustomed to driving the Strip mid-morning, but he accepted driving anywhere in Vegas took time. Finally, the female voice from his guidance system instructed him to turn right onto East Charleston Boulevard. "Your destination is ahead on your right."

Norm Davis looked lonely on the corner of Del Amo. Luke pulled to the curb and reached to open his passenger door. Norm climbed in with his bouquet.

"Luke, I'm really sorry," Norm offered, climbing into the car with his bouquet of flowers. Their first stop was a metro police station on West Oquendo Road, just off the Strip. Luke escorted Norm to the front desk to make a report of his car being stolen. They had to call the Desert Exotic Sports Cars to get the temp license plate number as well as the car's VIN for the report. While Norm talked to the desk officer, Luke went and introduced himself to the watch commander.

When they were finally back in Luke's car headed for the Silver Palace, Norm's bouquet was beginning to wilt. "You get back in your room and call your insurance company. Tell them they can get a copy of the stolen report by calling Metro," Luke suggested.

"Thanks, but I doubt they're gonna cover it. I only had the car for about an hour. Yesterday I was a winner. Today I'm a loser."

"What happens in Vegas, stays in Vegas," Luke said as the cliché came to mind.

"You think there's a chance I might get my Mercedes back?" Norm questioned.

Luke offered a smile as he wormed through the traffic. "This is Vegas, Norm. Chance lives here."

When they arrived at the Silver Palace, Luke walked with the solemn Norm to the fifty-second floor, where they found Dianna Jackson, the uniformed twenty-nine-year-old security officer, still posted at the door of the suite. She was surprised to see the two men.

"Norm, you okay? What happened?" Dianna questioned after a glance at Luke.

"I bought a car. I lost a car."

"It was stolen," Luke answered with a glance at Dianna and then turned his attention to Norm," If you'd like, I'll come in and explain things to Cleo."

Norm offered an open hand to Luke. "Thanks, but I own this one. I'll give Cleo the facts so she can give me, you know what." They shook hands. "You know," Norm continued. "None of this surprised God. All I have to do is figure out what He's trying to tell me."

"Maybe He just wants you to forget buying a car until you're back home," Luke suggested.

"Might be," Norm said, pulling a room key from a pocket. "I'll ask Him."

FOUR
ADD A FEMININE TOUCH

LUKE WAS surprised when he opened his office door to find Candice Harmon waiting in a chair in front of his desk.

"Gayle told me you were off property," Candice sat with her hands folded in her lap, dressed in her usual surveillance casual.

"Sorry to keep you waiting," Luke offered, rounding his desk. "It was Norm Davis, our slot jackpot winner from last night. He bought a new Mercedes Benz SL for two hundred and fifty. Drove it maybe eight miles before it was stolen. I gave him a ride to Metro. He made a report."

"Is he okay?"

"He's okay. Told me he's going to talk to God about it." Luke sank into the chair behind his desk.

"God would know who stole the car," Candice suggested with a quick smile, adding, "And this. It's about me talking to the GM last night?" Candice questioned carefully.

"Sort of," Luke granted, pushing back in his chair.

He was finding comfort in reading Candice's uneasiness. His attraction to her and their one-time kiss in his condo had him worried and cautious, but it was obvious she was looking at him as the director of security. A director who called her to his office for reasons she could only guess at. She was a subordinate and showing it.

Luke leaned forward into his desk. "I need your help, Candice."

"I'll do what I can," Candice answered.

"Let's share what's on the menu. The first is a trip to Dubai. The second is Lady Luck. The GM wants me to talk Luck out of the Eagles Nest. The Prince I'm going to pick up in Dubai is a big ticket. He's the priority. He usually brings ten or twelve big spenders with him. Selling that to the lady isn't going to be easy. And then there's three shifts of uniformed officers serving eleven thousand employees, and to that we add twelve hundred and thirty-six guests. Will something go wrong? Every day something goes wrong, and when it does, it comes to this office. Last night is an example. I had to come in, review everything, videos had to be validated, gaming commission notified, the machine inspected, winner interviewed."

"I'm sorry," Candice defended. "I had to call you."

"That was policy, but what if it happened while I'm in Dubai or busy getting our headliner out of the penthouse? The GM knows devoting time to Lady Luck and going to Dubai creates conflicts. He authorized me to hire an assistant, an assistant director, a number two." Luke paused.

Candice bit her lip and laced her fingers together.

Luke studied Candice. "You're it, lady. I'd like you to become my assistant director of security."

Candice was shocked. She sat erect, hands clasped together. She was uncertain about what to say. Luke waited. Finally, she spoke. Her tone was sober. "Yes, Luke, I'd like to be your assistant."

"Good." Luke granted Candice a smile. "Here's the plan. You moved into surveillance from uniform, so you know the drill for the whole department. I'll put Gayle in the loop and put out an email notifying everyone of your new position. Call engineering, tell them you need a desk, chair, lamp, a laptop, whatever, and you need it all now. There's room in here. They can help getting a phone line, a computer, file cabinet, anything you need."

"And while you're doing all that, think what we can tell Lady Luck. She has to move. She's out of the Nest, and the Price from Dubai is in."

"Got it," Candice agreed.

"I'll put Gayle in the loop. After you talk to Engineering, find out what room Lynne Strong is in. She's Luck's right hand. She might be the place to start."

Candice seemed eager for the challenge. As Luke moved for the door, she called to him, "Luke."

Luke paused and looked to her.

"Thank you." Candice moved an open hand to her heart.

"You're welcome." Luke returned her smile. "Now, fasten your seat belt."

Gayle Turner was at her desk when Luke reached surveillance. He knew Gayle was aware of the meeting in his office. He sat in the chair beside Gayle's desk. The two had a solid relationship. Luke knew he didn't have to sell Gayle, all he had to do was tell her.

Gayle had a savvy look about her. The fact her Vegas path had once led to a role in the MGM Grand Chorus line showed. She would have made a good assistant but her role as surveillance supervisor was critical. Luke hoped she would understand. Gayle took the lead. "How did your meeting with Candice go?" she asked.

"It went well," Luke answered.

"I saw this coming," Gayle suggested. "The Palace is growing, cheats are getting more sophisticated, guests more demanding. You need help."

Luke was surprised. "So you read the cards."

"Candice is good in here, but the job isn't big enough for her. It's called ambition. I understand why you want her. We'll miss her, but she'll do you good."

"You amaze me, Gayle."

"Don't forget that," Gayle said with a smile.

Candice was behind Luke's desk, telephone in hand, when he returned to his office. "Come on, put a number on it," she said into the telephone. She made notes on the desk. "Is that number negotiable? Okay, I'll get back to you. No, no press. I'll let you know." She hung up and looked to Luke who sat down in one of the chairs in front of his desk.

Candice was excited. "Look at this."

She swung the computer monitor on Luke's desk to face him. The monitor showed a panoramic wide shot of a picturesque two-story mansion surrounded by towering palms and scrubs. Luke studied it as Candice continued.

"Six bedrooms, seven baths, a master to die for, a pool with a jacuzzi, privacy guaranteed in a gated community, a stocked bar that comes with a bartender and a twenty-four-hour maid. The kitchen is manned by a private chef from Austria, and all this stands high on a hill out at the Lakes."

"Help me out here. This is something you're selling?"

Luke questioned. Knowing Candice was a licensed realtor. She had sold Luke his condo.

"No, no," Candice said, stabbing a finger at the monitor. "I've used this place. It's not for sale. It's for rent. Special events, big weddings, it will be great for Lady Luck."

The idea straightened Luke in his chair. He leaned toward the monitor. "Why would she move there?"

"Because it's freaking beautiful, private and quiet," Candice answered enthusiastically. "All we have to tell her is we need to get work done in the Nest. Permit timing, you know. We'll have a limo take her out there and bring her back. She can take her entire staff with her. We could even send a uniform along."

"I like it," Luke said, warming to the idea. What's the cost?"

Candice gritted her teeth. "Fifty-eight thousand a night and we need it for seven nights."

Luke grimaced trying to do the math.

"That's four hundred and six thousand," Candice answered. "Figure another couple grand for fresh flowers and Hershey's chocolate. She likes candy. Make that sixty thousand."

"You've been here two hours, and you've spent nearly half a million." Luke smiled. "But I like it. I'll talk to the GM. You find Lynne Strong and sell her on it."

"Oh, the crew from the Bombardier called. They need you to stop by the airport ASAP. It's about your flight."

A knock sounded on the office door. Luke pushed from his chair and opened it. Two engineers waited with a low cart stacked with a desk, a chair, lamp, a laptop computer, a whiteboard, a telephone, and more. "This usually means someone got hired or fired," the gloved engineer holding the cart handle said.

"She'll fill in the blanks for you," Luke said with a glance at Candice as he moved into the hallway.

Luke was walking to the back-of-the-house elevator when his cell phone rang. It was the lieutenant from the metro police he had talked to earlier when Norm Davis reported his car stolen. "Lieutenant, what's up."

"Hey, Luke, I wanted to let you know one of our patrol units recovered the car your guest reported stolen this morning. It was the only silver Mercedes at a homeless encampment up on East Seria. They tell me the car smells but other than that it's still a brand-new Mercedes. There were eighteen people up there, but no one seemed to know anything about the car."

"Shocking." Luke smiled. "You guys do good work. Norm Davis will welcome your call."

"Just got off the phone with him," the lieutenant added. "He was pleased. So now you owe me one at the Eye of the Tiger."

"Call me when you're ready," Luke said as the elevator car arrived. He stepped in, joining four housekeepers, a server with a cart and several of what he guessed were admins. They were young, attractive. They made Luke aware of his age. He moved to the back of the car as its doors closed. Luke's cell phone rang again. Privacy was an issue, but he took the call as the elevator stopped and the admins stepped off. "This is Luke."

"Luke, it's Norm. They found my car."

Luke could hear the relief and excitement in Norm Davis's voice. "I'm very glad to hear that, Norm."

"They impounded it. Said it was in good shape. I'm going to have it picked up, cleaned up, and shipped back home." Norm's voice was filled with excitement.

"And promise you won't leave the keys in it again." Luke smiled.

"You got that, for sure. Listen, Luke, you were there when I needed you and that deserves a reward. Cleo and I talked. We're leaving today, but we're not leaving without giving you something. There'll be an envelope waiting for you at the front desk."

Luke sobered as the elevator stopped at the bottom floor. He followed the uniformed housekeepers off the elevator and paused in the hallway. "Listen to me, Norm. You can't do that."

"Yes, I can," Norm answered in a friendly tone. "You and the Silver Palace are sending us away with a ton of riches. We won't miss it."

"Norm," Luke answered, tightening the cell to his ear. "Listen to me. My friendship isn't something you can buy. I gave it to you. You want to leave me something, leave me the friendship we shared. And that won't fit in an envelope."

"Well," Norm answered after a thoughtful pause. "I'm not surprised. I'm a fortunate man for having met you, Luke."

"And I feel the same," Luke assured.

"Cleo's going to say she told me so. You take care of yourself, Luke Mitchel. May God light your path."

"You do the same, Norm." Luke ended the call, clipping the phone on his belt as he headed for employee parking. He decided Norm Davis was a winner before he hit the jackpot in slots.

Leaving the covered parking structure at the rear of the Silver Palace, Luke welcomed the sunshine and traffic. He decided if he had to describe Vegas, the word *alive* would fit. The streets were crowded with their usual crush of cars and buses. The sleek-looking Aria Express Tram rumbled by on its overhead rail. A man dressed as Batman was offering fliers to passing pedestrians. Luke found comfort in all of it as he pulled into the passing traffic. Was his newfound sense of wellbeing based on the fact he now had an assistant? A woman he could trust. A woman capable of filling in the gaps and making decisions. Hell, Candice had been there less than two hours, and she had a probable solution to the issue with Lady Luck. By now, the departmental email he had put out announcing Candice's promotion would have reached far and wide in the army of employees at the Silver Palace. Most would shrug and go about their day while those in security would react, smile, comment and prove more of a challenge. Most would understand the practical dimension of Candice's new role. Others would see it as his attempt to get in her pants. Luke was determined to convince all his need for help was real. Those assigned to security's three shifts knew how long his days were. He was confident the three watch commanders would support him. He hoped. KC King from the AM watch had made it known he wanted to stay there. He went to UNLV on his days off, working on earning a law degree. Mario Lopez from Days cared for his crippled wife and four kids, while Anakoni Stone, his Hawaiian PM watch commander, hoped to become a dealer. Others would say he picked her because she had a great set. So be it, Luke decided. She did have a great set.

The GM endorsed it, approved it, and the fact Luke was headed for Dubai would soon make it clear to all that his need for an assistant was real.

Luke returned his attention to the Flight Crew's call as he moved with the crush of traffic. It seemed they were all headed for the airport. What Luke wanted was an assurance the gate providing access to the area for private aircraft was alerted to get him through. The feminine voice on the telephone advised Homeland

Security wouldn't allow uninspected vehicles inside the fence. She instructed him where to park, even provided a space number, and added he should walk to the gate, and who had been informed he was coming. A white and blue van would be dispatched to pick him up. Luke didn't like the answer. "You do know I'm the director, don't you?" he asked.

"Yes, I know who you are, but again, let me tell you the security protocols for the airport are set by Homeland Security," the feminine voice defended. "Please give me a call when you reach the gate."

Luke didn't like the answer, but accepted it. He had been director of security at the Silver Palace for over two years but had never been to the busy airport on business or seen the aircraft the Silver Palace owned. VIP Flights were the business of guest relations. Dubai, it seemed, wanted it different. The difference was money. As Greg Larson told him time and time again, it was the math that ran Vegas.

The GM read Luke's internal email announcement on Candice Harmon's promotion to assistant director of security as he sat in his office with the head of cash ops, the director of housekeeping and human resources. Larson smiled, wondering how long it would be before Luke got into Candice's pants. The accidental death of Luke's fiancé worried him. The director of security was key to the success of the Silver Palace as it was in every casino in Vegas. Either your director of security was honest, transparent and focused or your house of cards collapsed. Odds were important, but integrity ruled. Larson was pleased with Luke's decision. It proved he liked women, and he was focused on getting the job done.

Larson was bored with his meeting. Someone in cash

ops, according to human resources, complained about housekeeping's new uniforms. "You can see their tits, nipples and all," James Bergman, the thirty-eight-year-old director of human resources, said. "At least that's what started our investigation. A complaint from an unidentified aide in cash ops made the complaint."

"So, who said this?" Caroline Summers, the head of cash ops, questioned.

"I can't answer that," Bergman answered. "The caller has a right to autoimmunity. I can tell you it was a female."

The GM fought an urge to smile. He was finding the complaint coming from the thirty-eight-year-old director of human resources, a professed and obviously gay man, humorous.

"Unless you point a finger at who this unidentified woman is complaining about," Sonora Perez, the chunky Hispanic head of housekeeping, answered sharply, "how can we fix it? We just got our new uniforms. We modeled for the GM. You're talking about one of my girls. And guess what? They all have tits. They all wear the same uniform I'm wearing. No one's complained about my tits."

Larson looked at her breasts. They were large. He avoided any eye contact.

"This is Vegas," Caroline Summers, the graying head of cash ops, suggested. "People pay a lot of money to see tits. You had complaints from any of our guests?"

"No," Bergman answered defensively. "But corporate policy dictates when an employee complains of another employee inappropriately exposing themselves, in this case breasts, an investigation must follow."

The telephone on the GM's desk began vibrating on his desktop. He gathered it and looked. A text message read, *Leaving for Boulder*. He knew the sender was Naomi, his estranged wife. He closed the telephone and looked at the three gathered in front of his desk. "All this could be blamed on buttons. Allow me to suggest this. We have surveillance get up close and personal with housekeeping."

"Housekeepers selected will never know we're looking at them. We look and then we meet, again, say in five days."

Two of the three seemed relieved and pushed out of their chairs and headed for the door. Bergman followed reluctantly.

"Surveillance is probably already looking," Caroline Summers complained as she led the three from the office. The GM was out of his chair, gathering his jacket.

Greg Larson thought about where he was going after he climbed into his Maserati in employee parking. Tammy Larson, his eighteen-year-old daughter, was in rehab at Out of the Shadows Ranch near Boulder. He would be meeting Naomi there, and the three, Larson, his estranged wife, and their daughter, would be sharing a private dinner. Larson tried but couldn't remember, as he gunned his car toward the interstate, the last time the three of them had gathered to share anything. The best he could do was the memory of him and Naomi standing over the unconscious Tammy after her third near-fatal meth overdose. Their daughter, colorless, oxygen tube in her nose, breathing faintly, lay near death in the hospital ER. Both Larson and Naomi wept silently. It was Larson who dared to take Naomi's hand in his. His gesture prompted her into his arms. He held her awkwardly for nearly an hour. He wondered if her weeping was amplified by the memories that were haunting him. Neither spoke of the encounter, but it changed them both.

Naomi was talkative again. And Larson listened. They talked of her birth. Bringing Tammy home from the hospital. Her first words. Her first steps. Neither talked of the bitterness of their separation or their pending divorce.

Greg justified leaving Naomi eleven months earlier by declaring the love they once shared, the decades of love, was gone and to be replaced by silence and eventual separation. The reality was Greg Larson was having an affair with his director of human resources. She was Black, beautiful and different. Larson rented a condo they shared, but Charlotte Jonhson was gone now. His life had gotten a little complicated with Tammy's arrest for prostitution and possession of meth. It got even worse when she OD'd. Charlotte was now Rooms Director at the Cosmo and now they both worked at trying to forget each other.

It took Larson over forty minutes to get to the Out of the Shadows Ranch in Boulder. He hoped the busy drive was worth it. Naomi Larson's Mercedes was among the cars in the parking lot. He found his estranged wife waiting in the front lobby of the sprawling ranch house.

Naomi offered Larson a smile and gestured him to sit beside her. The big room was active with small groups sitting around tables talking. Others brought in trays filled with water and ice. It was active, alive, but strangely quiet. The voices were subdued and occasionally mixed with laughter. Naomi spoke softly after Larson sat down beside her.

"They told me Tammy is the one preparing our dinner." She sounded pleased.

Larson granted her a smile. "That's a surprise," Larson answered.

The place was unnerving. The power usually filling

him with a sense of strength as a GM faded as his eyes searched for something familiar, something to hold on to. There was little. The walls were a faint white and empty. The only thing Larson's eyes found was a cross hung above the door he had just entered. Christians, Larson decided, were primarily takers. They were always looking for, searching, begging for money. This place wasn't any different. They knew he had money. He knew Tammy being there was no cheap date. He wondered if Naomi had paid them. He hadn't seen a bill. He knew one was coming.

A server arrived in front of them. Larson guessed she was another rehab patient. She was young, blonde and her neck and arms were covered with too many tattoos to be anything else. Her voice, manner and smile were sincere. "Mr. and Mrs. Larson. I'm Shirl. I'll be showing you to Tammy's dining room. If you would follow me, please."

The tattooed blonde escorted Larson and Naomi across the wide room, passing those at the tables, talking quietly. They moved down a quiet hallway until reaching a closed door. "Have a pleasant time with your daughter," she said, rapping lightly on the door. The girl moved away quietly.

Larson and Naomi were exchanging an anxious look when Tammy opened the door. She looked vibrant, healthy and filled with enthusiasm.

Without hesitation, Tammy stepped into her mother's arms. Larson watched with a smile. Could this be Tammy, the colorless girl he had seen lying on a hospital gurney? She was dressed in faded jeans and a loose-fitting blue blouse. She reminded him of her look on graduation night. Tammy released her mother, gave

Larson a smile and pressed herself into his arms. "Love you, Dad," she whispered into his neck.

Larson returned the hug, realizing he was holding a young woman who was once his child. He kissed the top of her head. Her dark hair smelled fresh and clean. Releasing her father, Tammy's eyes went to both of them. "Come in. Please, sit down. I've prepared broiled chicken and rice. Dad, you're going to love the green peppers. They're fresh. I grew them in our garden."

Tammy's remark stuck in Larson's head. What was the claim of *our garden*? Whatever they were doing with Tammy, in spite of her wellbeing look, worried him. They had convinced her this place was now somehow hers.

The oval table was set for three. Prepared dishes sat waiting. Glasses had been filled. A white tablecloth was smoothed beneath all. A candle flicked in the center of the table. Tammy gestured her mother and dad to chairs at each end. She helped her mother with hers. Tammy sat between the two. She reached and took the hand of both parents.

"Shall we pray?"

Now Larson was convinced his daughter had been captured by the cult that ran the place, but it wasn't the time for a challenge. He closed his eyes and bowed his head. Tammy's hand was warm in his.

"Lord," Tammy began. "We gather to share our daily bread for which we are thankful. We also thank you for the love that binds us together. Thank you, Lord, for your love and guidance. Amen. Please," Tammy added, gesturing to their waiting plates.

"You prepared this?" Naomi questioned with a smile as she cut into her chicken.

"Yes," Tammy answered confidently with a smile.

Larson wondered if they had given her drugs. "I needed a little help on how long to broil the chicken. The chef saved me, but the rest is all me."

Larson exchanged a glance with Naomi. He could see they were both surprised at Tammy's new persona. The three ate their chicken. Tammy was right. Larson enjoyed his cuts of fresh green pepper.

"You know," Larson confessed. "I can't remember the last time the three of us shared dinner?"

"I can," Tammy answered. "It was when we took the motor home and drove to Reno. I can't remember where we stopped, but Mom and I gathered wood, you built a fire, and we cooked hot dogs. Dad, you found some marshmallows. It was fun."

"Lemme see," Naomi speculated. "You would have been about fourteen, I think."

"I remember we heard a growl in the darkness, and we decided it was time to be in the motor home," Larson added.

"And I locked the door," Naomi added.

Larson nodded agreement. "Yes, you did, but not many bears carry a set of keys."

Smiles and laughter filled the air as they talked and remembered. They remembered lives together. There was Tammy's struggle with geography in eighth grade, her first kitten and its refusal to use a sandbox, Naomi's attempt at becoming a blonde, and Larson's plan at building a trap for coyotes. He caught a skunk instead. They talked through the chicken and Larson's second round of green peppers. There was no mention of divorce or drugs. None seemed in a rush to go there. They talked until Tammy left the room and returned with three slices of cake. And then it got awkward.

Tammy started it. "I've changed," she said with a look at both of her parents.

"We noticed," Larson offered as if he were trying to get over his suspicions.

Tammy reached an open hand to both parents. Naomi took her daughter's hand without hesitation. Larson looked at the two, and then, to the hand Tammy offered. He grasped it in his.

"My life has changed," Tammy began, "I'm now following Jesus Christ. He is my Lord and Shepard. He forgave my sins and saved me from an early death. I love you and so does He."

Larson awkwardly withdrew his hand from Tammy's. He noticed Naomi did not. Mother and daughter now joined their free hands, covering one another. Tammy continued, "There's little you don't know about me. You gave me life. You raised me. You saved me. You brought me here."

"You are our life," Naomi assured, releasing Tammy's hand.

"Here, at Out of the Shadows, I've found a new life," Tammy said, clasping her hands in her lap. "In sharing my life's story with others, I've been asked who you are. I thought about that. Prayed about it and found I know what you are, but I don't know who you are. Dad, I know you're the general manager of the Silver Palace. That's what you are, but I don't know who you are." Her eyes moved to find Naomi's. "Mom, it's much the same for you. I know you're a beautiful woman, you live in a mansion on the hill, you once worked in a resort."

"More than one," Naomi added with a smile. Larson wasn't smiling.

"More than what you are, I need to learn who you are," Tammy continued. "What are your dreams? What caused the divorce you're in? Are you happy? What do you believe?"

An awkward silence followed. Tammy waited. Her newfound confidence was showing as she looked from her mother to father, waiting, hoping. Larson and Naomi exchanged looks.

Finally, Naomi spoke. "Tammy, you've asked very difficult questions. Questions whose answers I still struggle with."

"And I understand that," Tammy answered. "But without answers, I'm not a daughter you trust. I'm a spectator who can only guess at what's going on. I can't help you with your dreams if I don't know what they are."

Naomi looked again to Larson. She wanted help, but he was annoyed with Tammy's candor and testimony claiming Christian conversion. He wished he was at the Silver Palace. There, he'd be in charge. How was all this linked to his daughter's addiction?

He said the only thing that came to mind. "Tammy, what went wrong between your mother and I is private. It's none of your business. You need to accept that."

"I understand it's private, but I'm in the middle," Tammy defended. "Dad, you moved out of the house. I came to your condo and found you living with a Black woman. Is that why you left Mom? I need to know why."

"How about this," Larson answered defensively. He was angry. "We didn't ask you why you used meth? Where you got it? You're the kid. We're the parents. You know what you need to know. The rest is private, and that's called none of your business."

Tammy nodded her understanding. Naomi was holding her breath. Tammy continued, "Dad, I'm sorry I upset you, and you're right. I'm the kid. Your kid. I wouldn't exist without you. You created me. You changed from husband and wife to become mom and dad. We are family. Nothing can change that. Nothing. All I want is to know who you are."

Larson's patience was gone. The girl had changed. She looked like Tammy, but she was a near stranger. A person wanting to pull back the curtain on secrets. He bolted out of his chair. "I'm done with this. I'd say good night, but I'd be lying. Put that in your book of truth." Larson moved for the door.

"Greg," Naomi called in desperation.

"Dad," Tammy cried. Larson ignored both of them. He grabbed the door open. He stepped out and slammed it hard behind him.

Larson marched down the short hallway and crossed the main meeting room where the tables were crowded with patients and counselors who were reacting to the noise of the door slamming.

Larson saw their looks as he hurried across. "You can all go to hell," he growled.

FIVE

FLY, FLY AWAY

LUKE FOUND the numbered parking space he had been directed to outside a high hurricane fence with a barbed wire apron on the private aircraft side of Las Vegas's busy airport. He walked to a nearby guard house just as a blue and white minivan arrived inside the fenced gate. He pulled off his badge to show it to the bearded man in the guardhouse but was pointed to a nearby walk-through gate. As he approached it, a lock buzzed, and the gate swung open.

"Are you the woman I talked to?" Luke questioned as he climbed through the side door of the van.

"That would be me," the brunette answered with a smile as she twisted from behind the steering wheel of the van. She was attractive, near his age, with green eyes and brunette hair twisted up in a bun suggesting she wore a hat. She was dressed in a blue zippered jump suit with a colorful shoulder patch that read Silver Palace Air.

Luke closed the side door of the van. "Is the pilot here today?"

The brunette glanced at the rearview mirror as she pulled the van in gear. "Yes," she answered. "That would be me. I'm Captain Garrison. You can call me Kim."

Kim surprised Luke. He felt a flush of embarrassment. He was glad he was sitting behind the woman. "I'm Luke Mitchel. Call me Luke."

"Hello, Luke."

Kim drove the van through a maze of parked aircraft. Most were large jets. One had the name and logo of the *Los Angeles Dodgers* on it. Finally, the van stopped at the side of a long, sleek twin-engine jet that glistened in the sun.

"This is the ride to Dubai. We call her the Silver Bullet. Come on, I'll show you around."

Luke followed Kim out of the van and joined her at the nose of the Silver Bullet.

"She's named appropriately," Luke suggested, marveling at the long-swept winged craft fitted with two large jet engines positioned near the rear of the fuselage.

"Built by Bombardier," Kim said with hands on her hips. "She's a Global 8000 business jet. The fastest civil aircraft since the Concorde, with a top speed of Mach 0.94. First business jet to break the sound barrier. She went supersonic with a NASA F-18 chase plane observing."

Luke heard the words, but he had no idea what Kim was saying.

Kim led Luke along the glistening silver fuselage as she continued, "The Silver Bullet can do eight thousand nautical miles nonstop."

"We're nonstop to Dubai?" Luke questioned.

"Flight time from Vegas to Dubai is about sixteen hours," Kim explained. "That's with a flight speed of five hundred miles an hour. We won't do that. I like stopping in the Azores. Little island about fifteen hundred miles west of Portugal. We'll still be seven thousand plus miles from Dubai but we're doing round trip. Azores gives us all a chance to buy some fuel, get out, breathe some fresh air, stretch our legs."

"I'll welcome that," Luke agreed.

"Once we pick up the package in Dubai, it's back to Vegas. The nonstop flight time from Dubai to Vegas is nineteen hours and forty-seven minutes."

"Can we do that?" Luke questioned.

"No," Kim answered. "We'll touch down in Ottawa, buy some fuel and then it's seven hours to Vegas. Depending on the weather."

"This round trip thing is not going to happen in one day, is it?" Luke asked.

Kim glanced at her watch. "Dubai is eleven hours ahead of us. Do the math." She led the way to a stair-step jetway positioned beneath an open cabin door.

"I'll leave that to you," Luke answered, following Kim up the jetway stairs and admiring her bottom in her snug flight suit.

"Holy shit," Luke exclaimed as they stepped into the main cabin.

The room was carpeted. It reminded Luke of a living room in one of the penthouses at the Silver Palace. There was a rounded plush coach with pillows and throws. Ornate-shaded lamps stood positioned on tables at each end of the coach. The windows were covered with custom drapers. A round glass cocktail table decorated with a bouquet of artificial flowers separated the coach from two comfortable-looking recliners. A mirrored stocked bar with bottled liquors and logo glassware flanked the rear wall.

"This is the living room," Kim said.

"Yes, it is," the awestruck Luke agreed, still looking.

There was a rack of magazines near the recliners, a large flat-screen high-definition television framed the wall near the bar, beneath it was a custom-fitted refrigerator, and a shelf filled with CDs stood beside the frig.

"The coach folds down into a queen-size bed. If needed," Kim added. "We've got four bedrooms. One with a near king, and three lessors. Let me show you." She led Luke into a hallway with soft ambient lighting and elaborate wooden doors on either side. Kim opened the first and stood aside to allow Luke a look.

Luke stepped to the open door. A decorative custom bed with a cluster of inviting pillows filled the carpeted room with its curtained windows. Small tables on either side of the bed held shaded ornate lamps. On one of the tables sat a telephone. Again, there was a flat-screened television. Two hooks on the paneled wall held logoed robes from the Silver Palace. An open door revealed an en suite bathroom with a sink and shower. Closet doors lined the walls.

"So, this one is mine?" Luke questioned, still looking around the room.

"You wish," Kim answered, leading Luke to another door at the end of the hallway.

Again, she opened the door. Luke stepped by her to look into the room. Luke noticed Kim's scent. It was subtle, but it made a favorable impression. His eyes surveyed the room. The bed looked as if it matched the singles at the Silver Palace. The room was compact but inviting. A single table lamp stood beside the bed. The window was curtained.

"The other two match this one. I suggest you pick the one behind me. It's as far from the Prince as we can get you. In the event he's watching TV or something."

"Got it," Luke agreed.

"And beyond here," Kim continued, opening a door at the end of the shaded hallway, "is our kitchen." She stepped inside and motioned Luke in. Luke, once again, stepped in and looked. It was compact but state-of-the-art, with built-ins and storage.

"Impressive," Luke said, looking around.

"Our chef is also our butler," Kim explained. "He's an all-around *let me do that* kinda guy. And over here is our crew bathroom," Kim said, opening a door to reveal a sink and toilet.

"How big is your crew?" Luke questioned.

"Me, co-pilot, chef…and you."

"And the four of us are flying halfway around the world." Luke's anxiety was showing.

"Not until tomorrow. You need to be here at three a.m.," Kim answered. "Bring your passport and clean socks."

———

CANDICE HARMON SPENT her afternoon creating a new space, her space, in the director's office. She now had a telephone and a computer on her desk. She answered all of the calls. There were many. Valet called, they wanted, needed, additional parking spaces. The GM had directed them to call. She told them a survey would have to be done. Then, there was a heads-up from day watch at the employee entrance. A housekeeper had been caught carrying twenty-two bottles of shampoo and sixteen bars of soap hidden on her as she tried to check out for the day. The contraband was confiscated and the head of housekeeping notified. The housekeeper would be terminated. The card room manager called, he recognized a cheat playing Twenty-One. He wanted to know why facial recognition missed him. He wanted the cheat out. Candice passed word to the day watch commander. Get it done. She then called Gayle Turner and tactfully asked how the cheat was missed? Gayle promised an answer before the day was over. Engineering called to report forty-seven hundred dollars' worth of brass was missing from their workplace atop tower two. She passed word to Lopez, the day watch commander. A report had to be made. She knew who would have to investigate. She would. The new assistant director of security was already thinking they needed a full-time plain clothes detective. The answer was clear. She was it.

Candice now understood why Luke Mitchel needed help. She thought it was about their one-time kiss. She knew he was attracted to her. It was mutual, but regardless, the reality was Luke Mitchel was about to abandon her and fly off to Dubai. Until his return, she was in charge. She wasn't finding it easy.

Quite the contrary. She had gone to the PM watch roll call to introduce herself and establish her authority. The majority of the officers seemed pleased. They understood the challenges of the department, although after they were dismissed, Anakoni Stone, their burly uniformed Hawaiian PM watch commander, who Candice thought was a friend, approached with a smile and said, "So, you're now in the boss's office. What's next? You move into his condo. Do his laundry, make the bed."

Candice knew she couldn't ignore it. She leaned close to Stone with an expression he knew was serious as officers left the room. "Get this, Anakoni. You're talking to the assistant director of security. That makes me your boss. You ever say anything like that again, to me or anybody else, your ass is grass. I'll burn you so bad you won't be able to find a job, not even back in Hawaii. Understood?"

Stone studied Candice's expression for a moment before he nodded silent agreement. Candice marched away.

————

GREG LARSON WAS in his Maserati speeding toward Vegas when the monitor on his dash flashed. His estranged wife was calling. No surprise. He had stormed out of the rehab ranch after Tammy, with her new so-called Christian conversion, became demanding and insulting. They could all go to hell. He had a better relationship with his daughter when she was a meth freak. Fuck religion. He pressed an auto answer button on the steering wheel.

"Okay, Naomi, so I left in a hurry. You still there?"

"No, it was time," Naomi's voice said on a speaker. "Although Tammy's worried about your anger. Greg, is there somewhere we could talk?"

"I have to stop by the Palace," Larson answered. "You wanna meet at the White Blossom? It's private."

"Tell the head waiter to expect me," Naomi suggested.

"See you there."

The White Blossom was the best of the six fine-dining restaurants at the Silver Palace. The head waiter recognized the GM when he approached.

"Good evening, Harold. I'd like something private, quiet. My wife will be joining me." His reference to Naomi as his wife echoed in Larson's mind. Naomi was his estranged wife. The world knew they were separated.

Everyone at the Palace knew he was living with Charlotte Johnson, the Silver Palace's former director of human resources. Larson gave quick thought to explaining the circumstance, Charlotte was gone, Naomi was on her way. Fuck it, there wasn't enough time in the world.

Harold, the head waiter, dressed in a black suit and tie, nodded as he gathered leather bound menus from his polished podium. "I have the pond available, sir. If you'd follow me, please."

Larson knew where the pond was. It was an isolated table near a large, wide open window overlooking a spacious pond filled with soft lighting, quiet instrumental music, flowering lily pads and white, well-fed, well-behaved geese. The room was busy and crowded with well-dressed guests, but the table was far from others. A candle flickered on the table. Harold pulled out a chair for Larson.

"I'll have a tall Jack and Coke. Make it a double." Larson smiled as he sat down. "It will prepare me for my ex." He was providing a CYA (Cover Your Ass) for his earlier slip, or was it a slip? He allowed his mind to question. Harold nodded and moved away.

Larson was finishing his second drink when Harold escorted Naomi to the table. He sat her across from Larson. "May I bring a drink for the lady?" he questioned.

"Yes," Naomi answered. "White wine, please. Your choice, Harold."

Harold bowed and moved away. Larson looked at his estranged wife. He allowed the thought, she was attractive. Makeup was subtle, fresh.

Her hair was pulled back and tied up with a ribbon matching her dress, which fit well over what was still a

Vegas figure. Damn, he thought, as if it were the first time he had seen her.

"I haven't seen the pond in some time," Naomi said with a smile to Larson.

"Me too," Larson lied. He had had dinner there with Charlotte Johnson only a week before.

A server arrived with Naomi's wine. "I'll have another," Larson said as the glass was sat in front of Naomi. The girl smiled and moved away.

"All right, cutting to the chase. I'm sorry," Larson said, downing what was left of his drink. "But she pushed too hard. I couldn't take any more of the Tammy's Jesus stuff."

Naomi sampled her wine before she spoke. "Let's see," she mused. "Jesus or meth? Which one do you think is best for our daughter?"

Larson tried to find more in his empty glass, just as his third arrived. "Tammy has to learn there are limits. Her questions were unreasonable."

Naomi sampled her wine again. Larson downed half of his third drink.

"Greg, I didn't know the answers either. Maybe that's what we found so difficult, but whatever it was, the fact is our daughter, the little girl arrested for prostitution, the meth freak, the girl that laid in front of us in ER wearing an oxygen mask, she's the one that prepared dinner for us tonight. She even remembered how you like fresh green peppers. Where did that come from?"

Harold approached the table, hands clasped together. He offered a smile to both. "Will you be dining this evening?"

"No thanks, just drinks and conversation," Larson answered.

Harold bowed and backed away. A pair of the white

geese swam close on the other side of the low open window. They honked several times and swam on.

Naomi smiled, and looked from the geese to Larson. "I heard they mate for life."

"All right," Larson said, surrendering to Naomi's remark. He shook the ice in his drink glass and looked to her. "Jesus wins. Meth or Christianity? It's a trick question. I'll go back soon. Hope Jesus is busy somewhere else and tell her I'm sorry, but she has to learn there's limits.

"Don't we all," Naomi said, looking at her husband. "Tammy's just excited. She's found something to believe in, hold on to, other than drugs. That's a good thing. She wanted us to be a family tonight, and we were. A family she prepared dinner for." Naomi extended an open hand across the table. "Greg, promise me you'll go back soon."

Naomi's open hand surprised Larson. He hesitated. She was wearing her wedding ring. Larson reached and took her hand in his. His eyes went to hers. "I promise," he said, grasping her hand tighter. They hadn't touched one another in nineteen months. The pair of geese honked behind them. Larson smiled as the memory flooded his mind. "Remember when we went to see Elvis at the Westgate? Remember his song? You don't know what you've got, 'til you lose it."

"I remember," Naomi answered with a subtle smile.

———

LUKE WAS HOME. Packing for his trip didn't take long. An electric razor. The Marine Corps taught him better, but he needed it for practical purposes. Pre-shave, after-shave, toothpaste, although he thought they probably had it on board, and as Kim suggested, socks. He tried sleeping. Three a.m. wasn't that far away but sleep was evasive. Memories kept taking him back to the Far East. The last he had seen of it was from a crowded C-17 Glob Master as it roared for take-off from a dusty field in Afghanistan. He shot and killed men not far from the field. Now he was on the eve of flying to the Far East, only this time it was to pick up an Arab and bring him, along with his money, back to Las Vegas.

Life at times was pure shit, Luke concluded. He hoped a call to Candice would end the thoughts. He grabbed his cell and dialed.

Candice answered on the third ring, "Hi, Luke, you flying?"

"Don't rush me. I'm still waiting. Tell me about your day."

"You don't have that much time," Candice warned. "But the good news is Luck has agreed to move. You were right, Lynne Strong was the answer. They'll make it happen tomorrow morning."

"Don't forget the time. You have to be back for the weekly staff in the morning."

"I won't forget," Candice said, feeling the rush of the day. "I'll be out of here as soon as I get rid of a noisy right-to-carry at the front door."

"Be careful, girl," Luke cautioned, ending the call. He wished he was there.

Candice found two officers at the front entrance flanking an annoyed-looking forty-year-old standing with an irritated-looking blonde with folded arms. Candice acknowledged the officers and then deliberately softly to the armed man who had been detected by electronic screening. "Sir, your CCW license gives you a right to carry a concealed weapon just about anywhere in Nevada, but here in the Silver Palace, like every casino, it's different. We're private property, and that gives us a lawful right to turn anyone, gun or not, away. I'm sorry, you're welcome, but your gun isn't."

"Well fuck," the man said, matching Candice's tone. "So if I leave my gun in my room at the Signature we can come back, and these dudes will get out of my way?"

"We'd welcome that."

The unshaven man nodded, took the arm of the blonde standing with him and turned away. Candice granted a smile to the two officers as her cell buzzed. It was Gayle Turner, the surveillance supervisor.

"Candice, glad I caught you. I need you to come look at something?"

"Be right up." Candice took a back-of-the-house elevator to the surveillance level. Gayle Turner was waiting at her desk in surveillance. There were three monitors with live images on the desk.

"Sit down," Gayle urged. "Let me show you what Jan spotted a couple minutes ago."

The three monitors displayed different live images of a young man and woman in country dress, playing a slot machine. "Watch the guy's belt buckle after she plays," Gayle urged.

They watched as the woman smiled, looked around, then inserted a bill and pulled the handle on the slot machine. As the slot spun the woman leaned aside, allowing the man to step closer as he adjusted his cowboy size belt buckle and pressed on it. A sharp, brief, intense light flashed at the machine. The spinning video on the face of the slot immediately stopped.

Candice looked at Gayle. "He's all ours. What do you want to do?"

"I'll give the slots manager a heads-up. Then have security bring them both up to our screening room. The buckle is an illegal device. It's now ours. I'll ask them a couple questions, where they're staying, ID, and take pictures of both. Send the pictures all over town and then throw them out. They're done gambling in Vegas."

"Works for me. Send me a copy of everything."

———

AT BEST, Luke snoozed. He got up, dressed in his best black tee shirt and tan jacket, and double-checked to make sure he had his passport, birth certificate and driver's license. He pushed it all into his shaving bag and headed for the door. He was surprised at how light traffic was until he neared the airport. There, it slowed and jammed with cabs, buses of every size, and an endless line of limousines, SUVs and rental cars to be surrendered. Luke was glad he was going to the private side of the airport. There, he found his numbered space, locked the Tesla and headed for the gate.

This time waiting in the van was a young crewman who introduced himself as Jeff.

"Customs is next," Jeff explained as he drove Luke to the field office of US Customs.

Their wait was short. Jeff stayed at Luke's side as he dug out his passport, driver's license ID and birth certificate. Luke was given a form questioning the purpose of his trip. *Business*, Luke penciled in. More forms asked for the aircraft's identification, destination, anticipated route, date of return, amount of currency he carried, and the number of the Visa he had for Saudi Arabia. Jeff, a veteran of the Customs Office and its protocols, provided all the information. When they finished, Jeff hurried Luke to the van.

"Come on, bro, we've got a plane to catch."

Jeff drove directly to the waiting Bombardier Global 8000 jet. There, he gave the van to a groundsman who drove it away. Luke stared at the glistening swept wing Bombardier bathed in light from a circle of high-intensity lamps positioned around the craft. Crewmen in coveralls worked atop a wing with a long heavy fuel line leading from a tanker truck. The truck with its pumps running, filled the night with noise. Hooded generators were parked near the rear of the fuselage with heavy cables reaching up into the jet engines. A man in what Luke guessed was a flight uniform walked with another in coveralls as they moved around the landing gear. Both carried clipboards as they looked up into the undercarriage with flashlights. Preflight inspection, Luke guessed.

"Make yourself at home," Jeff suggested. "I got some loading to do."

The jetway stairs were still in place. Luke climbed to the open door of the cabin. It was quieter inside. Luke was sitting his gear in the lounge when he heard a female voice behind him. He turned and looked. The door to the cockpit stood open. Kim was in the pilot's right seat. Luke was awed by the instrument panel spread in front of her with its clusters of illuminated instruments, live video screens, rows of buttons and switches, and more.

"I copy, ground control, frequency two-one-nine six-point four-point. Contact after engine start," Kim said into a microphone she wore. Her fingers punched numbers into a radio panel in front of her.

"Morning, Captain." Luke smiled, leaning into the open cockpit door.

The busy Kim was surprised. She offered a glance and then returned her attention to a preflight list strapped to her right leg. "I'm a little busy. Would you wait in the lounge, please."

Luke nodded, although Kim didn't see it. He was surprised, but he did as ordered. He turned to the lounge. He thought about closing the door to the cockpit but decided not to. If she wanted the door closed she would have said so. He chose one of the soft recliners. It swiveled. He turned to a window and parted the curtains. The fueling crew was finishing their work. The wheeled lights were being turned off and pulled away. The uniformed man Luke had seen inspecting the craft came aboard. He glanced at Luke.

"You must be the guy going with us to Dubai," he said, offering a hand to Luke. "Ron Trepp, I'm your co-pilot." They shook hands. Luke guessed the man was in his early thirties. He liked his friendly attitude. "Buckle up for take-off," the man added, turning to the cockpit where he climbed in and over into the left seat across from Kim.

Luke watched until Jeff appeared from the hallway leading to the bedrooms and kitchen.

"Time to close some doors," Jeff said, moving by Luke to reach and pull the cabin door shut with a thud. He locked it and looked to the cockpit. "Hatch is closed and locked," he called.

Co-pilot Trepp raised a thumb in acknowledgment.

"You a crew member?" Luke questioned as Jeff moved past him for the hallway.

"Chef and butler," Jeff answered without a pause as he moved down the hallway.

"All aboard, prepare for take-off. Engine start," Co-Pilot Trepp's amplified voice announced on a speaker. The cabin door stayed open. Luke was glad. He watched as hands made practiced moves over switches, buttons and throttle controls and then the subtle sound of the turbines turning over reached Luke.

He reached and found the seat belts hidden in fluff on either side of his recliner. He fastened the seat belt and tightened it. He noticed Kim and the co-pilot pulled shoulder straps over their heads for fastening.

"Engine one up and running." Luke heard Ron Trepp say to Kim as he watched the cockpit instruments. Then he added, "Engine two up and running. Brakes still set. Ready for taxi."

Luke could feel vibration and noise from the engines.

"Brakes released." He heard Kim announce as the big craft moved.

Luke watched, alternating glances out the side window and then into the cockpit. Lights, aircraft and buildings slide by as the Bombardier taxied its way through the maze to the runway. Luke knew they were getting close when he saw other aircraft with their landing lights on as they taxied by or passed in a flash heading down the runway. He could hear the thunder of their engines. He instinctively tightened his grip on the recliner as he watched a Southwest airliner ahead of them disappear down the runway. The Bombardier swung into position with growls from its engines. The brakes squeaked as it halted into position and waited. Luke heard the radio command when it spoke in the cockpit.

"Zero-one-six-six, you are cleared for take-off."

The brakes thudded as they were released. Luke saw Kim's hand push the throttle controls hard forward. The engine noise turned to thunder. Wheels turned and vibrated. The aircraft surged forward, pushing Luke back into his seat. The noise and rumble increased until the nose rose into the darkness.

"Landing gear up," he heard Co-Pilot Trepp announce. Luke felt the thud of the mechanism folding beneath him. He turned his chair to look out the side window.

"Wow," Luke mouthed quietly as he looked at the lights of nighttime Las Vegas sprawling in every direction beneath them. He lived in this city, he worked in this city, and he bragged of knowing it well, but he'd never seen it from nighttime air. He was awestruck.

There was Mandalay, the Luxor, New York New York, Paris, Bellagio with its fountains, Caesar's the green of the Grand, the towers of the Silver Palace, the Cosmo and the unbelievable ever-changing illuminated Sphere, all joining to fill the night with color. Then the Bombardier banked, climbing, seeking altitude and speed, and the city beneath suddenly disappeared.

"Damn," Luke said aloud. He lived and worked in the magical maze beneath them, but he'd never see it at night. As a director at the Silver Palace, he could do it all, anytime. He heard the helicopters every night, but he had never been on one. Luke often felt fortunate and sophisticated with life on the Strip, but for the moment, he felt much like a tourist.

SIX

THE PRINCE AND THE CITY

LUKE MITCHEL WAS no stranger to flight. The Marine Corps had provided lots of it. Mostly in crowded, noisy, open-doored helicopters but some were in bigger troop transports, and that combined with commercial flights, made him comfortable in the air. Hell, he preferred flying. On the ground, they shot at you. Luke found the control for the recliner and before Kim had the Bombardier up to forty-two thousand feet in growing sunlight over Colorado, Luke was asleep in the soft chair.

Candice arrived at Luke's office before Day Watches scheduled briefing. She planned to attend. The majority in security knew who she was but they would be curious about if anything might change. Unlocking the combo on the door of Luke's office, she wondered how long she, and everybody else would stop thinking of it as Luke's office. She turned on the lights and computers before sitting down to look at the digital PM and AM logs on the computer. She had no sooner found them when the telephone rang. It was the multiple internal consoles. Candice glanced at it. It was the GM's office.

Candice gathered the receiver. "Good morning, this is the assistant director." She wanted her tone professional, businesslike.

"Candice," a familiar female voice said. It was Jackie Fallon, the GM's executive assistant. "The GM just buzzed me. He said the weekly meeting started ten minutes ago and you weren't there. Engineering raised some question about stolen brass. The GM would like you to attend."

"Oh, shit!" Candice bolted to her feet. She had forgotten Luke's mention of the meeting. "Yes, of course. I'll get right up there."

Candice hung up, grabbed papers from her desk to provide an appearance of business and moved for the door. Waiting for a back-of-the-house elevator added to her nervousness. An elevator finally arrived. It was full of smartly dressed female assistants arriving for the new day as well as uniformed housekeepers and a server with a breakfast cart. On the elevator, she smelled the aroma of coffee. It reminded her she hadn't had any. In surveillance someone always made a fresh community pot. She wondered what Luke did for coffee. She wished he was there. The elevator made two stops before reaching the seventh floor where the management staff meetings were held. When she got off the elevator, she rushed to the conference room. The double doors were closed. It added to her anxiety. Should she knock or just go in? Candice opted to go in. The GM was standing at the head of the long conference table. There were a dozen-plus managers seated around the table. Most had coffee. All of them looked to Candice as she closed the door.

"The race will put us at a hundred percent," Greg Larson continued after a glance at Candice. "I suggest we move poker tables one through six and park Ken Dillon's number eighty-six car right there."

Candice spotted an empty chair between a gray-haired lady she knew was the head of cash ops and the younger director of rooms near the end of the table. She nodded an apology to both as she squeezed into the chair between them. She deliberately turned her papers upside down on the table in front of her.

Larson went on, "Guests can take pictures, touch the car, smell the tires, drink, and gamble. We're working at getting Ken to stop by in his racing garb. Stay tuned." Then, leaning his hands on the table, the GM looked past others to Candice. "Candice, engineering had a question."

"Yes, sir," Candice managed as her heart raced.

James Matthews, forty-something with dark hair and glasses, was on the far side of the conference table, not far from the GM. He took off his glasses and rocked forward to rest his elbows on the table to look down the table to Candice. The others seemed to follow his lead. Curious eyes turned to her. "I was hoping Luke Mitchel would be here this morning," Matthews said.

Silence followed. Candice wasn't prepared. The quietness prompted her response. "The director of security is away on business," Candice said apologetically.

"We sort of guessed that," Matthews countered. "But the thieves are still here. They got almost eight grand of my brass. You working on that, or should I just call our insurance company?"

A ripple of laughter came from around the table.

"A report of your loss came in late yesterday," Candice answered with a glance at the GM. She was hoping he would intervene, but he seemed among those waiting on an answer. "A security supervisor took a formal report yesterday." Candice added, "An investigation has been initiated."

"And what has this initiated investigation found?" Matthews pressed soberly, lacing his fingers together on the table.

Candice decided she was dealing with a prick. She strengthened her resolve and straightened her back. She shuffled the papers in front of her and returned Matthews's look. "Discussion of our investigation in a forum such as this wouldn't be proper. You can be assured the loss has our attention. We'll keep the general manager informed. He'll decide what and when a discussion is appropriate."

"Thank you, Candice," the GM said, ending the exchange. "All right, let's hear from human resources. Tell us about your recruitment strategies?"

Candice allowed herself a deep, careful breath.

———

IN THE PLUSH main cabin of the Bombardier, the uniformed Kim woke Luke by pushing on his shoulder. He opened his eyes to find she was carrying two paper cups of coffee. Kim offered one of the cups to Luke as he straightened the recliner.

"Special latte Jeff brews," Kim said, sitting down on the couch across from him. "Heavy on the caffeine to keep us awake up front."

"Thanks," Luke said as he sampled his cup. "Sorry, I keep falling asleep."

"Time zones will do that. The Bullet rides smooth, doesn't she?" Kim suggested. "We're about forty minutes from the Azures. Winds are being user friendly. We're at thirty-eight thousand, making five hundred and ten knots. You hungry?"

Kim was being much friendlier than she had been earlier. Luke was pleased. "Hungry, what have you got in mind?" he questioned.

Kim rocked forward to rest her elbows on her knees. Their conversation was easy. There was little more than a slight steady vibration in the Bombardier's cabin. Noise from the engines was far behind and faint.

"There's this little snack shop next to the terminal. They have this great sandwich. Portuguese something. You gotta try it. I'll buy while they pump gas. I've even got some of their funny money from the last time we were over."

"Count me in." Luke smiled.

"Good." Kim smiled, pushing to her feet. "Me and my latte have to get back to work before Ron moves over into my seat."

"How long have you been doing this flying thing?" Luke questioned. He wanted to know more about this attractive user friendly uniformed beauty.

Kim paused, seemingly not bothered by the question. "Air Force Academy got me ready for F-thirty-five's," Kim explained. "Flew them for a couple years. Mainly in the Med. Found Southwest paid more than the Air Force and there was a lot more legroom in their cockpits."

She glanced toward the open cockpit. "Ron was a passenger on a flight from Vegas to San Diego. Think he's got a skirt down there. Anyway, Ron tells me he flies for the Silver Palace, and said they were looking for a pilot. Here I am."

"No." Luke smiled. "Here we are."

"You'll have to fill in the blanks for me when we have

our sandwich." Kim paused and smiled. "I just remembered its name. The Bifana."

"That was what I was just going to say," Luke teased as Kim moved for the cockpit, latte in hand.

———

Naomi Larson reasoned her sense of urgency to return to Boulder and the Out of the Shadow's Rehab Ranch to see Tammy was linked to motherhood. Reality or not, she was in her car headed for Boulder. She wasn't doing anything that would surprise or anger her estranged husband. Thinking of Greg as estranged no longer seemed to fit. There were no longer disputes over custody, they were talking to each other rather than attorneys, and they held hands at the pond. Naomi wouldn't allow thoughts of where it all might lead, but remembering her hand in Greg's had kept her awake much of the night. Naomi parked her SUV near the ranch house. She didn't have to look for Josh Logan. He came out to meet her in the parking lot.

Josh reminded Naomi of a hippy. He was thirty-something with long hair, too long, pushed beneath a Western hat. Boots, faded jeans and an oversized tee shirt added to his persona. "I understand someone got a little loud last night," Josh said from under the brim of his hat. Naomi was thinking of how to explain Greg's loud hasty departure, but Josh read her hesitancy and added, "This is not an easy path you're on. Things that fall apart are not always easy to put back together."

"Is Tammy all right?" Naomi questioned.

"We talked after you left. I think she'll be glad to see you. I believe she's out near the barn, feeding chickens."

Naomi found Tammy. They hugged. Naomi wiped

away tears. Tammy hid hers. They sat in the shade inside the open barn where six horses were housed. It was hot and smelly, but neither seemed to care. Tammy fit the scene in sandals, jeans, and a tied-up blouse. Naomi could only be described as looking out of place. They sat on stools facing one another as others worked feeding the horses and shoveled away their waste.

"Your father's a man with power and responsibility," Naomi offered, pushing hair from her daughter's forehead.

Tammy nodded agreement. "For me, he's dad. I love him. I wish I didn't know what I do."

"Last night, you talked about forgiveness. You have to forgive him."

"Have you, Mom?"

"I'm working on it. When I was pregnant with you and your dad was a front desk agent at the Hilton, I used to watch a show with Pat Robinson called *The Seven Hundred Club*. Pat said life was like planting a seed. Seeds were small, planted in dirt. They had to be watered. Then, patience, but eventually the seed would push up out of the dirt, grow and blossom. I don't know why it stuck in my head, but it did. You planted a seed last night."

"Maybe we're both waiting on a blossom, Mom," Tammy answered.

———

TWENTY-SIX MILES and a world away Greg Larson and Paula Marks, the rooms director from the Silver Place, were attending a meeting on the Strip at the Paris Resort and Casino. The strategies for the Formula 1 Las Vegas Grand Prix Street Race would be discussed. The meet was held in a guarded ballroom. Cameras and recording devices were prohibited. The chairman of the Race Planning Committee made the invitation list short and exclusive. The forty-some movers and shakers in attendance would be deciding how billions would be divided.

Greg Larson, among the privileged and powerful, had a plan. His plan would result in the Silver Palace making billions of dollars. The plan was on Larson's mind but so was another reality of the meeting and that was Charlotte Johnson, the rooms director from the Cosmopolitan. More than a rooms director from one of the Silver Palace's major competitors was the fact Charlotte Johnson was his ex-lover. They had discretely shared life and love in Larson's downtown condo for eleven months. The end came shortly after Tammy Larson's life-threatening struggles with meth emerged. Charlotte, perhaps wisely, saw the handwriting on the wall when drugs drew Tammy's mother and father into their joint effort to save Tammy's life. Charlotte told Greg Larson goodbye and not only moved out but moved on. Larson knew when he came to the meeting that Charlotte would be there. Charlotte Johnson was not hard to find. She was tall, Black and Vegas beautiful. Seeing her made Larson's thoughts, worries and concerns with an estranged wife and a daughter fighting addiction quickly yield to the excitement and passion he had shared with Charlotte. It was passion, love, and laughter. They didn't have to think about the past. They lived in the moment. They were living the Vegas life. Not a history of decades and years. It was clean, fresh and compelling. Larson yielded to it.

Charlotte was at a pre-meeting free bar when Larson approached her. "If I remember, it was a vodka martini."

Charlotte accepted her drink from the bartender and granted Larson a smile." You remember well."

"I remember important things," Larson added before he looked to the bartender. "Jack and Coke, please."

"How's your daughter doing?" Charlotte questioned after sampling her drink.

"Well," Larson answered, picking up his drink. "You know I've been meaning to reach out to you."

"Really, I seldom miss calls," Charlotte answered.

"I thought perhaps it was best I wait until I saw you."

"Now you see me," Charlotte said.

"I believe you left something important at the condo."

"Oh, and what would that be?"

"You'll have to come see," Larson suggested.

"I'm sure I left all the keys behind," Charlotte smiled.

"You don't need a key if the door is unlocked," Larson suggested, raising his drink to his lips.

"My, my." Charlotte smiled seductively. She walked away, offering Larson a glance and a smile as she joined a group of others.

Larson knew the look, at least, he hoped he did. The door would be unlocked.

———

CANDICE'S DAY was long and challenging. She had painted herself into a corner with the comment she made at the GM's weekly staff meeting. "We'll keep the GM informed," she promised while looking at the director of engineering, but as a newbie, late for the meeting, she was really talking to the GM. Now the clock was ticking, and she knew to find something. A refugee from surveillance, Candice knew the starting point was there. She met with Gayle Turner, the supervisor of surveillance. Gayle was more than a friend, she was a sister and ally.

Gayle knew how to make it happen in surveillance. After Candice's plea, they met at Gayle's desk in the surveillance unit. They started at the time engineering discovered missing brass fixtures from their inventory gathered on the top of tower two for the Silver Palace's new glass-sided pool. The missing fixtures led to the discovery additional brass was missing to a total nearing ten thousand dollars. Candice had an inventory of the missing brass. It was not parts you could stick in your pocket. Together, Candice and Gayle watched video recordings of the stockpile of brass, boxed and stacked with other building supplies.

They ran the videos backward from the time of the reported loss until the time it was carried onto the rooftop by a team of four engineers. Six cameras covered the rooftop where the brass was stored. Candice and Gayle looked at all of them. They found the engineers picked their noses, adjusted their balls and one of them even urinated in a bucket, but none took anything from the stash of building supplies. It was time-consuming and boring, and after several hours of reviewing, the two gave up. They had found nothing. Candice knew reporting the engineer had urinated in a bucket when they had nothing would not be wise.

"I've got an idea," Gayle said, getting out of her chair to walk around her office, stretching her legs.

"I'm listening," Candice answered, holding her chin with an elbow propped on Gayle's desk.

"Let's look at who signed for the brass when it was delivered," Gayle suggested. "What if what we're looking for was never delivered? What if someone got their hands on it before it was delivered?"

Candice bolted straight. "I like that." She shuffled through the paperwork gathered by Sergeant Lopez when he took the initial report. Candice found what she was looking for. "Here it is," she said to Gayle. "Engineer by the name of Shawn Gleason signed for the delivery six days ago. Hummele's building supplies delivered it."

Gayle slapped her hands together. "So we find that and have a look."

Their work began. The task was daunting, but again, cameras filled in the blanks. They found the video of the truck making the delivery. They watched as the engineer, identified as Shawn Gleason, met the truck at a back-of-the-house loading dock. A second engineer arrived and helped unload the delivery. It was staked on the dock where Gleason counted the boxes but opened none. He signed a slip the driver presented and then the truck pulled away. The delivery consisted of assorted boxes, various sizes, and all obviously heavy.

One of the engineers walked away to return with a powered open-wheeled lift. The two men stacked the boxes onto the lift.

The review challenge grew as Candice and Gayle now had to track a variety of camera recordings following the two engineers and their stacked lift as it crossed through the back of the house to an elevator and up to the top of tower two. One of Gayle's on-duty surveillance agents, a thirty-four-year-old blonde refugee from Twenty-One, joined in the search for recordings but their collective review showed the inventory from the truck arrived on the rooftop without ever being opened.

Their earlier review of recordings had revealed no one had tampered with the delivery until the engineers working on the roof could not find the brass parts they needed. Thinking they were stolen, security was called, and a report was made. Now it was clear the brass parts were likely never delivered. Engineer Gleason did not inventory the delivery. The missing brass clearly belonged to the truck making the delivery, but the supplier could and would shun responsibility by displaying a delivered inventory list signed by Engineer Shawn Gleason. It wasn't a theft, after all, just a fuck up. A fuck up that took nearly five hours, but Candice was breathing easier. She had the answers she needed for the GM, and to her satisfaction it wasn't an answer Director of Engineering Tom Matthews wanted.

———

LUKE AND KIM had their Bifana, a Portuguese sandwich, shortly after the Silver Bullet landed in the Azores. It didn't turn out as they hoped. They ordered the sandwiches from a takeaway window with the hope of sitting down to play and getting to know one another. Luke had seen enough of Kim to decide she was fascinating, with or without her captain's uniform. Their first issue was noise. It seemed every jet flying that day was landing in the Azores and wanted to park near the terminal's sandwich shop. Luke was waiting for the jet engines to fade when their co-pilot, Ron Trepp, reached them. A tire pressure gauge for one of the nose wheels was indicating it was low and fading. Luke knew what it meant. He was left without Kim, but he had two Bifana sandwiches, although Kim's had a bite out of it. Luke took them both on board to Jeff the Chef, who claimed he knew how to save them.

"You just tell me when," Jeff urged.

The issue with the front tire was resolved with a

pressurized spray of flat fixer provided by the Portuguese ground crew. They were back in the air with more fuel in less than three hours. After they were at altitude, Kim left the cockpit to join Luke in the forward lounge.

"Depending on weather, and we've got some cloud cover," Kim told Luke, "We should reach Dubai in about seven hours. To get to the Emirates, we have to be careful about what we fly over. There's a few Middle East countries we need to avoid."

"Seven hours," Luke suggested. "Gives us time to finish our sandwich."

"Ready when you are." Kim smiled.

Circumstances in the Middle East, better known as *war*, made the final leg of the Silver Bullet's flight to DubaiDubai in the Arab Emirates, a piece of navigation put together hastily in the cockpit. More important to Luke it kept Kim busy in the cockpit. Once again, their sandwiches were put on hold. Luke felt a change in their airspeed and sensed they were descending. He turned his chair to the window. The clouds had surrendered to the heat of the desert as Dubai came into view. Luke had seen Afghanistan from the air. Dubai was different. The city was a maze of towering glistening glass spikes reaching into the sky, laced with a maze of freeways leading nowhere. As the descent continued, Luke saw the spike of Burj Khalifa, the tallest building in the world. It towered into the sky, surrounded by a mix of others with designs announcing he was looking at what had to be among the richest cities in the world. The city was a sharp contrast to its surrounding desert landscape. The sprawling urban expanse was a patchwork of modern architecture and innovative designs. Clusters of shimmering skyscrapers with their glass facades reflected the sunlight and the deep blue waters of the Arabian Gulf.

"All crew prepare for landing," Ron Trepp's voice announced over the craft's speaker system. "Seat belts fastened, please." Luke fastened his seat belt as the Bombardier banked hard left. His view of the city disappeared. When the wings leveled, Luke's view yielded to the tops of passing warehouses, busy roadways, and jammed parking lots. Luke thought it looked as if Dubai was catching up with Vegas.

The landing was smooth, and the Bombardier was soon one of many aircraft crowding the busy airport. Luke watched as they taxied to a space between two larger jet aircraft. He glimpsed a groundsman giving signals and then they stopped.

Jeff appeared and unlocked the cabin door. "Welcome to Dubai." He smiled.

The air outside was hot, dry and inviting. A set of stairs was pushed to the open cabin door. Luke followed Jeff down the steps as a black limo arrived and pulled to a stop. Luke wondered if it was Jamal Hassan, the twenty-nine-year-old they would take to Vegas. He was surprised when two men in dark suits wearing turbans climbed from the limo and approached.

They were young and sober. "We are looking for Luther Mitchel," the older of the two announced.

Luke wondered if the two men were armed. They had a persona that suggested they were. "I'm Luke Mitchel," he answered.

The Turban that spoke gestured to the limo. "Come with us, please."

"Why?" Luke questioned. His suspicions were growing.

"Minister Hassan would like to speak with you." The Turban then added, "He should not be kept waiting."

Luke detected an English accent when the man spoke. He knew they were referring to the oil kingpin Greg Larson had mentioned. The uniformed Kim and her Co-Pilot Ron Trepp joined Luke and Jeff as they stood facing the two suits.

"What's going on?" Kim questioned.

The Turban answered, "Luther Mitchel will be going with us." It was as much a warning as an answer. He gestured to the car. "Get in, please."

Luke looked to Kim and the others. He was worried, but he didn't want Dubai or the oil minister to become an issue. "I'll be back." Luke forced a smile and moved for the limo. The two Turbans flanked his walk to the car.

SEVEN
OIL AND WATER

EIGHT THOUSAND, one hundred and forty miles to the west, Greg Larson sat waiting in the living room of his three-bedroom condominium eight blocks off the Las Vegas Strip in the quiet Angel Park neighborhood. He had taken a Viagra forty minutes earlier, and as he told Charlotte, his front door was unlocked. His drug and memories were both ready psychologically. The pleasures Charlotte had once brought him filled his mind. She was an exciting woman who knew how to pleasure him. He was hungry for her body. When they made love, she preferred the dominant position. He welcomed it, thinking of the minutes ahead. What should they do first? Charlotte was coming with the knowledge that they would make love. Should they, would they, talk first? Larson decided talk could wait. They both knew what tonight's reunion was about. Who needed casual talk about her role as the Rooms Director at the Cosmo. She was a beautiful Black woman, and he wanted her naked against him. Was the fact she was Black part of the allure, or more importantly, was it the allure? Was that it? Powerful White man in a city driven by sex attracts and seduces a Black icon. Was Charlotte just another prize to set on the shelf in his masculine mind? No, she was the epitome of sex and femininity. He loved her. His thoughts stabbed at reality. Was their pending reunion just two people getting laid? Would there be, could there be a reunion without sex? Wasn't getting laid called making love? That's what he and Charlotte were about to do. They were going to make love, and it was nobody's business but theirs. Naomi didn't need to know, and it sure as hell wasn't any of Tammy's business. The kid was smart. What was with her? Honor roll throughout high school, then lying about going to college, arrested for prostitution. A drug addict. Now a Jesus freak. Maybe that was a good thing.

Larson deliberately turned his thoughts away from his estranged wife and his daughter. They had no business in this night, he assured himself, adjusting the erection growing in his crotch. Come on, Charlotte! His eyes went to the phone on the cocktail table in front of him. Why wonder when she was going to open the unlocked door? He was confident the look he got from her when he made the invitation was positive. So why not call her? He hesitated. What would he say? *Hurry, I got it up.* He was uncertain, wary.

———

LESS THAN NINE MILES AWAY, in a distance that had to be measured in more than the miles, Naomi Larson, wrapped in a robe, sat on her adjustable California king-size Sleep Number bed in the sprawling five-bedroom mansion atop a hill off East Sahara in the gated community of Palm Grove. She stared at the cell phone laying near her feet. Earlier, she sat on the patio watching the sprawling lights of Las Vegas spread before her on the desert floor. She remembered feeling alone while the city below was filled with life and laughter. She bathed, but the loneliness didn't wash away. Now, wrapped in her robe, she tried getting lost in the bedroom's flat-screen TV. HGTV was the best of her search but the couple trying to find their starter home in New Jersey held little interest. She wondered if the fact they were young, in love and starting a new chapter in their lives was what turned her off. She didn't know or care. She traded them for quiet, but the quietness proved challenging. The answer came easy. She was alone in it. Naomi thought of Tammy. Just thinking of her daughter made her smile. She could still smell the bar where they had sat and talked. More than talk, they opened their hearts. The one-time distance between mother and daughter was gone. Now they were not only of one mind, they were of one heart. Tammy thanked Jesus. Naomi thanked God. Whoever played a role in pulling Tammy away from the swamp of meth she had sunk in, had her appreciation. If that was Jesus, as Tammy claimed, Hallelujah. Greg would be pleased to learn Tammy's accusations weren't meant to pry into his private life. She just wanted her father close. She wanted to fill in the blanks. Most of all Naomi was relieved Tammy looked forward to her father's return. Wouldn't Greg Larson want to hear that? It was a reason to call him, although even the thought of it made Naomi's heart race.

Greg would answer, she would tell him about Tammy, but the reality was she hadn't dialed his private cell in nineteen months. Why was she doing it now? She was still the estranged wife. The finality of their divorce moved closer every day. Their daughter was in rehab.

Tammy's appearance on a prostitution charge was only six days away, but Naomi confessed in the silence of the master bedroom, she wanted to hear his voice. Greg Larson was much more than Tammy's father, or the general manager of the Silver Palace, he was her husband. He had been her husband for decades. Ironically, Tammy's drugs had not only impacted her life, it had spilled onto Tammy's parents, who were involved in a bitter, hate-filled divorce. Parents who now admitted their child was what they made her. Parents who now had hope. Parents who now knew there was someone else in the family. Jesus. Tammy made it clear. Jesus was in. Maybe that was what was changing Naomi. She didn't care. The curtain had been pulled back. She and Greg had a reason to talk. Talk that brought smiles and hope. Maybe it wasn't too late. Tammy had survived. Why couldn't they? All Naomi had to do was reach for the cell phone, but she paused as tears welled in her eyes.

———

IN DUBAI, Luke Mitchel was driven to the Emirates Towers on Sheikh Zayed Road, where the dark limo drove into underground parking. Luke's two escorts spoke to one another in a language he didn't recognize. A private elevator took the trio to the forty-eighth floor, where Luke was escorted into a windowed combination office and comfortable lounge.

"Please, be patient," one of the Turbans suggested, and they left the room.

Fascinated by the view of Dubai, Luke walked to a window. There was a towering, upside-down horseshoe-shaped building towering in the distance. Luke was fascinated by it, but he was anxious. He knew he was in the presence of substantial wealth. The irony, Luke decided, was this was how first-time visitors to Las Vegas felt. Overwhelmed, awestruck. His thoughts were interrupted by a door opening near a bar at the end of the room.

The man entering wore a dark mustache and beard which matched his balding hairline. Luke guessed his age as early sixties. He was dressed in a suit and tie which made Luke conscious of his sports jacket and black tee shirt.

Luke was greeted with a smile and an open hand. "You would be Luther Mitchel, director of security from the Silver Palace."

The two men shook hands. "I'm Akeen Hassan." The suit and tie smiled. "I'm Jamal's father. Please have a seat."

The two men sat in comfortable padded chairs facing one another.

"And you would be the Minister of Oil for the Arab states," Luke said, returning the man's smile and proving he, too, had done his homework.

"I think between the two of us, you have the more interesting position," Akeen suggested.

"Yes," Luke answered. "I am a fortunate man."

"I appreciate you coming to pick up Jamal for his trip to Las Vegas."

"My pleasure," Luke assured.

"I wanted to meet you," Akeen said, rocking forward in his chair. "I want assurance my son will be safe in your city. In the past, as I suspect you know, Jamal was not alone during his visit to Las Vegas. I sent two trusted individuals with him who set boundaries."

"Yes, I remember them," Luke answered.

"Jamal was uncomfortable with them. I surprised him

with this trip after his recent challenging time in Iran. He is excited to be going, but this time he insisted that he decides who will accompany him. So, he will be traveling only with those he invites. As a result, I must ask your umbrella of safekeeping be extended to ensure his wellbeing."

"Minister, I am not a police officer," Luke defended.

"But you once were."

Luke smiled. The minister had also done his work. "True, but my authority is limited to the Silver Palace. I assure you Jamal will be safe while our guest, as all guests are, but when he leaves our property, he, like others, are free to do what they like."

"The cost of his wellbeing is not an issue, you understand. We are not talking about money."

"I understand," Luke defended. "And I'm not addressing the costs." He was becoming suspicious of the minister's concerns. Luke could see it. He was talking with a worried parent. A parent that knew their child's habits. "What should I protect Jamal from while he is our guest?" Luke tried to lead the man.

"I hear your country is troubled with drugs," Akeen suggested cautiously.

"Drugs are a problem. As they are in most of the world, but we try keeping drugs off property."

"I'm glad to hear that. I would appreciate a close watch on Jamal. He, like most young men, has been lured into trying drugs. As his father, I don't want him harmed or have him become an addict."

"I understand your concern," Luke said candidly. "As his father, you've talked to Jamal?"

"Yes." Akeen nodded. "He knows our culture prohibits drug use, but I won't be with Jamal, and your town has a reputation for being a place with few limits."

"I know my town well, Minister. We will take care of your son while he's our guest, but when he goes into his room and closes the door, what he does in there is his choice."

Akeen pushed to his feet. Luke did the same. The minister extended an open hand again. Luke took it. The minister held Luke's hand in his.

"I enjoy a certain measure of wealth and power. I can only hope Jamal has listened to my words. I feel better now that I have met you."

"And it was my pleasure meeting you, sir."

———

GREG LARSON TRIED SITTING and waiting. It only seemed to make the time drag slower. Where the hell was Charlotte? Waiting was beginning to soil the idea of their lovemaking. This was somehow turning from passion to guilt. Another lie for Tammy and Naomi. It was none of their business in the first place. His erection was troubling him. He headed for the hall bath. There he urinated. Pleased with his growing erection, he zipped and moved to the sink to wash his hands. It was there he saw his image in the mirror. He studied the face looking back at him. It had guilt and lies written all over it. Tammy would know. So would Naomi. He was a liar and a cheat. It didn't matter that nearly eleven thousand employees were under his command. He was the general manager of one of the most successful casino resorts in Las Vegas, but he was also the man who took a Viagra and now awaited the arrival of a woman other than his wife. Adultery. Explain that to your daughter the next time she prepares dinner. And Naomi, he wouldn't even have to confess it to her, she'd see it on his face.

"Fuck!" Larson growled at his image in the mirror and turned away.

In his living room, Larson gathered his cell phone from the cocktail table and dialed Charlotte's number. His heart was racing.

"Hello," the familiar feminine voice answered.

"Charlotte, it's Greg. I just got a call from the casino. They just found some marked cards in Twenty-One. I've got to go in."

"What? I'm almost there. Can't security handle that?"

"Yeah, normally, but Luke Mitchel's in Dubai. This is all mine."

The cell went quiet. Larson could hear traffic noise as he waited. She was driving. He chewed on a lip.

"You prick, you're lying," Charlotte answered angrily. "There's no marked cards, just an asshole who can't make up his mind. Allow me to help, Greg. Take a fucking hike!"

A dial tone sang in Larson's ear. He dropped the cell phone to the carpet, sank into a chair and covered his face with both hands.

———

GAYLE TURNER WAS at her desk in the surveillance unit when Candice arrived. "We got work to do, girl," Candice said, waving a handful of papers in the air.

Gayle turned her attention from the three monitors on her desk as Candice sat down beside her. Candice read from the reports she carried.

"Three days, four complaints. Car clots. Compounding it is the fact all four cars belonged to guests. Listen to this, a pair of hiking boots, a set of leather gloves, two sets of sunglasses, suntan lotion, two pairs of black high-heeled shoes, six Taylor Swift CDs, and a sun hat. None of it over the top in value but all from four vehicles in guest parking. That's four guests that won't be coming back." Candice pushed the reports in front of Gayle. "Find them."

"We'll have to reach back a couple days. Take some time. See who's out there. Can I set up a bait car?" Gayle questioned.

Candice pushed out of her chair. "You can use a bear trap if you want to. Director of rooms complained to me. We've had to pay out on all this. Find this dick."

Gayle picked up the reports and began thumbing through them. "You think it may be more than one thief?"

Candice was moving for the door. "You tell me."

After Candice was gone, Gayle looked to the glass wall that separated the supervisors' desk from the array of large video screens delivering colorful real-time images from every corner of the Silver Palace. Five surveillance agents, dressed casually, sat at a long curved control desk as they watched the images on the screens. Gayle keyed a button on an intercom. "Nancy, Calib. Come see me."

A moment later, Calib, a thirty-year-old with a buzz cut, opened and held the glass door open for Nancy, a shapely twenty-nine-year-old in jeans, as the two entered to join Gayle.

Gayle pushed back in her chair and looked at the two. "I hope neither of you have plans for tonight."

––––––

THE SAME TWO Turbans that brought Luke to meet the Minister of Oil returned him to the airport. As soon as

Luke climbed out, they drove away. A fuel truck with two attendants were refueling the Silver Bullet. Jeff, the Butler/Chef had a cargo door open where he worked with a vendor loading food and beverages from a truck. Co-Pilot Ron Trepp was doing his walk-around inspection with a clipboard in hand. The uniformed Pilot Kim Garrison was at the open driver's window of a van parked under a wing of the Bombardier. Luke, walking to the steps leading up to the open cabin door, noticed the van had what looked like official emblems on it along with the word Customs imprinted on it in several languages. He paused to watch the activity. The Customs van pulled away. Kim looked to Luke, smiled, and walked to him.

"I don't see any oil stains," Kim said, looking Luke up and down.

"We bonded," Luke said. "He asked if our pilot was really a woman."

"You know women are allowed to drive cars now," Kim said.

"Explains all the one-way streets," Luke added.

Kim glanced after the Customs van that was now some distance away. "Customs asked about you. They wanted to see the visas of everyone that came in on the plane."

"Sorry about that," Luke suggested. "Is it a problem?"

"Not anymore," Kim explained. "I told them the Oil Minister wanted to see you and then they seemed to lose interest in you and your visa."

"Thanks for that. Looks like as soon as Jamal gets here with whomever he invites to join him in the sly, we can get out of dodge."

"Jamal's already here," Kim answered. "He arrived just

after you and the Turbans drove away. First thing he asked was, what time do we take off?"

Luke looked to the open cabin door. "Is there anyone with him?"

"Oh, yeah," Kim answered as she smiled and walked away to join her co-pilot.

Luke took in a deep breath and turned to the stairs. He was shocked by what he saw as he stepped into the plush cabin. A long-haired brunette sat straddling a male with her legs folded on either of the man, as his hands pushed a pair of panties and shorts down over her exposed buttocks. Moans of pleasure and eagerness came from the two.

"Hey," Luke barked.

The brunette reacted by twisting herself away from the man. She pulled up her panties and shorts as she looked to Luke. She looked young. Her makeup was heavy. The man slouching in the recliner was twenty-nine-year-old Jamal Hassan. He offered an apologetic smile to Luke as he straightened himself in the chair. "You must be the security guy my dad wanted to see."

"That would be me," Luke answered soberly. "And since you're in here, I know someone has shown you around. We have bedrooms. Understood?"

Jamal nodded agreement as he straightened himself even more in the recliner. "Girl's name is Veronica. She's from the UK. I invited her. That okay with you and my father?"

Two more girls appeared from the bedroom hallway. They were as young as Veronica. Both were dressed provocatively. Seeing Luke, they paused and glanced at Jamal. He accepted their lead. "These ladies would be Lydia and Wendy. Both from someplace in Australia."

Luke was running ahead of the introductions. He

knew what the three women were. In Vegas, they wouldn't get past security at the front entrance. Here, they had obviously endeared themselves to Jamal. Luke knew he had to set ground rules.

"We'll soon be airborne," Luke said soberly, making sure he made eye contact with all four. "You know where we're going, Vegas. Our airplane is comfortable but small. That means we treat each other with respect. Everybody understand that? Respect."

Jamal looked from Luke to the girls. "Ladies, would you give me a minute with the warden?"

The three girls all smiled at Jamal's remark and moved into the hallway and bedrooms. Jamal waited until he heard the doors close. He rocked forward in his chair, wiped lipstick from his mouth and looked to Luke. "You earn what, maybe the better part of two hundred thousand? Tell you what. I'll double your pay. Cash. All you have to do is find a private place to be, somewhere where you won't be embarrassed or annoyed and stay there until we get to Vegas.Then you can go back to being the dick you really are. Two hundred cash. Deal?"

Jamal's words stung. Luke glared at him. Jamal was no longer the wealthy son of the oil minister for the Middle East, or a spike in the cash flow for the Silver Palace, he was simply a young smart ass who thought he owned the world. Luke stepped to Jamal, reached down, grabbed the front of his shirt with both hands and jerked him to his feet.

Holding the kid's face only inches from his own, Luke spoke in a low, threatening tone. "I make the deals, kid, and yours sucks. You know what you are? You're a fucking passenger. You give me any shit, I'll drop your ass ice in Iceland. You understand me?"

Jamal swallowed and forced a nod. Luke released him, and he fell into the soft recliner.

"Okay, if we come in?" Kim asked, leading her co-pilot into the cabin. They were both reading the tense situation. Luke stepped away from Jamal who sat gripping the soft arms of the recliner.

"Sure," Luke answered with a glance at the two before his look returned to Jamal. "We were just talking about our flight to Vegas."

Jamal nodded acceptance again. Kim looked at Jamal's shirt which was pulled from his belt line into a wrinkled mass of cloth beneath his throat. She looked to Luke's sober face and connected the dots. "Get ready. Engine start in about ten minutes," she said, turning to the open cockpit.

EIGHT
PIECE BY PIECE

SLEEP WASN'T an option for Greg Larson after his call to Charlotte Johnson. He knew he had done the right thing, but it wasn't something he could ever share with Naomi or Tammy, or anyone else for that matter. So why did he do it? Was it the right thing if someone else got hurt? The answer was yes. Charlotte's ego may have been wounded, but she was strong. She would recover quickly, and she would move on and so would he. He just wasn't certain what his path might be, or where it might lead, but he did know the quiet loneliness of the condo that was doing little more than presenting haunting realities. It was not the place to be. He put on a tie in a bathroom and then found a jacket before heading for his car.

The streets of Vegas were quiet for Larson's drive to the Silver Palace. He saw a couple walking hand in hand and wondered how long they had been married. Last he'd heard, Vegas had fifty-six wedding chapels. Marriage, what was the promise...*in good times and in bad times.* He decided this night was a bad time.

———

GAYLE TURNER, the surveillance supervisor, knew where the keys to the Silver Palace's fleet of six upscale Mercedes Benz were kept. She watched them being hidden all the time. All you had to do was push on the spring-loaded lid for the gas tank and it sprang open, providing an excellent place to hide a key. Hidden, that was, with the exception of the surveillance staff. Gayle chose the Mercedes at the end of a line of six cars. Who would miss one shiny new G Class Mercedes Benz that cost one hundred and forty-nine thousand dollars? Gayle recovered the hidden key and climbed into the car carrying a backpack she'd borrowed from Lost & Found.

She drove the big car down the employee's exit ramp where she made a U-turn and drove back up the ramp to turn into guest parking. There was an empty parking space close to the elevator that, by design, took everyone to the casino level. There, they could decide to gamble or take another elevator to the upper-level guest rooms. Gayle eased the big silver Mercedes into the parking space. Once satisfied with how the car was parked, she ran the driver's window halfway down. Then, digging in the backpack, she pulled out a pair of men's Cartier sunglasses worth four grand. The sunglasses were followed with a new iPhone, two Snickers candy bars, a pair of Givenchy Spectre sneakers and a Montblanc ballpoint pen. She positioned the collection strategically on the center divider, the driver's door panel and the floor on the passenger's side. Satisfied, Gayle smiled, climbed out and pocketed the keys. She heard the screech of tires echoing in the vast concrete caverns. Gayle hurried toward the elevator.

Driving his Maserati into employee parking, Larson

saw a security officer look at him as he passed. He looked in his rearview mirror and saw the officer talking on his radio. Soon all of the three thousand six hundred and fourteen employees on duty in the Silver Palace would know the GM had arrived. Although, being recognized was comforting. He was the man in charge, the man everybody watched. Would they know what he had done? Did his face show it? Larson climbed out of his car. He was home. This was his place. Here, he would never hear, *Take a hike*. Here, he was more than boss, here he was the general manager.

Larson shared an elevator with a server and his cart, a young housekeeper and Gayle Turner, the supervisor of surveillance. Gayle Turner was the only one of the three Larson recognized. He offered Gayle a smile. "How's the house this evening?"

"Busy," Gayle answered with her own smile. "Nothing unusual other than the incident the incident in Twenty-One."

The elevator stopped on the casino level. Larson glanced at Gayle as he stepped off. "Copy me on the report," Larson said as the doors closed.

———

CHOOSING the card room proved right. The room was busy. The noise was familiar and comforting. It was electronic chimes from slots mixing with voices and subtle background music meant to calm the nerves of the losers. A uniformed count team of security officers pushed a four-wheeled cart from one table to another, collecting the Drop. The Drop was oil for the gears running the Silver Palace. The Drop Team deployed during the early morning hours when crowds were at their thinnest. Larson watched them from where he stood on the side of the card room. His thoughts were on the revenue collected. Proving his heart belonged to the Palace, he counted the card tables and active slots and factored in twenty-four hours. His estimate was sixteen million. Add another near twenty from food services, rooms, and entertainment. Thirty-six million per day. He studied the mix of card tables, thinking of rearranging them to create an aisle, a carpeted corridor, where the shapely attractive servers would walk. Having a player thinking about anything but the cards in front of him was a good thing.

Larson finally looked to the card room podium. He was pleased to see Tom Roberts, the card room manager sitting at a counter inside the raised podium near the center of the room. Roberts, in his mid-thirties, looked like a male model, and unlike most of the card room staff, had a PhD in Mathematics. Roberts taught at UCLA before giving in to the allure of odds and Vegas. Lacy Ramias, the attractive night manager, was with him. Her presence explained why Roberts was in so late. He and everyone else in the rumor mill knew they were lovers. Larson made a path through the tables to the podium. Lacy spotted Larson's approach and alerted Roberts. He stood and granted a smile to the GM.

"Good evening, Chief. You get called in because of the fight."

"No, just curious about who's doing what," Larson said, knowing he was teasing the two. He leaned an elbow on the podium rail. "Tell me about this fight."

Roberts gestured to the steps leading up onto the podium platform. "Would you like to come up?"

"No thanks," Larson said, glancing at Lacy's snug jacket and matching pants. She looked more like an escapee from a chorus line than a card room manager. He returned his look to Roberts. "Tell me about this fight."

Roberts glanced at his watch. "About an hour ago, Twenty-One table number twelve. This guy's sitting in the number two chair, woman beside him elbows his drink. Tall whiskey sour. It gets the cards in front of him, and the rest goes into his lap. He looks like a horse pissed on him. Pure accident. Couple servers are right on it, but the guy goes fifty-one-fifty. The lady's a fifty-nine-year-old guest. The guy calls her a bunch of bitches. He's using profanity and he's loud. Player on the other side of the lady tells the mouth to calm down and shut up. That doesn't go well, so the mouth pushes the guy hard. Surveillance will tell us who threw the first punch. The mouth gets hit and says hello to the carpet. He comes up with a bloody nose but still cursing."

"About then, two security officers and a supervisor arrive," Lacy Ramias added. "They separate the three. Take them away. Clean-up did their thing, and we went on with the game."

"Then, KC King calls me," Tom Roberts continued. "Turns out the mouth wants to sue us, and wouldn't you know it, he's a councilman from Los Angeles."

"Sorry I missed it," Larson said with a look at table twelve, but his interest was really about how long the table may have been out of service.

"Security and surveillance will have reports waiting for you," Roberts suggested.

"I'll have a look," Larson said, stepping away from the rail. "Everything else all right."

"Strong night," Lacy offered. "You'll like the Drop."

Larson nodded his appreciation and walked toward the back of the house.

He understood he was talking to two young managers about a fight in the card room, but they had lust written all over them. Once, it wasn't so different for him, Larson decided, but now it was. Instead of aching for the touch of a loved one he was torn between an estranged wife, an ex-lover and a daughter who chose Jesus over meth. Larson found his way to employee dining. The dining room wasn't crowded. Larson went through the buffet line primarily to see what was being served. He chose a cup of coffee and an empty table. By habit, he took the cell phone from his belt and laid it on the table. He was enjoying his anonymity. He looked at people, avoiding a look at the cell phone. The phone was haunting him. He had used it to call Charlotte. Now, it was begging him to call Naomi. He went back to people-watching. What he saw surprised him. Employees, including housekeepers, an engineer, a dealer and a server, were all discretely pushing food from the buffet into backpacks, large purses, and their pockets. Cookies, slices of pork, fresh fruit, and cereal was being pushed, jammed, and hidden to be soon carried out the door.

How could security miss all this? Larson asked himself. Bottom line, he concluded, was they probably did it, too. Everyone was aware of the eat-before-you-leave phenomenon. Housekeepers were notorious for it, but Larson hadn't seen or heard of the sneak food away issue. Watching it discretely and carefully, he soon realized he wasn't watching rich people. These were hard-working men and women who were doing it because they, or someone they knew, was hungry.

"Holy shit," he whispered aloud, knowing he had to do something.

Larson's reliance on math took the challenge. He saw the F&B, Food & Beverage budgets every week. There were no abnormalities. He visited the Employees Buffet on a regular basis. There had never been an issue or complaint and then he realized that was the answer. There was no problem. The realization made him smile until his cell phone vibrated and danced on the tabletop. It would be security, surveillance or Luke Mitchel's new assistant wanting to tell him about a fight in the card room that he already knew about.

"This is Larson," he said, using his GM tone.

"Greg," a familiar feminine voice said softly in his ear. Larson was shocked. It was Naomi, his estranged wife. He bolted straight in his chair.

Larson's surprise showed as his mind raced, grabbing at the worst-case scenario, "Something happened to Tammy?"

"No, no, Tammy's fine. I saw her today. I'm sorry I didn't mean to alarm you."

"It's been a long…" Larson chose not to complete the thought. "You saw her today. How is she?" He allowed himself to relax in the chair.

Naomi was again on the patio outside her master bedroom. She paced in the darkness in her robe as she talked, glancing at the distant glow of light from the Strip. She had given in to her urge to call her estranged husband, but now that she had, she wasn't sure what to say. It was as if she were on the Titanic. As long as they talked, their words would keep the ship afloat.

"She's fine. We sat in the barn and talked. Did you know they have horses there?"

"They call it a ranch."

"Logical," Naomi granted. "Tammy and I talked. She's sorry she pushed so hard after our dinner. She loves you, Greg. Will you go see her? She needs her dad in her life right now."

"Yeah, I will. I've learned problems can't be solved by running away from them. Did she ask you to call me?"

There was an awkward pause before Naomi answered. "No, she didn't ask me to call. Calling you was my idea."

Larson felt a compulsion for candor. "Get this," he said, leaning his elbows onto the table, "I'm in employee dining. I couldn't sleep. All I could think of was calling you."

"To ask about Tammy?"

"Sure, that's what I'd say…but the truth is, Naomi." Larson stopped, almost choking on his words.

"Greg, remember how we sat and talked while Tammy made dinner ready for us? Just you and I."

"Yes, I remember."

"I'm awake. You said you can't sleep."

"Yeah, go on."

"What if you came over and we talk. Just the two of us. I could make a pot of coffee."

"I'll be there in twenty-five minutes," Larson answered enthusiastically, pushing out of his chair.

———

THE SILVER BULLET, the Bombardier belonging to the Silver Palace, was at thirty-seven thousand feet, traveling at five hundred and forty-eight miles an hour. They were forty-two minutes from touching down in Canada for refueling for their final sprint to Las Vegas. Luke Mitchel sat in one of the recliners in the cabin's front lounge. He was trying to find something on the flat-screen television. So far, all he had found was heavy Irish accents on a talk show, a French drama set in the Middle Ages, and a show from Iceland demonstrating how to can steamed fish. Where was HGTV or National Geographic? He was turning off the TV when Jamal appeared in the mouth of the hallway. Luke hadn't seen the kid since their face-to-face exchange before take-off in Dubai. Jamal appeared to be playing by the rules. There had been no noise, no laughter, no sight of him or the three girls. Luke was worried. Had his angry outburst and getting physical with Jamal created an issue?

Luke thought this could be his first and last trip on the Silver Bullet. Jamal's father had juice, lots of it. The kid may have called him. Luke could be out of a job when they touched down in Vegas. He regretted creating a problem for Greg Larson, the man who saved his life, but he didn't regret getting in Jamal's face. Luke looked at Jamal.

"Can we talk?" Jamal asked, leaning on the doorway of the hall. Luke noticed he was barefoot.

"Sure," Luke answered. Jamal was a tough read. Jamal stepped into the lounge and moved to the second recliner. The two men sat facing one another.

"It's rare anyone disagrees with me," Jamal said to Luke.

"Thank the Marine Corps, or maybe the LAPD," Luke answered soberly.

"You made me think about why people fear me." Jamal clasped his hands together. "They're not afraid of me, they're afraid of my father."

"And you're just realizing that?"

"I know the business of oil. I understand how it influences the economy. I help with difficult negotiations. I have a black belt in karate," Jamal offered. "I can take care of myself, but nothing I do can change who my father is?"

"You sure you want to?"

"No," Jamal answered. "But it's not easy being Kareem Hassan's son. I can't get out of his shadow. I'd like to be me, be my own man, but at times, he makes being Kareen Hassan's son very easy."

"We can't pick our parents. Guess you're just going to have to get used to it. You're rich."

"You won't tell my father about earlier."

"I won't if you don't."

Jamal extended an open hand to Luke. "I'm sorry about my conduct. May we be friends?"

Luke understood Jamal's open hand was driven more by his desire to be in charge of the situation than having anything to do with friendship. Friendship between the director of security from the Silver Palace and the son of one of the richest men in the world seemed unlikely but not impossible. Luke took Jamal's hand. "So, what's the plan when we get you to Vegas?" Luke smiled as they shook hands.

"My father sent me to Iran to take all their money," Jamal answered. "Maybe that's why he sent me to Vegas."

————

TWENTY-ONE HUNDRED AND eighty-six miles west of the speeding Silver Bullet and at a much lower altitude, Candice Harmon, wearing panties and a loose-fitting pajama top, was awake and feeding her tropical fish. She tried sleeping but knowing surveillance was baiting a car clot kept her awake. It wasn't a major crime. It wasn't likely it would ever be anything more than routine, but it was happening on her watch. She was in charge. Luke was away having a ball in Dubai. Drinking, partying with a bunch of rich Arabs while she finished another sixteen-hour day. Was this why he picked her? Did he really need an assistant?

Candice opened a slider and walked onto the balcony of her third-story condo. The night was warm and quiet. No, it was hot. She smiled as the cliché came to mind, *"But it's a dry heat."* Thinking of the heat made her think of how Luke had turned up the heat. She once again asked herself for the real reason he chose her. Was it the fact they had kissed? Only once, but they both knew they wanted more. Damn fate for killing Luke's girlfriend the day of their kiss. Wasn't that in and of itself an acknowledgment of their attraction for one another, but now, as his new assistant, what was to become of their relationship? Could he, could she, expand their one-time kiss into a discrete, secretive work romance? Hell, there were those already saying she got the job because she had a set of great tits. Why the hell hadn't Gayle called? When would Luke be back? Candice decided a drink would help, but then thought better of it. She'd soon be back at work.

———

Six miles away on the Las Vegas Strip, the darkness of night was washed away by miles of colorful digital lighting illuminating the towering glass facades crowding the skyline. Among them stood the two towers of the Silver Palace. Its new glass-walled roof's edge pool, aptly named, *The Edge of the World*, was lit and alive with a variety of couples deep in the illuminated water crowding the glass wall for a look at a world seventy-eight floors beneath them.

In the Silver Palace's surveillance unit, its supervisor, Gayle Turner, sat, arms folded, feet up on her desk, leaning far back in her office chair, eyes closed, sound asleep. Her work day was in its eighteenth hour. There were three monitors on Gayle's desk. Each displayed a different image of guest parking. The first was a wide shot from a ceiling-mounted fixed camera showing a wide shot of row after row of parked cars. A second camera showed a wide shot of the parked and baited Mercedes Benz. The third was a wide angle that included the Mercedes and the nearby bank of elevators. There was no movement on any of the monitors until the elevator doors opened and a masked man wearing a hoody pulled over his head stepped out of an arriving elevator. The hooded man looked young, frail. He looked to his left and then right before moving toward the rows of parked cars. Suddenly, Calib Meyers and Nancy Rollins, the two surveillance agents assigned to the project, having seen the hooded figure on their larger screens on the other side of the glass partition, burst into the room.

"Gayle, wake up." Calib pushed Gayle's shoulder.

Gayle opened her eyes, dropped her feet to the floor and looked as Nancy Rollins pulled the monitor showing the parked Mercedes into their view.

"He showed up about sixty seconds ago," Calib said as they watched the monitor. The hooded, masked figure walked to the partially open driver's window of the Mercedes. He paused and looked around.

Gayle reached and grabbed a radio sitting on her desk. "Gate Keeper Thirty, surveillance 10, we've got a suspect in guest parking. He's wearing a mask and a hoody."

"Thirty here, surveillance," a filtered male answered. It was KC King's voice, he was the AM security watch commander. "Ready when you are."

"Look at that dick," Calib said in astonishment as they watched the hooded figure open the driver's door of the Mercedes and climb in.

"Wait, wait," Gayle urged as she tightened the camera's focus on the Mercedes.

An interior light blinked on. The hooded silhouetted moved, reaching, searching, looking, and then he lifted the backpack into view. He slid out of the car, backpack in hand, and moved for the elevator.

Gayle keyed the radio again as they watched. "Okay, thirty, he's all yours."

The hooded figure stepped into the elevator and disappeared. Gayle punched several keys on her keyboard and the image switched to an elevator door at the rear of the card room just as the uniformed KC King and two security officers arrived. Impatient, KC King punched at the buttons for the elevator. The elevator light blinked, and the doors parted. A bewildered-looking server pushing a food cart looked at the three security officers poised to leap on him.

"What?" a confused Gayle Turner said as she and the surveillance agents stared at the monitor. The image was silent, but KC King motioned the two officers onto the car.

"Where in the hell did he go?" Calib said in disbelief.

Gayle went back to her keyboard. Punching the keys she found a PTZ, Pan-Tilt-Zoom camera. She swung it to follow KC King, who walked quickly along the back of the card room. Ahead of him, the server pushed his cart through double doors into the back of the house. KC was not far behind.

The controls on the keyboard rattled again. Another PTZ brought up an image of the kitchen. Gayle swung it quickly to find KC and the Server. KC opened the top of the food cart, reached inside and lifted out a dark hoodie.

"Hooray," Calib shouted. "We got the sonofabitch." Nancy Rollins was all smiles. She patted Gayle's shoulders from where she stood behind her.

KC King reached into the cart again. The young server stood frozen. KC came up with a pair of sunglasses. He pushed them onto the face of the young server. Again, KC went into the cart. This time, he lifted out an iPhone and a pair of sneakers. He held them up for the camera as the other two officers arrived. KC spoke to them, and the server wearing the crooked sunglasses was quickly handcuffed.

KC King smiled and held a thumbs up for the camera he knew was watching.

NINE

SHOW ME THE MONEY

GREG LARSON AWOKE to a colorful desert sunrise as it reached through the bedroom window of the master bedroom of a house he remembered belonged to his estranged wife, Naomi. Greg sat up and swung his feet to the floor. He was naked. His clothes were scattered over a nearby recliner and the floor with his shorts tangled in a sheet near the foot of the king-size bed. He reached for his shorts as he glanced at Naomi's side of the bed. She was gone. Greg grabbed his shorts and hurried to the master bath.

Images from a night just past came rushing back as Larson relieved himself. He hadn't been in the house since Tammy's first arrest. After Naomi's invitation to *just talk,* he drove up the hill to the gated community, sped through the streets to the cul-de-sac where he found Naomi, dressed in a robe waiting at a back door with Sparky, her big Rottweiler. The dog barked once as Larson opened the gate. Naomi quieted him. Larson smiled as he reached Naomi. He was about to speak when she surprised him by taking him by the shoulders and kissing him. Surprise yielded to passion. Naomi's robe fell away as they crossed the kitchen. She was nude. Larson's jacket met the carpet along with his shoes in the hallway as their gasping embraces took them into the master bedroom and onto the bed. The big dog followed. Naomi chased him away.

They made love until they were both exhausted. Then they talked in the darkness. The darkness helped draw them close. Naomi told more about what she was calling her *barn talk* with Tammy. Tammy's Christian experience, from Naomi's point of view, was providing a wall separating her from a past she wanted to forget, while offering a new life, filled with hope, at least while she was still hidden from the world at the Out of the Shadows ranch.

Naomi ran a nailed finger over the silhouette of Larson's bare shoulder as she told him she believed there was value in forgetting and forgiving what was past.

"Can you forgive me?" Larson questioned carefully.

"I already have," Naomi answered, pulling him to her.

They slept after that. At least Larson did. Sleep came as he thought of how he might tell Tammy that Mom and Dad were putting the pieces back together.

He had no toothbrush or anything else to make his morning comfortable. Larson rinsed his mouth with cold water, used one of Naomi's hair brushes, felt his unshaven face as he looked in the mirror, and then put on yesterday's shirt and tie.

Larson found Naomi in the kitchen. She was wearing the same robe as when he arrived. Somehow, she looked rested and attractive. "You've got time for coffee, haven't you," she suggested with a smile.

Larson sat and waited as Naomi poured two cups. He noticed his was a familiar mug he had used for years. It had a fading Hyatt logo on it. A pendulum clock ticked on the wall beside the refrigerator. Larson looked around the familiar room. It felt comfortable, familiar. He remembered buying the house, when they moved in, excited with their ten-year-old daughter, the big party Naomi put together, the feel of the sun out near the pool. Somehow, it had all faded. Now, ironically with their eighteen-year-old daughter scheduled to appear in court on a charge of prostitution, while fighting meth addiction, the family was seemingly born again. Larson smiled at the thought as Naomi sat his coffee in front of him and sat down across from him.

"Wanna tell me what you're smiling at?"

The big Rottweiler came in, wagging its tail as it crossed to Larson and pushed its big head up between his legs. Larson smiled and petted the dog's head. "Nothing, just the smell of your coffee," Larson answered as his eyes found Naomi's. She returned his smile. Words weren't important.

———

CANDICE WAS NOT happy when she arrived at the Silver Palace in the morning. The day before had been filled with incidents with three counterfeit ten-dollar bills finding their way into the count room, an accidental discharge of a firearm in the men's locker room, an eight-year security veteran was suspended for three days and two cards, a queen and a jack had been found by a server on the floor beneath Twenty-One table number six. None of it was exciting but it all took time. The new assistant director of security had to be there, had to ask questions, had to make sure the answers were truthful, had to assign follow-up when needed and then write the needed reports. She doubted anyone read them. They would be forwarded on the company net to the concerned department heads for follow-up, endorsement, or recommendation, but by the time she finished the reports, which took hours, the rumor mill usually came in first. As a result, some of those concerned forwarded comments and suggestions, which required even more writing and follow-up.

She granted the officer at the employee entrance and another at the elevators a nod of acknowledgment and went straight to her office, no Luke Mitchel's office, on the third floor. The telephone on her new desk was ringing after she unlocked the door.

"Good morning, this is Candice. How may I assist you?"

"Candice, it's Luke. I'm told we'll touch down in forty-eight minutes."

"In Las Vegas?" Candice was surprised.

"No, we're going to land in Palm Springs."

"What! Palm Springs?"

"No, dummy, I'm kidding. What happened to your sense of humor."

"It got lost in guest parking yesterday."

"Okay, save it. Tell me about it at lunch?

"Employee dining, right?"

"Make that forty-seven minutes."

Candice was glad Luke called. Someone was thinking of her. It helped. She smiled as she sat down and turned on her computer. The word RESTRICTED in bold red print appeared on the monitor.

It was followed by a warning. *The Following Report concerns theft by an employee and must be considered Confidential.* Candice raced through her read of the incident. The baiting of the company Mercedes Benz, the server in his hoodie and mask. His capture and arrest by KC King. The report was written by Gayle Turner, her boss in surveillance. That was until her promotion to assistant director. This reeked of jealousy. Candice knew of the baiting setup. She helped make the plan. She had been deliberately ignored and being ignored pointed a finger directly at Gayle Turner. Bolting out of her chair Candice decided, friend or not, this couldn't stand. She was going to have a piece of Gail Turner's ass. She'd show her who was boss.

Candice marched to the surveillance unit, practicing the words. She couldn't use profanity, and she had to be rational. Gayle had violated the chain of command. That was the point she would use to justify her anger. The bitch. Candice jerked open the door to the supervisor's room expecting to find Gayle Turner sitting there. She wasn't. Nancy Rollins was.

Candice was careful with her question. "Where's Gayle?"

"She left just minutes before you got here," Nancy explained, "nineteen hours. She wasn't doing anybody any good by staying longer. She was going to call you about the car clot, but Calib and I said we'd put you in the loop. She said to tell you the report went nowhere but to your desk. Have you seen it?" Nancy's excitement was showing.

"Quick read," Candice answered.

"Let me get Calib in here and we'll fill in the blanks."

Candice felt the cell phone she carried on her belt beneath her jacket vibrating. She signaled Nancy to wait as she looked at the caller ID. It was the GM's office calling. "This is Candice."

"Candice, it's Jackie. The general manager would like to see you."

Candice took a breath. "I'll be right up."

Greg Larson was standing at the wide window of his office, cup of Starbucks in hand, looking at the panorama of the Strip when Jackie stepped into the open door of his office. "Sir, Candice Harmon is here."

Larson turned from the window, went to his desk and sat down as Candice entered.

"Close the door, please."

Candice closed the door. "Good morning, sir."

"Have a seat, miss."

Candice sat down in one of two chairs in front of the GM's desk.

"You catch any thieves in the past twenty-four hours."

"Yes, Sir. We caught the car clot that's been pouching guest parking. It was Glen Simpson. A twenty-four-year-old server. Been with us for eight months. I'll forward the video and report to you."

Larson sipped his coffee and then set it aside to rest his elbows on his desk. "There's bigger fish in the sea," he said soberly. "For the past two weeks we've suffered a two percent spike in losses. Do you know what that means?"

"I understand losses. I didn't know the percentage."

"I'll tell you what it means," Larson said soberly. "It means every week, eighty-eight thousand dollars is going out the door. That's about twelve grand a day. How much money did this car clot have on him?"

"I'm sorry, sir, I don't know."

"I'm betting he's what we might call a chicken shit thief. And while you were directing resources to catch this chicken shit thief, others you didn't know about were stealing a big chunk of change. In short, young lady, you've got to find out what the fuck is going on. I want results and I want them soon. You got that?"

"Yes, sir."

"So, get out of here. Go do it."

————

THE BOMBARDIER BELONGING to the Silver Palace, known as the Silver Bullet, touched down at Harry Reid International Airport in Las Vegas between a take-off by a Southwest flight and a landing by a United Air Lines flight full of eager faces convinced they were about to become winners. The Silver Bullet was cleared to taxi to the private side of the busy airport, where a ground crew waved it into assigned parking. Luke was pleased to see a chauffeur waiting beside a glistening black limo. Greg Larson had covered the details. Luke waited at the bottom of the jetway, where he shook hands with Jamal. "Good Luck, Jamal, remember you're in a strange land."

Jamal took Luke's hand as he looked around, listening to the thunder of the jets filling the shy. He looked excited. The three girls traveling with him crowded around him. They were sharing his excitement. "There are no strangers to this land. Just winners and losers."

Luke returned the smile and gestured Jamal to the waiting limo. "I wish you luck."

"Thank you, Luke."

Jamal and the girls were quickly into the limo. Jamal waved as it pulled away. Luke returned his attention to the jetway as Kim Garrison came down the steps in her uniform, "Maybe next time we can make the sandwich thing work," Kim suggested.

"I hear they make a pretty good sandwich at the Eye of the Tiger," Luke suggested. "Say seven o'clock."

"Thanks, but Ron and I are off to Mexico tomorrow and the FAA has this thing about sleep."

"Then after Mexico."

"For sure," Kim added with a smile.

Luke offered a hand to Kim. She took it. "You fly a mean plane, lady. You made it a pleasure. Promise you'll call when you're back from Mexico."

"As they say in Vegas. Bet on it."

Greg Larson and Tom Roberts, the card room manager, were waiting at the front entrance along with a bellman and Linda Hawkins, an attractive guest relations officer, when Jamal's limo arrived. The chauffeur, as instructed, had called. There were handshakes, smiles, and a photographer whose pictures would be sent to a waiting father in Dubai.

Jamal accepted an invitation to have a drink at the bar with the GM and the card room manager but declined going up to his waiting penthouse and chose the high stakes poker room instead.

There were already two players at the table Jamal chose. They were playing Texas Hold 'Em. He sat down and offered the attractive brunette dealer a smile. "Deal me in, next hand, please."

The balding gray-haired player at the table owned a fleet of crab boats in Alaska, while the other, a thirty-year-old with a dark beard, mustache, and ponytail, was a screenwriter from Hollywood. Jamal was dealt his two-hole cards. He studied them and then watched the reveal of the five cards turned over, one by one, skillfully by the dealer.

When the hand of cards were all exposed, Jamal bet a hundred thousand dollars on his hand. The crab fisherman folded. The screenwriter stayed. His three jacks won. His yelp at winning brought the curious to surround the table. The crowd grew as Jamal bet two hundred thousand on the next hand. He lost again. This time to the crab fisherman's two pair. An attractive, busty server arrived at the table. Actually, sent by the card room manager. She asked all if they would like a drink.

Jamal ordered a Red Bull vodka. "And I'd like you to stop by the Sports Book," he added. "Tell them I'd like you to bet half a mill on whatever team, you pick, scoring a run in the next ten minutes."

The server went away excited. The crowd around the table grew buzzing with speculation and awe. Jamal won the next hand of Hold 'Em. He pulled the winnings in front of him. The dealer smiled and dealt another hand. The server returned. She pushed through the crowd around the table to Jamal's shoulder. "We won! I mean, you won." She was trembling with excitement. "A million freaking dollars!"

"Where's my drink?" Jamal questioned soberly.

"Oh," the young server said as she turned, disappearing into the crush around the table.

———

GREG LARSON HAD one thing more important to him than the two percent revenue loss or the high stakes Texas Hold 'Em drawing a crowd in the card room and that was his daughter Tammy. He was in his Maserati trying to keep it at the posted speed limit as he sped toward the Out of The Shadows Rehab Ranch in Boulder. He hadn't called to set an appointment. They could stuff appointments. He was paying them. He was betting a surprise would be more impressive to Tammy. He hoped, although he had little idea what he would say that would make her welcome him. Maybe this Jesus thing she was into would help. He knew he couldn't tell her about his spending the night with her mother. He'd leave that to Naomi. Today was about father and daughter. Screw what the words might be. What was more important was the fact he loved her, meth, Jesus and all.

Larson's polished Maserati drew attention as he parked amid the dusty SUVs, pickups, and aging sedans.

Josh Logan, dressed in faded jeans and cowboy boots, met Larson on the front porch of the ranch house at the rehab facility.

"I'd like to see my daughter, Tammy," Larson said as he met Logan on the steps.

"I'd like that too," Logan answered, "but Tammy's been missing since roll call this morning."

"What! Why the hell haven't you called me? Where did she go?"

"Your daughter's eighteen years old, Mr. Larson. No one's a prisoner here. I just got off the phone with your wife."

"Jesus Christ," Larson complained. "We're paying you to baby set our daughter and you fuck it up. What are you doing to find her?"

"I might ask you the same," Josh answered. "As to what we're doing. We're praying for her safe return."

"Bullshit!" Larson complained, turning away. He was back in his Maserati headed for the interstate when he dialed Naomi. "I just talked with Josh Logan. He said he called you. What the hell's going on."

"I was going to call you, but I didn't want you troubled at work," Naomi explained emotionally. "Josh said Tammy left a note. She went looking for a friend, a girl with bad withdrawals. He was hoping they'll both come back."

"Oh, that'll work. Why didn't that prick tell me that. Have you tried calling her cell."

"At least a half dozen times. It rings. She can see who's calling. She won't answer. At least she's missing because she's trying to help someone. Josh is praying, hoping they'll both return."

"Good for him. We've been down this path before, Naomi. Last time we hoped, we found her near death in an ER."

"Greg, hope is all we have."

"I have to get back to the casino. Promise you'll call me if you hear anything."

"Of course," Naomi answered, then apprehensively, she asked, "Will I see you tonight?"

The line was quiet for an awkward moment before Larson spoke. "We've got a high roller in house. Son of an oil baron. It may be late."

"That wouldn't be a first," Naomi answered, trying to be lighthearted. "Time is on our side, Greg."

"But you'll call if you hear anything."

"I promise."

———

LUKE MITCHEL HAD BEEN GONE for less than seventy-two hours but speed, time and walking on foreign soil made his return to the Silver Palace feel surreal.

"Got everything under control?" Luke smiled at the two uniformed officers at the employee entrance. One had just checked the briefcase of the cashier on her way out.

"How was Dubai, Chief?" the older of the two officers asked.

"They've got more desert than we have," Luke answered. "But I like ours best."

Luke headed for a back-of-the-house elevator. He found himself basking in the Vegas phenomenon of *who cares what time it is*. The chimes from the distant slots and the wide-sprawling busy kitchen filled with shouts, aromas and the clatter of pots and pans, brought him relief. He expected to find Candice in the office he now shared with her, but it was empty. There was evidence she had been there.

On her new desk, in addition to a computer, monitor, desk lamp and a variety of reports and printouts, was a paper cup with a lipstick stain, and the air had the faint scent of Oscar de la Renta. Again, it was comforting. He was home. He smiled, thinking he now had the challenge of deciding which woman smelled best, Candice or Kim, the flight captain. Luke turned to the door. He knew where Candice would be.

The surveillance supervisor's office was crowded. All three monitors on Gayle Turner's desk were focused on the high stakes poker room where Jamal sat playing Texas Hold 'Em. The crowd around Jamal had grown to a thick half-circle. So had the pile of cash in front of him. Candice was in a chair beside Gayle watching. Standing behind the two were surveillance agents, Nancy Rollins and Calib Jacobs. Frick and Fratt, the young Oriental duo, who surveillance relied on for, *don't ask, don't tell*, undercover work, were on either side.

The six, much like the crowd they watched, were mesmerized by Jamal's betting. Luke opened the door and stepped in. "Do I need a ticket?" he questioned, looking at the collection of faces.

"Welcome home." Candice smiled.

Calib and Nancy took the cue from Luke's look and

moved for the glass door leading into the array of wide multiple video screens. Frick and Frat offered Luke a smile and headed for their *cave*, which was an enlarged closet full of electronics at the rear of the surveillance complex.

"Here, take mine," Candice said, getting up, offering Luke her chair.

"No, no, stay," Luke declined. "I've sat through too many time zones."

"We're watching the package you brought us," Gayle said. "He beat you here from the airport. He's playing Hold 'Em. He's won the last four hands and that's not counting the mill he got from a server making him a bet at Sports Book."

Luke studied at the monitors. "He's got deep pockets. He stays in long enough the odds will shift to our favor."

"How was the Silver Bullet?" Candice questioned. "We noticed Jamal arrived with three young lovelies."

"Jamal was quiet. I didn't get their names."

The telephone on Gayle's desk rang. She picked it up. "Surveillance, Turner." She listened for a moment then said, "Got it, thanks." She hung up and looked to Luke and Candice. "That was Tom Roberts from the card room. Jamal just bought everyone in the crowd a drink. I could hear their cheers."

"That'll add to the crowd size," Luke suggested.

———

GREG LARSON WAS BACK in his office. He was watching the action in the card room on a large flat-screen on the wall of his office as three scantily clad servers brought trays crowded with drinks and began passing them out to the smiling crowd. Jamal looked to the crush of admirers as he raised his glass. There was no audio with the on-screen images, but Larson knew they were cheering. Jackie, his executive assistant, was at his side.

Larson shook his head and looked to her. "Get me the card room manager and the MOD."

The GM left the flat-screen image play as he returned to his desk. It wasn't long before Jackie appeared in the open door of his office. "They're here."

"Send them in."

Charles Roberts and Jack Lester entered the office as if they were both walking on ice.

"Sit down, guys. Who's the guest relations officer assigned to Jamal?"

Lester chose to answer. As the on-duty MOD, he was responsible for the moment. "That would be Shirl Conners."

"Get her up here," Larson ordered.

Lester pulled out his cell and dialed. "Shirl, come up to the GM's office. Yes, right now."

The three waited. Larson's fingers drummed the glass on the top of his desk. They sat silent until Jackie escorted the guest relations officer into the room. She was an attractive thirty-two-year-old blonde dressed in heels and a form-fitting gray suit.

Tom Roberts offered his chair to the girl.

"It's all right, I'll stand."

Roberts accepted and sank into his chair.

Larson studied the blonde for a moment before speaking. "How long have you been in guest relations?"

"Almost three years," the blonde answered, showing no anxiety.

"Three years. Then you know our protocols and practices regarding VIPs and our card room. Today, you ignored your experience and allowed the circus going on in the card room to become a real issue. You could have asked for help. Why did you permit a crowd of onlookers in the card room? And worse than that, you permitted him to buy drinks that would incite everyone, but worst of all, why did you allow a server to make a bet for him in Sportsbook? That's not only a policy violation, it's a crime. Do you have any idea what you cost the casino today?"

"I simply don't care," the blonde answered defiantly. "Jamal hired me as his cultural assistant. I'll earn three times what you pay me, and I'll no longer have to answer questions about my bra size or the color of my panties. I'm done, I quit. Bet on that." The blonde turned and marched out.

The three men were speechless.

TEN
COME ONE, COME ALL

IT HAD BEEN A WHILE, but Tammy knew from talking to Janice, before the girl fled from rehab, that they both frequented the same meth dealers. At first it just gave the two girls a common denominator, a bridge to build friendship on, something to talk about, and then Janice was discovered missing at lights out. Tammy worried about her all night. Janice had used longer, heavier, and Tammy knew if she didn't find her, the County Coroner would. Tammy got up before daylight, wrote a note, and walked away.

Tammy was twenty-six miles from Vegas, but it only took one truck driver to fill the gap. The trucker was only six years older than she was. They talked about TV, movies, dope, Jesus and parents before Tammy was dropped where Boulder Highway ended at Fremont Street. The trucker was on his way to the Hard Rock with a couple hundred thousand dollars' worth of whiskey. Tammy's cell phone had kept vibrating. She recognized the callers. Five from her mother. Two from her father and three for the ranch. She finally turned her phone off. They could all wait. Tammy was pleased. She was only five blocks from a meth dealer she and Janice had bragged about.

Walking the streets, past cheap motels, a liquor store where two homeless shared a bottle, and a used furniture store with a large dog barking inside its front door, made Tammy feel free. The fact she was running from rehab, even if it was to find a friend, another addict, made the streets comfortable. Plus, she felt she wasn't alone. Jesus was with her. He cared about Jan, too. Tammy enjoyed a flirtatious look from an older man who passed in the opposite direction.

She knew she was walking in the right direction when a young Black man leaning on a car at the curb questioned her. "You looking for something, girl?"

"Yeah, the corner of Meth and Meth."

"How about a little blow? Save you some money."

Tammy smiled, shook her head. "No thanks, color me boring." She kept walking.

"Turn left next corner. Half a block down," the Black voice called. "Tell Wanda James says hello."

Tammy raised a hand and waved it in appreciation.

———

PACING in his office at the Silver Palace, Greg Larson glared at his cell phone. All he was getting from calls to his daughter was *the voice mail box for the number you called is full and can no longer accept calls.* Larson concluded Tammy's claim that she was now following Jesus hadn't improved her manners. He pushed the cell back in a jacket pocket, and although weary of watching the flat-screen tv, he went back to the image of Jamal Hassan playing Texas Hold 'Em. The kid kept winning.

He had already bought the blonde from guest relations, and he tipped the server who made the Sports Book bet for him a hundred grand. The house was down five mil with the Sports Book factored in. Larson had an idea. He didn't like it, but he didn't like how Jamal and his crowd of curious were turning the card room into an amusement park, either. He knew the house would get him, but for now, the circus had to end.

"Jackie," Larson shouted at his open office door. "Get Tom Roberts and Lester up here."

"Yes, sir, and sir, Luke Mitchel is here."

"About time he showed up," Larson growled. It was a tease. He knew Luke would hear him.

"Sonofabich," he growled, glancing at Jamal raising his hands in victory again.

"You know," Luke said, entering the office. "Cursing is prohibited in Dubai."

Larson looked to Luke. "This isn't Dubai. It's Vegas." He studied Luke for a moment. "What's with this five o'clock shadow thing?"

Luke sat down in one of the chairs in front of Larson's desk. "You ever tried an electric razor on an airplane?"

Larson returned to the chair behind his desk. "You were supposed to bring our Arab friend here so we could make money."

"He's on a streak," Tom Roberts, the card room manager, said, leading Jack Lester, the MOD, into the office.

"Just wanted to check in," Luke said, pushing out of his chair.

"Stay, you need to be in the loop on this." Larson looked to the two men from the card room. "Don't bother sitting down, gentlemen. This won't take long. I got a call from the manager at Mandalay. He'd like Jamal to come over for dinner in the Foundation Room, sixty-three floors above the Strip. He'll have a terrific view of the Silver Palace from there. Tom, you whisper it in Jamal's ear. He'll like the idea. Use our limo."

Roberts nodded agreement.

"Lester," Larson continued, "as soon as Jamal's gone, get the spectators the fuck out of our card room. We're not the poker channel. And when he's back, no spectators. Don't let it happen again, maybe, unless he invites them in. Got it?"

"Got it," Lester assured.

"Here's the biggy, and I'm talking tits. This is Vegas, where people pay to see tits.

"We're going to show Jamal a set of tits that will make him feel like a twelve-year-old looking at porn on the net. I want them young, firm, and in a lace bra beneath a white blouse that's as thin as his imagination. In addition to tits, I want blonde hair, blue eyes and a Viagra smile, and I want all this sitting across from Jamal, the next time he sits down to play Hold 'Em."

"That's Penny Nichols on AMs," Tom Roberts answered without hesitation. "She deals Twenty-One, but she can deal anything. I put her on AMs because she won't hide her nipples. In addition to a great set, she's got a smile to go with them. She's hard to ignore, if you know what I mean."

"Call her," Larson urged. "She's now a Floater. Give her a room. She's on call. All overtime. Next time Jamal sits down in our card room she's across from him. Go make it happen. His dinner is getting cold at Mandalay."

"I'm on it," Roberts answered, moving for the door. Lester followed him. Luke looked to Larson with a smile when the two men were gone. "Penny Nichols? She sounds like a good bet."

"Don't you have some kind of an emergency to take care of," Larson said to Luke as he picked up his telephone. "And while you're doing that, shave. Bill," Larson said into his phone, "Listen, I'm sending over Jamal Hassan. Yeah, that guy. We told him you invited him to the Foundation Room for lunch. Why? Because you owe me. Remember that suite you wanted for your mother-in-law?

"Yeah, well, call it, payback. He'll be there within the hour. And, of course, I appreciate you thinking of this."

Larson hung up and returned his attention to Luke, who smiled and pushed out of his chair. "Right, I'll go shave."

"Why haven't you told me about Penny Marshal?"

Luke was moving for the door. "I don't ask about who you date, so guess what?"

Luke asked for and got a room. He knew with Jamal in-house, his phone would be ringing. The Silver Palace was at eighty percent occupancy with an expected sell-out for the upcoming weekend. As a result, the room Luke got was on the eighth floor. It had two twin beds and a view of the kitchen's large exhaust blowers. Housekeeping was kind in providing him a razor, shaving cream, and a toothbrush. Luke tossed his jacket, took off his holstered Beretta APX Compact pistol with its fifteen-round spare magazine, sat on a bed, pushed off his shoes and ordered a hamburger with onions and an order of fries. He was told there would be a delay because they were busy.

A black tee shirt was added to the pile on the bed, and Luke headed for the small bathroom to shave. He was shirtless and half-shaven when a knock sounded at his door.

"Come in," Luke shouted from the open bathroom.

Luke expected the knock was an announcement that his room service order had arrived. He was surprised when Candice appeared in the open bathroom door. Shirtless, with half his face and neck covered with shaving cream, he glanced at her. "You don't have a hamburger on you, do you?"

Candice leaned on the open doorframe and studied Luke. "I'm staying in too. My room's a queen on the eighteenth. Much nicer than this."

"I got here late," Luke answered, rushing his shave.

Candice seemed in no rush to move from the doorway. "You know, I can't remember the last time I saw a man shave."

"Might be because most of us do it in private."

"I think you missed a spot right here," Candice said, pointing to a spot on her own cheek.

———

AT MANDALAY BAY'S Foundation dining room, sixty-three floors above the Strip with its unparalleled view of the evening lights, twenty-nine-year-old Jamal Hassan was making a lasting impression on those dining around him. The three girls he brought from Dubai had never been to Vegas, but he now had Shirl Conners, his new blonde, shapely cultural adviser who knew the town well. Shirl was no longer dressed in her conservative guest relations wardrobe. Now she wore a low cut, form-fitting, head-turning, short blue dress bought by Jamal at the Silver Palace's sheek She-On dress shop for eight hundred dollars. They had enjoyed an impressive lobster dinner and as dessert was served, Jamal instructed Shirl to tell their waiter he would be picking up the tab for the six tables full of diners surrounding theirs. That was after telling the surprised young waiter he would be receiving a thousand-dollar gratuity.

"I don't like being alone during the night," Jamal told Shirl. "Would it be rude to tell these folks they're invited to a party in the Eagle's Nest at the Silver Palace?"

Rude or not, Shirl made the rounds of the tables. Sixteen people accepted. Only a couple in their sixties declined, but they, like many of the others, came to the table to thank Jamal. The manager, alerted to the plan, ordered a small bus. An extremely comfortable one with its own bar and bartender. The Plush bus driver, at Jamal's urging, provided a tour of the night time Strip. A call from Mandalay to the Silver Palace alerted them the bus was on its way.

TAMMY LARSON WAS among those in Las Vegas who didn't like the darkness. The lights of the city lit the night sky but the street Tammy was on had few. She was only five blocks off Frontier Street, but the distance had to be measured more economically than by city blocks. She had walked most of the day. She found three meth dealers. None were impressed that she was in rehab or that she had found Jesus. One dealer told her Jesus had His own casino. He suggested she look there for her friend. The last meth dealer she talked to, a skinny man with too much ink, who did business from his aging van, offered Tammy a sniff to promote his stash. At first she declined and walked away. She was hungry, tired and worried. All the shit feelings she had when she didn't use.

Tammy turned around and went back to the skinny man with the ink. "Okay, sign me up for the freebie."

The man smiled and prepared a smeg of white powder on a cigarette paper inside the open door of his van. "You gotta do it inside, girl," the Ink said as he pushed the van door wide. He offered the paper to Tammy. She climbed into the van and accepted the paper. She took a deep breath and then sucked the powder up her right nostril. A flush of warmth traveled from her face to her feet. She raised a hand and looked at it. It looked far away. A stiff arm pushed her further back into the van. She heard the van down close and then someone was pulling at her clothes. A roaring buzz filled her ears.

———

CANDICE SAT in the cushioned chair in Luke's room. He sat on one of the beds to eat his hamburger. Candice accepted an offer to share french fries. They both picked a canned Diet Coke from the small fridge in the room and talked shop. It was really a way for Luke to judge how Candice was doing in her new position.

"Fill in the blanks for me while I was partying in Dubai."

"Engineering found human waste in our new roof top pool," Candice answered.

"Come on." Luke grimaced. "I'm eating my burger."

"You asked." Candice continued. "Two slip and falls. One in a guest tub. No merit to it. They wanted a free room. We gave it to them. The one at the pool. Kid spilled his iced drink. Dad slipped on it, went down. Broke his elbow. I showed them our video of it. No liability on us. We comped their room. Kitchen helper suffered a burn from a spill of boiling water. Got his legs and feet. He'll be off for a couple weeks. His fault. Guest was found carrying a small, secreted TV from the bathroom of their suite. Security at the rear guest entrance caught it. TV recovered. Couple was banned. And KC King caught one of his own smoking a joint out on the receiving dock with a housekeeper. Both suspended, referred to HR. I was late for the GM's Staff meeting. Jackie called me. Told me to get up there. Engineering had a beef about some missing brass. Surveillance saved it. No theft. Supplier shorted them. The biggy was the car clot haunting guest parking. Gayle and I produced a plan to bait him with property from Lost and Found in one of our company cars. It worked. Young server. He's gone. Video is waiting on your computer, and I did an electronic sweep of the GM's office with Frick and Fratt."

"You were busy," Luke suggested, taking a last bite of his burger. He was pleased with Candice's summary as well as her poise.

"There is more," Candice said. "GM called me to his office. I wish I had made notes."

"Forget notes. Use the small recorder. It's in the bottom right drawer in the office. What did the GM want?"

"He wants us to plug a hole in the Titanic. He claims we're losing twelve grand a day. That's eighty-plus a week. He claims he did the math and there's a two percent loss in revenues, and he wants it fixed."

"The GM does rely on the math. Did he give any specific examples?"

"No, just a *get out of my office and go fix it.*"

"Got a plan?" Luke questioned.

"Thought I'd attend roll call briefings around the clock," Candice suggested. "Put the troops in the loop. More body searches out back. Get housekeeping to get better at reporting losses. Towels, rugs, clocks. Anything a guest might carry away."

"Do it," Luke agreed. "The losses the GM is talking about don't all belong to us, but we've got to CYA. Let's talk about our VIP plan. While Jamal is in house, I'm going to call this home. How about you and I doing twelve and twelve? You do eight a.m. to eight p.m., and I'll cover dark thirty."

"You got the best part."

"That's because I'm the boss."

————

THE VIP PLUSH BUS, with its Twenty-One passengers and a bartender, made its way up one side of the nighttime Strip and down the other. The ride presented an up close and personal look at what made the Strip famous as well as providing time for the bartender to serve all aboard. The bus finally arrived at the front entrance to the Silver Palace. They arrived an hour ahead of Lady Luck's evening performance. Jamal had VIP seating for the show, but he had his Cultural Aid invite all to join him after Luck's show for his *Hello Vegas* party to be held atop the Palace in the Eagle's Nest. Shouts of approval and applause followed.

————

IN THE QUIET of the Silver Palace's surveillance unit, Luke, Candice and Gayle Turner were crowded around Gayle's desk with its three monitors, watching the excited guests scramble off the bus and head inside.

"It's going to be a long night," Luke suggested.

———

TAMMY LARSON WAS AWAKENED when she was pushed out of the van onto the sidewalk. Everything was spinning. She felt nauseous. She propped herself up into a sitting position.

"Cover yourself, girl," an older woman snapped, walking by with her dog. The dog pulled on its leash, trying to reach Tammy.

Tammy realized she could feel her bare buttocks on the cement walk. She noticed her panties were pushed down. They were torn and stained. She reached and pulled her jeans up from her knees with effort. Trying to stand, she realized her blouse had been unbuttoned. Her wrinkled bra was pushed beneath a breast. On her feet, Tammy began to feel the pain between her legs. The pain was deep inside her. She swayed, trying to balance, squinting to see where she was.

Tammy, staggering to the wall of a closed tire shop, brushed at her buttocks to push away dirt from the sidewalk. She found her cell phone was still in a back pocket.

"Jesus, help me," she cried.

Cars sweep by on the street. A middle-aged couple hurried by, giving her an annoyed look.

"Please, Jesus, please," Tammy mumbled. Her hands shook as she tried to see the numbers on her cell phone.

———

Thirteen miles away in the foothills of Red Rock Canyon in the gated community of the Valley of the Sun, forty-eight-year-old Naomi Larson sat with her still legally estranged husband, Greg, the GM of the Silver Palace. Together, they sat on patio recliners outside their twenty-nine million dollar, five-bedroom home setting on a fully landscaped acre. The gates for the neighborhood kept away lessors but not the pain and anguish for the parents of a missing eighteen-year-old daughter who was also a meth addict recently arrested for prostitution and currently missing from rehab after several near-death overdoses.

Naomi and Larson sat looking at the spread of the distant lights of Las Vegas reaching far into the desert night. The big Rottweiler lay between them. Larson's jacket hung on the back of his chair. His tie was loose. Naomi was again wrapped in a robe. The hour was late. The five-bedroom house behind them no longer seemed like a home. Part of it was missing.

"When I left the casino, I drove down to Fremont," Larson said to the darkness. "I didn't know where to look, but I had to look. Vegas has been home for a long time, but there's a city out there I'd forgotten about, and somewhere in that city is our daughter."

"God, I hope she's all right. I called all her friends," Naomi added, pausing as she reached across and took her husband's hand in hers. "Greg, we did this. We gave Tammy everything but our hearts."

"I wanted success. I chased it, found it, only to find I had abandoned what was really important," Larson said, squeezing his wife's hand.

Naomi made no effort to wipe away the tear tracing down her cheek. The darkness didn't erase her anguish, but it hid her sorrow.

———

LADY LUCK'S show was a sell-out, and as the big crowd spilled out into the casino, the elevators quickly filled with those invited to the Eagle's Nest, the palatial penthouse on the Silver Palace's seventy-third floor. Jamal Hassan, the twenty-eight-year-old son of the Oil Barron of the Mid-East, one of the world's richest men in the world, was its current occupant. Jamal invited more people into the car adding to those already crowding around him. They pushed and shoved onto the private elevator reserved for the penthouse.

"We'll be back to get you," Jamal shouted to those left behind.

Uniformed watch commander KC King stood soberly watching the excited faces crowd onto the elevators. Lola Martinez, his assistant, stood at his shoulder.

"See any familiar faces?" KC asked, studying the crowd.

"One. six-forty-seven-f. Blonde, thirty-something. Sandy Walls. We put her off for soliciting around the bar in the card room. Two or three weeks ago. Tonight, she came in with an older guy, along with the gang from Mandalay. Bet on a date for hire. The average in there tonight must be thirty at the most," Lola Martinez suggested. "Sex, drugs and rock and roll."

———

THREE FLOORS ABOVE, Luke Mitchel sat beside Gayle Turner in the surveillance supervisor's office. The three monitors on Gayle's desk showed different images of the elevators and those awaiting the private car for the penthouse.

"Party before cards?" Gayle questioned.

"Remember, last time Jamal was here, he only played during the day. Nights were reserved for partying. House will make a buck or two with the crowd in the penthouse. They won't be drinking Dr Pepper."

"Or smoking Newports." Gayle smiled in agreement.

———

GUEST SERVICES HAD ARRANGED for a trio to provide music for the party. A twenty-year-old bottle of Santory was sent by the GM along with three trays of snacks and finger foods courtesy of Chef LeBlanc. The party got loud when Jamal turned shot drinking into serious betting. The twelve-foot high ceilings were clouding with a marijuana haze.

Room service delivered more alcohol along with anything and everything found on the room service menus. The private penthouse elevator continued making runs to the casino floor to pick up those waiting. The number in the penthouse grew to over thirty. It was noisy and loud, and in the center of it, smoking a joint with a glass of Suntory in hand, Jamal Hassan cheered on a shapely thirty-year-old,

"Take it off," Jamal shouted.

Cheers followed.

"I'll give you a thousand for that blouse," he added.

More cheers followed.

"Come on, take it off."

Luke grew weary of watching the surveillance images of the doors to the penthouse, the carpeted hallway and the smiling faces on the private elevator. Although, the image of a couple turning a kiss in the hallway into a passion, usually reserved for privacy, resulted in security being alerted. KC responded and quickly led them away. Leaving surveillance, Luke made the rounds of the card room. There always was a surge after a show, and Lady Luck was proving her worth. Twenty-One, Keno, Pai Gow, Craps and Poker were all busy, but with Tom Charles on the Managers Podium and two other managers moving from one game table to another, all was under control. Luke went from the noisy slots and the busy card room to the back of the house's noisier kitchen. The surge from the showroom was not only eager to gamble, they were hungry. Tall white chef hats, aprons and stained uniformed shirts all worked at the spread of busy grills and ovens. The clatter of pots and pans and shouted commands amazed Luke. Out of what seemed to be chaos came a variety of the Strip's finest foods. The Silver Palace's seven crowded restaurants, all with waiting lines, coupled with orders coming from over the thousands of rooms, proved the kitchen got it right.

After the card room and kitchen, Luke checked in with housekeeping, engineering and the cash cage. Every busy area of the casino had attentive, uniformed security officers. Luke found the officers comforting.

He noted visitors and guests simply didn't see the security officers. That was a good thing.

It was fourteen minutes past two a.m. and in the Eagle's Nest, the Silver Palace's premier penthouse, thirty-three invited guests, along with four members of Jamal's personal staff, were doing their best to make the night memorable. Jessie Kingsley, a thirty-two-year-old from Hunting Beach, was intoxicated. Drugs and alcohol. He and his wife Karen, whom he hadn't seen in an hour, were among those invited from Mandalay Bay's Foundation Restaurant.

Jessie was on an urgent search, but it wasn't for his wife, it was for a bathroom. The Eagles Nest had five, and Jessie, desperate to find one, found all five, and all were occupied. Nature gave Jessie little choice. He found a curtained door leading onto a balcony. Holding his crotch Jessie went onto the balcony, closed the door and urinated into a planted green pot. The night air was comforting, and as Jessie urinated on the plant, he looked at the view of the Strip stretching in front of him. Sounds from the street below reached up to him. It was quiet compared to the noise inside the penthouse. Jessie smiled, he was pissing on Vegas.

When done relieving himself, Jessie found he had urinated on one of his one hundred and seventy-six dollar Sketchers. His smile turned to anger. He looked at the green bush standing in the pot he had targeted. It was rimmed with urine and leaking from the bottom onto the floor of the balcony. Jessie growled and picked up the potted plant. Urine spilled onto his hands. He grunted and tossed the heavy planted pot over the rail of the balcony. It plummeted away into the darkness.

The urine-soaked potted plant fell fourteen stories from the seventy-third-floor balcony before it reached its *terminal velocity*, which in the dry desert air, was one hundred and twenty-eight miles an hour. It took only twelve seconds for the potted plant to smash onto the pavement, inches in front of a young, newly married couple from Mount Union, Pennsylvania. The impact sounded like cannon fire. It rattled windows and sent screams into the night. Sharp glass fragments from the shattered pot flew like bullets, denting into passing cars, breaking windows and flattening tires.

Martin Walters, the new groom, was hit in the face, hands and arms by chunks of flying glass. His wife Joan, struck in the hands and face, spit pieces of glass from her bloody mouth as she sank to her knees in shock. She screamed when she saw her husband stretched on the pavement with blood pooling around his head.

ELEVEN
BLOOD & MONEY

LUKE WALKED CASUALLY down the buffet line in employee dining, trying to decide if he was hungry or not. A heavy thud shook the wide dining room, startling Luke. He paused, listened. So did the near two hundred employees scattered at tables across the room. The compact radio on Luke's belt beneath his jacket brought a quick answer. "Explosion, front entrance," a female security officer's excited voice blurted. Luke bolted for the stairs at the back of the room.

KC King and three other officers were at the scene when Luke arrived at the front of the Silver Palace. He saw the man lying on the cement walkway. Blood pooled around his head. A hysterical woman was kneeling beside the man. She shook him, screamed and called his name. Blood dripped from her chin. KC King took the woman by the shoulders and pulled her away.

"Did you call nine-one-one?" Luke yelled to KC.

"Yeah, asked for two ambulances," KC answered, handing the hysterical woman to a floor manager from the casino. Luke went to the fallen man and kneeled beside him. Three more officers arrived on scene.

"Get everyone back," Luke ordered. "Put up some tape."

A car alarm filled the night with constant beeping from an SUV with a flattened tire and broken window. A taxi behind the SUV had a chunk of the broken pottery sticking in its indented front door. The couple in the cab had cell phones out, shooting pictures. Traffic on the Strip came to a halt in both directions. People climbed out of their cars, looking, pointing their cells for pictures. The sidewalk in both directions filled with shoulder to shoulder curious.

Sirens yelped in the distance. An ambulance snaked its way through the tangle of stalled traffic. Lights flashing, it drove on the sidewalk the final half block to reach Luke, KC and the fallen man. Close behind the ambulance came a fire truck, air horn and siren blasting as it drove down the center divider to reach the scene. Helmeted firemen scrambled off the big truck to hurry to the aid of the paramedics.

"I want pictures," Luke ordered with a look at a Black female officer. "Pictures of everything. You can't take too many."

The officer pulled out her cell phone and began the task as the sirens from another ambulance reached them. Chaos yielded to training and experience as security officers pushed the growing crowd of curious away, as wide orange vinyl tape with the warning, *Do Not Cross,* was stretched to keep them back. Two Metro PD Police Officers in yellow safety jackets arrived by bicycle. They were part of a team assigned to the Strip. The bicycle officers were quickly followed by a police car with two more uniformed police officers. They parked on the sidewalk and scrambled out.

Metro PD officers quickly assumed command, assisting the paramedics and firefighters as the unconscious young man was lifted by stretcher into an ambulance. His bride, still hysterical, was escorted to a second ambulance. Then, the officers began examining damaged vehicles, requesting ID from witnesses and victims.

Luke saw the blood-stained victims with cuts and clothes covered with shards of glass and plant shreds. The damaged vehicles and shattered pieces of pottery assured him they weren't dealing with a bomb. He looked up at the towering facade of the Silver Palace. He knew the balconies above him were all decorated with live potted plants. It was not a good conclusion. Another police car arrived. This one driven by a sergeant. The police were getting traffic on the Strip moving. One of the officers showed the sergeant the bloodstains on the sidewalk. Another officer pulled a piece of pottery from an indent on an SUV with a broken window. Luke knew the police would soon ask questions. Questions he had no answers for. He moved to KC King and said, "The Metro cops own the street. Let's get inside before they do."

"You thinking what I'm thinking?" KC asked.

Luke nodded agreement. "Yeah," Luke granted him. "Leave a couple officers out here to help. Tell them to get rid of the blood on the sidewalk as soon as Metro allows. Bloods not good for business. I'll meet you at the elevator."

"We going up to the Nest."

"Somebody pushed more than bird shit off a balcony."

Luke, KC, and two security officers rode the private

elevator to the Eagle's Nest penthouse. Music and laughter coming from the Eagle's Nest was loud when they stepped off the elevator onto the carpeted hallway on the seventy-third floor. Luke keyed his radio as they walked to the tall, ornate double doors of the suite.

"Surveillance, this is Gate Keeper Ten, get us images of everyone coming out of the Nest, and get us anything you can on what happened up front. Copy."

"Copy, Ten," Gayle Turner's filtered radio voice answered.

Luke clipped the radio on his belt and looked to KC King. "Do it."

KC exchanged a look with the two officers standing behind them. Then, with an open hand, he pounded hard on the ornate double wooden doors of the Eagle's Nest. The music, laughter and voices continued inside. The four men waited.

"Again," Luke urged with a glance at KC.

KC ponded harder a second time. Again, there was no response from inside. KC looked to Luke for direction.

Luke nodded. "Okay, open it."

KC King and Luke both stepped aside. KC looked to the two uniformed officers. "Go for it."

The two officers exchanged a look, took a breath, and shoulders down, charged the door. The crack from the wide double wooden doors was loud as splinters and hardware flew. The two doors exploded inward. Screams and shouts filled the air as the music stopped.

SIX POINT eight miles from the Silver Palace and seven blocks from the lights of Fremont Street, Tammy Larson sat on the cement in the doorway of a closed Walgreens

Pharmacy. She had no idea how long she had been there. She knew she slept after walking. Afraid the man in the van might return, she made herself walk until she collapsed. Tammy couldn't remember falling asleep. Was it sleep when you couldn't remember it? God was punishing her. She had willingly accepted the man's offer to try what looked like crystal meth. She was back to being what she once was. A desperate addict, a whore, alone on a street she didn't know the name of. She was alone, Godless, frightened and in pain. She reached for the stinging sensation in her crouch and found her jeans were wet. Tears welled in her eyes. She had peed herself. Occasionally, a car swept by. Then, a noisy diesel bus filled with seniors. Tammy thought about dying. Death would solve all her problems. Her parents would mourn, for a while. Her friends had forsaken her, or had she forsaken them? It didn't matter. She was told she had a friend named Jesus. Where was He? She couldn't blame Him. She was the one sucking dope up her nose.

"Oh, Jesus," Tammy cried, covering her face with her hands and then the cell phone she had pushed into a pocket gave its distinct doorbell chime. It rang a second time as she reached and grabbed it. "Hello."

"Tammy, it's Josh. Where are you? We're worried."

Tammy sniffed, wiped away tears. "I don't know," she sobbed. "There's a sign that says Walgreens."

"Does the sign have a number under it?" Josh questioned.

Tammy twisted and looked at the illuminated glass door. She read the numbers aloud, "One-four-five-six,"

"Do you know the name of the street?" Josh asked.

"No," Tammy sobbed. "I'm scared."

"You have a friend with you. You know that's true. Talk to Him until we get there."

"Please hurry," Tammy cried into the cell.

"We're on our way. Don't move. Stay right there. Promise."

"I promise," Tammy cried, and the phone went quiet.

Tossing his cell phone aside, Josh Logan went to Google on the laptop in his lap. He quickly had a list of street addresses for every Walgreens store in Las Vegas. "Got it," he said aloud, reaching to a lamp on a bedside table. His wife Crystal, lying beside him, stirred and sat up.

"Found her," Josh said excitedly, pushing the laptop aside to grab at the cell phone on the sheets.

Clark Nelson, Tammy's counselor from the Out of the Shadows Rehabilitation Ranch near Boulder, was with Karen Jacobs, a fellow counselor, lover, and friend. The couple had been driving the neighborhoods Tammy talked about when describing her addiction. They had been driving, looking, searching for three hours. They were in a Del Taco when Josh called them. "We're only a couple blocks away," Clark said excitedly.

———

GREG LARSON SAT on the king-size bed with pillows stuffed behind him watching a report on CNN about yet another hurricane forming in the gulf and expected to reach Florida within days. There were people with greater problems than his, Larson decided. Ironically, the images from the TV made him think of the storm that tore his family apart. Was it worse, more painful to lose your family or lose your home? He came close to losing both. He reached and patted the big Rottweiler lying between him and his sleeping wife, Naomi. He decided the storm that took Tammy away was worse than the one threatening Florida. Those in Florida could run or get ready for the storm while Tammy, a runaway missing in the night, haunted by addiction, left him and his wife, feeling powerless, worried and frightened. He and Naomi had talked about going in search of their daughter, but they had no idea where to start or where to look. He had called time and time again with no answer.

Accepting there was a void, a gap, a crevasse between them, Larson looked from the TV illuminating the bedroom to the ceiling. *God*, he said silently, *I'll do anything, give anything, go anywhere, if you'll just bring her home.*

Larson had no sooner finished his silent prayer when the bedside telephone rang. It was on Naomi's side of the bed. Larson reached across her and picked up the receiver. "Hello."

"Boss," Luke Mitchel's voice said in his ear. "There's been an incident with Jamal Hassan. The police are here. A guest at a party in the Nest tossed a potted plant off the balcony. There were injuries."

"Jesus," Larson growled.

"Greg," Naomi questioned, pushed up, looking alarmed, stretching the coiled cord pulled across her. "Who is it?"

"It's okay. It's work," Larson said to Naomi.

Luke, hearing Naomi's voice, and recognizing it, was surprised. He knew the two had been locked in a bitter divorce for months. He knew, well at least, he thought he knew. Greg Larson was sharing a condo with Charlotte Johnson, the Black beauty and former HR director for the Silver Palace. She was now the rooms director at the Cosmopolitan. She had tempted Luke with an offer to become the director of risk management at the Cosmo.

He had seen her a number of times at the condo she shared with Larson. Luke thought he knew the man, thought they were friends, close friends. Naomi's voice in the background, which he was certain sounded as if she were just awakened, was changing everything, most importantly, his trust.

"Okay, Luke. I'll be in," Larson said, deliberately wanting the exchange short. He handed the receiver to his wife and rolled off the bed in search of his shoes. "Something's gone south with our high roller. I've got to go in."

Naomi sat the telephone receiver back in its cradle. It rang instantly. Larson had moved from the bed to a chair where he worked at lacing a shoe. "Damn," he said with a look to Naomi, "tell 'em I'm on my way."

"He said to tell you he's on his way, Luke," Naomi said into the receiver.

"Miss Larson, it's Josh, from Out of the Shadows."

Naomi bolted straight in her sitting position on the bed. "Josh," she blurted. "What's wrong? Have you found her?"

Larson heard. He was quick to his wife's side.

"It's good news. We've found her. She should be here within the next twenty or thirty minutes."

"Oh, thank God," Naomi sobbed into the receiver.

"We're on our way," Larson shouted with relief. "Come on, get dressed."

———

UNIFORMED SECURITY OFFICERS had been summoned to the Eagle's Nest atop the Silver Palace to line up Jamal's guests from the penthouse to the private elevator. Jamal accepted Luke's suggestion to wait in the quiet of the suite's master bedroom. Shirl Conners, Jamal's newly hired cultural adviser, and former Silver Palace guest relations officer, was at his side.

"There's no basis for questioning Jamal," the attractive blonde cautioned before following Jamal into the master bedroom and closing the door.

Luke found the puddle on the balcony deck and a round stain where the potted plant had set. He knew one of the male guests was responsible, and there was only one way to find him. Every male had to be questioned. Luke quickly made a call to Candice. They needed help.

After his call to Candice, Luke put KC in the loop, "We've got to question every man that was in here before we allow them on the elevator. Did they take a leak on the balcony? When the answer is no, there has to be a follow-up question. Did you see anyone on the balcony?"

The arrival of the metro police sergeant, accompanied by a plain-clothed detective and the two policemen in yellow vests, changed everything. The sergeant and the detective were directed to Luke. KC moved away to allow privacy.

"You're the director of security?" the sergeant questioned.

"Luke Mitchel," Luke answered, offering the sergeant an open hand.

"Luke, this is Detective Hanson." They shook hands.

The sergeant looked around the palatial wide room, it was cluttered with cups, glasses, some empty, some not, dirty ashtrays, plates, soiled napkins, scattered pillows, a single high-heeled shoe, a hoodie, stains on the rug and a pair of men's jockey shorts. He returned his attention to Luke.

"Detective Hanson will be assuming the investigation."

Luke understood what the sergeant was saying. It was *get out of our way*.

"Valet out front said someone dropped a potted plant off a balcony," the detective added. "Fortunately, no one was killed."

"Agreed," Luke said. "Let me assure you we'll do whatever we can to support your investigation. It may be of little help, but for your comfort, I'm a refugee from Law Enforcement. The LAPD."

"LAPD," Detective Hanson said soberly. "Well, in spite of that, we may need help."

The detective's remark stiffened Luke. The sergeant and the detective both saw Luke's reaction.

"I'm just kidding," Detective Hanson smiled. "I've got a brother-in-law working Devonshire."

The door to the master bedroom opened, and the blonde Shirl Conners, dressed in a short black skirt, heels, and form-fitting blouse, stepped out and closed the door. She glanced at Luke and the police and moved for the front door of the penthouse which stood broken and open.

"Working girl?" Detective Hanson asked.

"No," Luke answered. "Cultural adviser to our VIP."

"That's the kind of culture I need," the sergeant added as they watched the blonde disappear into the hallway.

Luke led the two police officers onto the balcony, where he pointed out the wet stain on the deck and the impression the missing potted plant left on the surface. "The current tenant is Jamal Hassan," Luke explained. "He's from Dubai. Son of an oil baron. One of the richest men in the world. Jamal's in the master. He's cooperative. We've got video of everyone in and out of here tonight and maybe something from a fixed camera outside."

"You mean you may have something on who tossed the pot."

"Surveillance is looking. I'll keep you in the loop."

"We've got reckless disregard, assault with a deadly weapon," Detective Hanson speculated. "It's worse for you. The Silver Palace is sitting on a pile of shit. Even if we find the asshole who tossed the plant, those injured and those with damages aren't going after him, but they will be climbing all over your cash cage."

Luke knew the detective was right. He left KC King and two uniformed security officers outside the Eagle's Nest to answer any need for assistance. A second detective arrived, along with a photographer and a DNA specialist. Luke knew it was time to get out of their way. He briefed KC in the hallway, instructing him to get ID from any and all who had been in the penthouse, including housekeepers, servers, and members of the band.

Luke called surveillance as he headed for the parking lot. He spoke with Gayle Turner. They were still collecting video of those riding the private elevator down from the penthouse to the casino level and they had found a distant image of a figure on the balcony making suspicious moves just before the incident occurred. Frick and Fratt were working on an enlargement to erase shadows and glare in an attempt to identify the individual's wardrobe or face, and no, Gayle hadn't seen the GM arriving. Luke wondered what could be taking Larson so long. He reasoned hearing Naomi's voice in the background when he reached out to the GM earlier may hold the answer.

"There is someone here who wants to talk to you," Gayle said, passing the telephone to Candice.

"Luke," Candice's voice said in his ear, "Gayle brought

me up to speed on what's going on. I didn't think you'd want me upstairs with all those cops. How can I help?"

"You know what we need from surveillance," Luke answered. "Make it happen. Tell the GM I'm on my way to Sunrise to check on the injured. See if the police are done up front. If they are, get someone out there to clean up the blood."

"Got it," Candice assured. "Cell's on."

"Ditto."

———

SUNRISE HOSPITAL on Maryland Parkway was just six minutes from the Silver Palace. Luke was surprised when he drove out of the Palace's covered parking structure to find daylight on its way. Damn, he realized he hadn't slept since leaning back into one of the soft recliners in the Silver Bullet's plush lounge. Too many time zones and too much speed. Luke decided he had a right to be tired. As soon as he briefed the GM, he looked forward to dumping it all in Candice's lap.

Parking at the hospital was a bitch, made worse by the fact he was tired. Every parking space he found empty was posted, *Reserved—Physicians Only*. Luke gave up and parked in one, disregarding the warning. How many physicians drove a Tesla?

Luke flashed his gold and silver security badge at the nurses station in the ER. He made it quick, allowing the two young nurses behind the counter to think he was a metro police detective. "I'm looking for the couple that came in from the Silver Palace with injuries."

"This way, please," the younger of the two nurses said, leading Luke down a short hallway to a line of curtained cubicles. "Married yesterday. They're lucky they weren't killed," the nurse suggested.

Luke was surprised when the blonde Shirl Conners pulled aside the curtain on the end cubicle and stepped out. The nurse looked at both. "I'll let you two talk." She moved away.

"You're a little late," Shirl said to Luke.

"Maybe you're at the wrong place," Luke suggested.

Shirl led Luke away from the mouth of the cubicle. "I'll cut to the chase," she said, leaning a shoulder against the wall. "It's Luke, right?"

"Yeah," It wasn't a friendly tone.

"Not likely you've dealt with too many million-dollar lawsuits, so I'll keep it simple."

"How kind."

"It's not a good thing when something like this happens that could result in negative press for Jamal," Shirl continued. "So allow me to suggest I handle this."

"Last I heard, you were no longer an employee of the Silver Palace."

"You heard right." Shirl forced a sarcastic, short-lived smile. "I'm here on behalf of Jamal Hassan. Need I remind you oil has been around long before the Silver Palace, and oil will be around long after the Silver Palace."

"You said you were going to keep it simple. What are you doing here?"

"I'm here to check on the condition of newlyweds, Martin and Joan Walters. You'll be pleased to hear they're both doing well."

"Enough, lady," Luke said, leaning toward Shirl's face. "You're not a doctor or an attorney. You're not even guest relations anymore, but what you are, is done with the two people in there."

"Or what?" Shirl questioned, matching Luke's tone. "You're not a doctor or an attorney. You're a wannabe cop. You mess with those two kids in there, and I'll dump this whole thing in your inbox." Shirl pushed from the wall and marched away. Luke waited until Shirl was gone then he reached for the curtain of the cubicle he saw Shirl come out of. Joan Walters, wearing a Band-Aid beneath her right eye and a visible cut on her bottom lip sat bedside holding the hand of her husband Martin. Martin wore a stained gauze bandage wrapped around his head, a Band-Aid on his chin and another wrap of gauze over his right hand. He was awake, smiling, with his hospital bed raised to a near-seated position.

"You must be the police, Shirl said you would be coming by." Martin smiled as he adjusted the bandage on his head.

Luke chose to avoid the question. "Last time I saw you, either of you was in front of the Silver Palace."

"It's not the Silver Palace." Martin smiled, lifting his wife's hand. "It's a freaking gold mine."

"Look what we got for a wedding present," Joan raised her hand to show a fist full of one-hundred-dollar bills. "Do you know how many hundred-dollar bills are in a thousand dollars?"

"And that's just to cover costs til we get outta here," Martin added. "She said our hospital stay is covered, our room at Mandalay is covered, and they wanna move us over to the Silver Palace. All paid."

"That's impressive," Luke answered.

"And they want us to come over to Dubai for a visit." Joan again waved the cash. "And the best was her asking what our dreams were. You know, just married and stuff. I said someday we wanted to buy a house. Guess what? They wanna buy us a house in Mount Union."

"Shirl said when we get home, pick one out." Martin smiled, swinging Joan's hand. "Tell me Vegas ain't lucky."

———

THE DISTANCE from the Larson home near Red Rock to The Out of the Shadows Ranch near Boulder City was normally a forty-minute drive, but there was nothing normal about Tammy Larson being found and brought back from the street. Greg Larson made the drive in twenty-seven minutes. Most on the interstate didn't know they had been passed by a Maserati. They just knew a black car weaving in and out and around other cars had passed them, traveling well over a hundred miles an hour.

The morning sun was warm when Larson and Naomi parked among the SUVs, pickups and a tired-looking John Deere. All looked normal, with a big dog sleeping on the front porch of the ranch house and two young men in jeans and tee shirts digging a hole for a Palm setting in a pot nearby. What was different was no staff coming out to meet them. The big junkyard dog didn't bother moving when Larson and Naomi hurried inside.

Inside the ranch house's main room, the Larsons found the answer. Twenty-three people were on their knees in four different groups at tables spread across the room. It was eerily quiet. Naomi took her husband's hand and led him across the room. When they reached the hallway to Tammy's room, they saw the group waiting. Larson's heart raced with anxiety.

Naomi recognizes Josh Logan and Tammy's counselor, Clark Nelson. She didn't care about the two women or the bearded older man standing with them.

"Where is she?" Naomi demanded, intent on pushing through the four to reach the door to Tammy's room.

Josh Logan raised a hand to block her. "Naomi, this is our doctor. Listen to him, please."

Larson reached to take Naomi by the shoulders from where he stood behind her.

The doctor took the cue. "Mrs. Larson, I'm Dr. Steele. I was called when your daughter was found. My office is in Boulder, so I was here when Tammy was brought in. She's unharmed. She was emotional, but I believe she's in good health."

"I want to see her," Naomi insisted.

The doctor nodded agreement. "And we understand that, but before you go in you need to understand this is a young lady on the edge. She went back to the streets for twenty-four hours. She said she ingested drugs. I injected Narcan, tested her blood. White count is strong. Intoxication is fading. I've given her a sedative. She'll sleep for some time. It's important those around her are stable and supportive when she awakens."

"How long will that be?" Greg Larson questioned from behind Naomi.

"Another four to five hours. Depends on whether or not she had any sleep last night, and please, no emotions inside."

"The girl, her friend," Naomi pressed with a look at Josh, "the one Tammy went looking for?"

"She came back on her own last night," Clark Nelson answered. "Tammy knows she's here."

"We'll keep it all in mind," Larson promised, still holding Naomi's shoulders.

"Join us in thanking God she's safe," Josh added, hoping to lighten the moment. "God's got really great hearing, you know." He stepped aside and gestured the others to do the same.

Faint sunlight found its way around the curtained window in Tammy's room. Even more light spilled in when Naomi opened the door. Larson followed her in and closed the door quietly. Tammy was asleep on her side, face deep in a pillow. Naomi studied her daughter and then reached for her husband's hand. She squeezed it. Relief brought tears to her eyes. Larson gestured Naomi to a bedside chair. She moved to it and sat down carefully. He chose another at the foot of the bed. Naomi and Larson exchanged a look, a smile, as the noise of Tammy's breathing was the only sound in the room. It was comforting.

TWELVE

A ROSE BY ANOTHER NAME

LUKE WAS WORRIED. The early morning traffic in Las Vegas was bumper-to-bumper and slow. It added to Luke's frustration. Where the hell were all these people going? Luke's fatigue was growing. His encounter with Shirl Conners at the Morning Side Hospital left him feeling powerless. What was it she called him? A wannabe cop. What the hell was she talking about? He was the director of security at the Silver Palace. He was in charge of two hundred and seventy-two officers. The Silver Palace had six thousand eight hundred and fifty-two rooms. When at full occupancy, over ten thousand guests would entrust their safety and well-being to him and his staff. Security protected hundreds of millions in cold hard cash while providing close watch over ten thousand-plus employees spread over three round-the-clock shifts. Was that the work of a wannabe? Shirl Conners was a bitch. A good-looking one, but nevertheless a bitch. Why was she getting in the way? Money. No, it was more than money. It was to protect the rich kid, Jamal Hassan. The pot thrown from the seventy-third floor at the Palace had hit more than the pavement near two newlyweds. Jamal was at risk and how was the son of an oil baron protected? By hiding behind money. Money had more power than most. Especially more than a wannabe.

His plan was simple. By now, Luke expected he would find Greg Larson waiting for a briefing at the Palace. He'd take Candice along. That way, he would only have to tell the story once, and Candice would know exactly what the GM's reaction was and hear directly how he wanted to proceed. Proceed! Hell, it was over. Oil was floating on the water. Money solved it.

It wasn't money from the Palace. Was that good or bad? He wasn't sure. Whatever it was, Shirl Conners was still a bitch. Jamal could perhaps take the bitch back to the Mid-East with him.

———

CANDICE, looking fresh and attractive in slacks and a sleeveless blouse, met Luke when he came in from employee parking. Luke decided she looked better than Shirl Conners. Candice had been chatting with two uniformed officers at the employee entrance.

"Let's go brief the boss," Luke said as Candice joined him in his walk to the back-of-the-house elevators.

"If you mean the GM," Candice cautioned, "He hasn't come in yet."

"What?" Luke questioned with a glance at his watch. It was well past Larson's usual arrival time. "Where is he?"

"I thought you'd tell me that," Candice answered. "If he was here, you know Gayle would announce it."

Luke paused at the bank of the back-of-the-house

elevators. Dealers, servers, and housekeepers moved by and all seemed in a hurry. The elevators came and went. The memory of Naomi's voice in the background when he made the call to the GM earlier came to mind. Was a woman, an estranged wife, getting in the way? Ironically, Luke thought, his morning had been much the same with a woman in the way. Shirl Conners got in his way. Now, uncertain what to do, he was feeling like a wannabe.

"Police all gone?" Luke questioned with a look at Candice. In addition to looking good, she smelled good.

"Yeah, they took pictures, measured everything, got statements from seven employees, impounded the SUV that was damaged, looked at what surveillance had, collected lots of pieces from the broken pot. Said they'd be back later to pick up a CD. Did I mention they took pictures?"

Luke granted Candice a smile as an elevator arrived. Employees got off. Candice followed Luke onto the elevator. "And the blood out front?" Luke questioned as two housekeepers with a wheeled bucket and a mop got on with them. Two dealers, a server pushing a cart, and two engineers wearing heavy tool belts pushed Luke and Candice to the back of the car. The elevator climbed and stopped promptly on the main floor. The two dealers got off. The doors closed, and the elevator climbed.

"Engineering pressure hosed the blood. Sidewalk looks new. They also repaired the doors on the Nest, and by end of watch today, they plan to have every potted plant on a balcony bolted firmly to the deck," Candice gave into her curiosity and tapped the shoulder of the heavy-set housekeeper in front of her.

"Someone make a mess?"

"Five one-twenty-nine," the housekeeper answered

without turning. "Check-out guest took a crap right in the middle of the bathroom floor."

"Guess who didn't win," Candice suggested.

The elevator stopped. The doors parted. The engineers got off.

"I'm going to my room," Luke said as the elevator resumed its climb. He watched the digital lights indicating floors as they flashed on and off.

"Is that an invitation?" Candice questioned, fluttering her lashes.

The heavy-set housekeeper tried a discrete glance at the two. Luke saw it and chose to add to her suspicions. "I'm going to take a long hot shower. You wanna come along?"

The two housekeepers pressed their shoulders together.

"All right," Candice answered, "but we're not getting my panties all wet like last time."

The elevator stopped on the fifth floor. The two housekeepers pushed their wheeled bucket off the car. They glanced at Luke and Candice as the doors closed.

"You really going to shower?" Candice asked.

"Sleep first," Luke answered. "But you're going to wake me when the boss shows up."

"Got it," Candice assured.

———

GREG LARSON and Naomi sat in the dim light of Tammy's room, listening to their daughter breathing. Neither was paying attention to the time. Larson's right leg became an issue. Mussels on the back of his leg were beginning to spaz. He finally yielded to it by standing, but that made his foot uncomfortable. He looked to

Naomi. She nodded her understanding, and Larson opened the door quietly. Naomi followed him into the hallway.

"If it wasn't for her breathing, I'd freak out," Larson said, stretching and bending.

Naomi pulled her bag off her shoulder and rummaged in it. "I've got some Alprazolam. Would you like one?"

"I'll take three of them."

Naomi offered Larson a small ornate pill canister she lifted from her bag.

"I was kidding," Larson said. "I'll pass."

Naomi twisted the canister open and shook a tablet into her hand. She quickly moved it to her mouth. They found cold bottled water in the empty kitchen. They sat shoulder to shoulder on the steps of the front porch. After the darkness in Tammy's room, they welcomed the sunlight. Larson noticed the Palm he'd seen two men working on when they arrived. The tree was now in the ground, surrounded by a parapet of wet soil.

In the distance, a group of eight worked in a field filled with rows of small green plants. Strawberry plants, Larson guessed. Watching them made him feel like he was a million miles from Las Vegas.

"You're being quiet," Naomi suggested after a drink of her bottled water.

"I was far, far away," Larson answered.

"Silver Palace isn't that far."

"I was wondering where I could go, where we could go, leave all this behind."

"Tommy Smother's once said, everywhere you go, there you are."

"I was thinking about not going back."

"You should have accepted my Alprazolam."

"I can run, but I can't hide. I left my cell in the car. It's not like I don't have it all. We have all the money we need. We'll get Tammy through this. It's not like I'll ever be promoted. Don't need it. Don't want it. I like being with you and the kid. We should buy a ranch."

Naomi laid a hand on her husband's leg. "Remember when you were rooms director at the Signature."

"I remember. Guy was the biggest dick I ever worked for."

"And you quit to become a realtor. How long did that last?"

"Six, maybe seven months."

"This time, it's not an asshole at the Signature. This time, it's our daughter and drugs. A rock tossed in a pond creates a lot of ripples. What happens to Tammy affects both you and me. Look what it's done to us. Don't you think it will please her? If you walk away from the Palace now, who do you think Tammy will believe caused it?"

"That's your Alprazolam talking."

"I still have some."

Larson smiled, lifting Naomi's hand from his leg, he kissed it. "You know we're trying to put the genie back in the bottle. What if Tammy runs away again tonight."

"Running away and going out in search of a friend is different, you know," Naomi defended.

"And do some drugs while you're out there."

"We can't keep her in chains, Greg."

"You're right. Maybe the only way we can keep her, is by letting her go."

———

Jamal Hassan was pleased with the report Shirl Conners brought from the hospital. She talked about the cash she had given the newlyweds along with the promise of providing a path to the good life. It wasn't cheap, but Jamal had little interest in the accounting. He didn't care about the dollar amounts. It was like gambling. It wasn't what was lost, it was what was won. Shirl made no mention of her encounter with Luke Mitchel.

"Let's go play some cards," Jamal said, finishing a drink of Suntory whiskey. The six breasts he brought with him from Dubai and Shirl Conners were all smiles and eager to go, but where? They didn't care. They had spent several hours waiting, secluded in a guest bedroom in the Nest until the police finally got to them. The interrogations were brief. The girls knew nothing of someone going onto the balcony to throw a potted plant over the railing. Detective Hanson decided they were innocent, but he took his time interviewing them. He identified them on his notepad as Tits-1, Tits-2 and Tits-3.

The high stakes card room was protected by a pony wall that encircled the six tables inside, although the wide entrance had no gate, or obstruction to keep the curious away, but the world knew you didn't step inside unless the manager recognized your face, knew what room you were staying in, your choice of drinks, and the amount of cash you had on deposit in the cash cage. There was only one table in play. Five men ranging in age from twenty-four to seventy-three. One player's chair, directly in front of the dealer was vacant, reserved, awaiting the anticipated arrival of Jamal Hassan.

The trap was baited, all it needed now was a rat. Penny Nichols was thirty-two years old and more beautiful than she thought. She was a Vegas Icon. Blonde, blue-eyed, and friendly. Factor in Penny's genetic gift of having protruding nipples, which were difficult to hide beneath a dealer's thin shirt, and you had a woman who could make you forget how many jacks remained in a deck if one was showing. Why? Because most were fascinated by the two nipples staring at them. Penny, at the direction of the GM, was dealing Texas Hold 'Em and waiting.

Tom Roberts, the general manager of the card room was among those waiting. There were no clocks. Roberts's team of floor managers, like all his dealers, were prohibited from wearing watches. Time had no friends in Vegas. The card room was busy, but the really busy time would come as the afternoon hours gave way to darkness. Las Vegas, like the whore she sometimes was, loved darkness. Darkness changed timidity to boldness. Smiles became seductive as jeans with holes in their knees surrendered to low-cut gowns with thin straps. Bets doubled, cares faded, and luck became a friend. Into this world of chance, luck and odds came Jamal Hassan, his three imports and Shirl Conners. The card room manager sitting comfortably in his raised podium saw Jamal, the three girls and Shirl when they stepped out of the elevator. Jamal, to most, was a typical Vegas guest. Late twenties, well dressed, eager.

Two of the girls held Jamal's arms with the third and Shirl Conners following as they strolled into the card room. Tom Roberts picked up his cell and dialed. A moment later, Jack Lester, the floor manager in the high stakes card parlor, answered, "This is Jack."

"Jack, the package has arrived," Tom Roberts said. "I hope you saved him a seat on the bus."

"Seat saved," Lester assured. "He'll be right up front staring into the headlamps."

Jamal and the ladies were crossing the card room, moving through the Twenty-One tables, when something caught Jamal's attention. He paused and looked at the dealer.

She stood with her arms folded as protocol dictated when a table was idle. Hers was. She offered Jamal a smile. She was on the high side of thirty, hair pulled back into an attractive bun. Her makeup was flawless. She was more pretty than attractive. Her name tag read *Johnny*, and she looked like someone's older sister.

Jamal returned Johnny's smile. "You look ready."

Johnny unfolded her arms and leaned into the table. She added to her smile. "As they say in Vegas, ready or not."

Jamal accepted the challenge and pushed onto the center chair in front of Johnny. The deck of cards on the table lay face down in a fanned arch. Without looking, Johnny reached and pushed the fan of cards into a solid deck. She split the deck once, twice and on the third, pushed the cards skillfully together, all while smiling at Jamal and the four girls.

Jamal watched Johnny's skills with the cards before he raised his eyes to hers. "What's the maximum bet?"

"Fifteen thousand," Johnny answered.

"Let's get the floor manager over here," Jamal suggested. "I'd like to double that. I think I can beat you, Johnny."

Johnny raised a hand to get the attention of the floor manager. Her eyes went back to Jamal's. "Beat me? Many have tried."

Jamal reached and took Shirl's hand in his. "Shirl, go

to the cash cage. Bring back a hundred thousand. Nothing smaller than a Franklin."

Shirl nodded and moved away. Johnny, awaiting the arrival of the floor manager, studied Jamal for a moment. "So who are you, sir?"

Jamal leaned his elbows onto the table. "I'm not sure. You can help me figure that out."

———

IN THE SURVEILLANCE UNIT, three floors above the card room, Gayle Turner sat staring at the three monitors on her desk. Candice Harmon stood at Gayle's shoulder as they watched the three different images of Jamal and the young girls.

"Looks like Jamal traded Texas Hold 'Em for Twenty-One," Candice suggested.

"Shirl Conners traded her ass for more than that," Gayle answered, studying Shirl's image on one of the screens.

———

AT THE OUT of the Shadows Ranch, Greg Larson and his wife Naomi were back to sitting on the front steps. They had checked on Tammy three times. She had turned over but appeared to be still sleeping soundly. They walked to see the horses in the barn, counted chickens and chicks behind the ranch house and found two noisy pigs in a shed near a patch of green peppers before returning to the steps. Larson wasn't about to admit it, but he understood Tammy's fascination with the ranch. It was an interesting place, full of people her own age struggling with addiction, run by a bunch of leftover hippies who believed in Jesus. Maybe the *Spirit* Josh Logan talked about was what was making the steps at the front porch comfortable. Larson reminded himself, the alleged Christians running the place were making money off of those with serious problems.

In comparison, what he did helped people have fun and no one at the Silver Palace had to clean up horse shit.

"I'm going to check on her again," Naomi announced, pushing off the steps. "I'll only be a minute."

Larson watched two crows land on top of the barn. Ironically, Larson thought, Tammy's disappearance from the ranch resulted in him and Naomi finding they were still very much in love. How could that be explained to the kid?

Larson's thoughts were interrupted when Josh Logan opened the screen door on the porch. "Mr. Larson, your daughter is awake."

When Larson reached Tammy's room, he found Naomi standing outside the door of the bathroom. "First things first." She smiled as Larson moved closer.

The bathroom door opened, and Tammy, dressed in panties and a wrinkled blouse, bolted into her parents' open arms.

———

AT THE SILVER PALACE, Luke Mitchel was awake, too. He had slept, brushed and shaved. Strapping on his 9MM pistol and badge made him think of it. What was it Shirl Conner's called him? A wannabe. Well, the wannabe was about to leave the nest and go sting someone in the ass. Luke forgot most comments from women but let one of them call him a wannabe and he was obsessing over it.

Food would cover his obsession. Plan A, go down to employee dining, call Candice, once fed and briefed, they'd go in search of the GM. He had to be in by now. Luke grabbed his sports coat, slipped it over his black tee shirt and moved for the door.

———

When Jack Lester learned of Jamal's request to bump up the limit on bets in Twenty-One, he quickly went to the card room manager. They conferred, and Tom Roberts sent the challenge back to Jamal. "Bet whatever you want." Roberts knew the odds favored the house.

Shirl Conners returned to Jamal at the Twenty-One table with a bulging bank bag and an armed security officer.

"Let's start with fifty thousand," Jamal suggested.

Shirl dumped the currency from the bank bag onto the table and began counting. Johnny turned sober and dealt herself the first card, face up. It was a queen of hearts. She dealt the next card beside the first, face down.

Jamal watched as Johnny quickly placed two cards in front of him. They were both face-up, a jack of hearts and a seven of diamonds. Jamal studied the two cards for a moment, then looked to Johnny. "Hit me."

Johnny peeled another card from the deck and placed it face up beside the first two. It was a three of clubs, making her total twenty.

Shirl smugly pushed the pile of crisp currency toward Johnny, who turned over the card she had lying face down. It was a nine of spades. The three girls did what most young girls did in Vegas. They screamed, laughed and slapped hands together in the air. The noise and cheers did not go unnoticed. A circle of curious onlookers began forming behind Jamal and the girls. A shapely server, sent by the card room manager, arrived at Jamal's shoulder. She pushed a breast against him. Jack Lester arrived at the table and began counting out the winnings.

In the employee dining room, Luke sat at a table with a cheeseburger, french fries, an orange, and a Diet Coke. He was halfway through the burger when Candice arrived. She reached and took several french fries from Luke's plate and then sampled his drink.

"Tell me about Jamal," Luke urged.

"He's playing Twenty-One. So far, it's one to four. His favor. Fifty grand a pop. Gayle's doing everything but looking up his nose. He's got quite a crowd around him." She reached and took more of his fries.

"When we finish *our* lunch," Luke said, "we'll go find the GM and bring him up to speed."

"That might be hard to do," Candice cautioned. "He's not on property."

"What! Where is he?" Luke questioned with a final bite of his burger.

"Jackie Fallon belongs to our club. She doesn't know where he is either."

Luke picked at the dwindling supply of french fries on his plate as Candice pushed his hand aside and took more.

"When I called him last night," Luke said, pushing a fry into his mouth, "I heard Naomi's voice in the background."

"Get outta here. He's shacking up with Charlotte Johnson. You know, Black beauty. They've been lovers for months."

"What I heard last night wasn't an estranged wife. It

was just a wife. Here's my point," Luke explained, pushing back in his chair. "Just because you sleep with someone doesn't mean you have a future with them."

Candice pointed a french fry at Luke. "And just because you have a future with someone doesn't mean you're going to sleep with them."

"You had to steal my last french fry to tell me that."

———

IN THE CARD ROOM, Tom Roberts was facing a dilemma. Jamal Hassan had just bought the growing crowd around his Twenty-One table a free drink. Their choice. One savvy thirty-year-old ordered an Ono Cocktail. On the Strip, the major casinos sold the Ono for around ten thousand. Three other servers joined the first, and soon thirty-seven people were enjoying a cocktail while they watched Jamal make bets that took their breath away. The score was now four to eight. Jamal was winning.

———

TAMMY LARSON APOLOGIZED to her parents time and time again. Her tears and sobs were sincere. Tammy asked if she could have a private moment with Josh Logan. She wanted an update on her friend. Josh was summoned. Larson and Naomi went back to the steps on the front porch. Sitting shoulder to shoulder, they talked. Naomi had to wipe away tears.

"You know, since you won't let me quit," Larson suggested, "I'm going to have to go back to work."

"I can drop you there."

"Maybe we'll get Logan and his wife to take you up

the hill and then I'll set them up with a payback dinner at the Palace."

Behind the closed door of Tammy's room, she sat on her bed while Josh, elbows on his knees, sat in a chair, listening.

"I screwed it," Tammy confessed. "Back to the streets. I became what I was. It wasn't even difficult. The guy offered me meth. You know, try and buy. I took it and wham. He didn't force me. I did it."

"And that filled you with regret?" Josh suggested. "That's a good thing. Imagine if you felt no regret. Biological and physiological change takes time. Did you think you'd live the rest of your life and not sin? Jesus did what he promised. He forgave you. Not just the sins or mistakes from last night, last month, or last year. He forgives all of it, past, present and future. Do you love your parents?"

"Yes, of course."

"You know they've made mistakes, got things wrong. Do you still love them? Can you forgive them?"

"Yes."

"Love is the mountain we all have to climb. Jesus tells us to forgive others. Why? Because love is the key. Love is what took you to the streets in search of your friend. You give love and guess what? You get love. Jesus is your friend. He'll help you get it right. Bow your head," Josh urged. Reaching, he took Tammy's hands in his. "Lord, Tammy messed up, she knows it. She wants to make it right. Forgive her, guide her, love her and open her heart to love others. In Jesus's name, Amen."

———

AT THE SILVER PALACE, Jamal Hassan had become the center of attention, and he was relishing the spotlight. The crowd around him, pushing, shoving, standing on their toes while holding open cell phones, now numbered near fifty. Two Craps tables, the Texas Hold 'Em in the high stakes coral and several Twenty-One tables sat idle as Jamal provided the entertainment with his brazen betting and growing pile of winnings.

He had tipped his attractive server a thousand dollars, bought two more rounds of drinks for the crowd and relied on Shirl Conners to keep track of his winnings, and he was winning.

Tom Roberts, the card room manager, was also doing the math. And math ran the town. Played legitimately, Roberts knew Jamal's streak would soon run into a wall. The odds of winning at Twenty-One were forty-seven percent. Jamal, with his breath-taking bets was now well beyond that. Increase one number, and the odds changed. The crowd, the idle tables and Jamal's intent to hold the world around him could not change the percentages. Roberts was concerned they hadn't changed, but he knew they would. It was his card room, and no matter how big someone made the bets, percentage owned the game. Roberts was concerned, not worried. *Worry* didn't have a home in Vegas. Luck and chance were always talked about, but the odds owned the town. Roberts hoped the percentages would soon show up. He hoped Greg Larson would, too. Where the hell was he? He would feel better with the GM agreeing the math would turn it around.

The fact Jamal was surrounded by strangers who cheered his winnings against the house filled him with a sense of power and awe, but there were others. Others, who wanted more than his luck, they wanted his money.

Nic Wilson was a thirty-two-year-old pimp. He ran a pack of twelve women. They ranged in age from nineteen to forty-two. Some liked their women young, others, well, they claimed older women had more experience. Young or old, Nic's minimum for one of his Sensual Tour Guides was eight hours for twelve hundred dollars. He kept seven hundred for his management fees and paid the girls' five, plus any tips or winnings they may collect. The money provided Nic the good life, along with a five-bedroom mansion and three cars, but Nic's money was like Cotton Candy, just a taste wasn't enough. He wanted more.

Conventions, and Las Vegas had many of them, coupled with independent business meetings that had to be scheduled in Vegas, proved to be a reliable source for Sensual Tour Guide Services, but it wasn't enough for Nic.

He had to buy the tips and information he got from the reservations, guest services, valets, room service and others in the know, but he found advanced knowledge of conventions and meetings provided a valuable edge on scheduling his ladies. He also learned among those attending that there was a pecking order for discretionary money. The CEO of a company choosing Vegas had more to spend than the worker ants that got little more than a free room. Nic's tip on Jamal Hassan's arrival in Vegas came from the maintenance crew chief of the Silver Palace's company plane. Nic paid fifteen hundred for the tip. Jamal was picked up in Dubai, and he had money. Lots of money and Nic had a plan, a big one and it was for big bucks.

Nic planned on giving Jamal Hassan a *Rose*. This Rose was twenty-six years old. Her name was Rosie Martinez. She was an undocumented immigrant from Honduras with a slight Hispanic accent. She had a current Nevada driver's license, a birth certificate showing she was born in Austin, Texas, and an imaginary widowed mother living in Parker, Arizona. Rosie had a seductive smile, and a natural beauty enhanced with all the trimmings and allure Las Vegas could provide. Rosie went beyond attractive. She was the picture in your yearbook of the one that got away, she was the neighbor's daughter you knew you couldn't touch, she was young, she was innocent, and she was ready.

THIRTEEN
UNTIL DEATH DOTH PART

Rosie Martinez was playing a slot machine when Jamal and the four women with him sat down at a Twenty-One table. She waited until there was a crowd gathered around Jamal before she moved closer to watch him play. She not only watched and listened to Jamal she studied the four women with him. Rosie knew they were competition, a wall she might have to climb. The younger three were quickly identified as frosting on the cake. Tag alongs, window dressing, proof the young Arab liked women. The older one, handling Jamal's money, was smarter, more savvy, sophisticated, and alert, than the younger noisy ones. Rosie joined the crowd behind Jamal. There were five people in front of her, but like most crowds of spectators, there weren't lines or groups. Some stood shoulder to shoulder, but most were couples or friends hoping to get a look at what had to be *big* money. Rosie skillfully wormed her way through the crush,

"Excuse me, pardon me, sorry," she whispered, pushing with a shoulder or a breast. The breast worked best, and although it took her half an hour, she finished by moving directly behind Jamal. She waited on his next bet which he won. Jamal cheered and raised his arms in victory. The crowd cheered with him. Rosie took the opportunity, blaming the crowd surge. She pushed forward, shoving breasts up on either side of Jamal's neck with a hand on his shoulders. His neck felt warm on her breasts. She knew he would be feeling it, too.

"I'm sorry," Rosie said, leaning close to Jamal's ear. Her breasts were still pressed to his neck. She drew herself away carefully. Jamal not only felt the soft flesh on his neck, but her scent intoxicated him.

Jamal twisted in his chair. He liked what he saw. His smile proved that. Her voice matched her persona. She was Vegas, and the fish had found the bait. "No, no, not to worry," Jamal assured. "You brought me luck."

Jamal turned to the table and watched as Johnny turned over the first of two cards in front of her. It was a ten of hearts. Jamal glanced at Shirl Conners. Shirl understood and she pushed three stacks of hundred-dollar bills toward the dealer.

"Show time." Jamal smiled at Johnny.

Johnny's polished nails reached and flipped the first hole card. It was a queen of spades. Jamal studied it and looked to Johnny. "I think I can beat that."

Johnny reached and turned over her second card. It was a nine of clubs. A hush fell over the crowd surrounding the table. Jamal sobered. He turned over his cards. First, a queen of hearts, and then slowly, revealing, a queen of clubs. The crowd roared with approval. Rosie reached and grabbed Jamal around the neck and kissed his cheek. "I'm sorry, I meant well." She pulled away from him.

Jamal twisted Rosie, who looked shy and innocent. "It's break time. Would you join me for dinner?"

The three girls and Shirl Conners were not pleased. Shirl worked at pushing Jamal's winnings into a bank bag as an armed security officer appeared at the table. Rosie moved a hand to her heart as if surprised. Jamal slid off his chair at the Twenty-One table and extended a hand to Rosie.

Rosie hesitated, looked at Jamal's hand, then his face. "Yes, I would love that." She stepped toward Jamal and took his hand. He smiled and held it as he looked at the faces surrounding him. "Thank you, thank you all."

Applause and cheers followed.

In the surveillance unit, three floors above, Luke Mitchel and Candice Harmon stood at Gayle Turner's shoulders as she leafed through a thick photo album on her desk of headshots of known escorts and prostitutes. "I don't find anything in here that fits this girl."

"Then she may be what Vegas has a lot of," Luke suggested. "Good-looking women."

Gayle and Candice exchanged a smile, and both looked to Luke and spoke in unison, "Thank you."

———

GREG LARSON and his wife Naomi were waiting on the front steps at the ranch in Boulder. Larson looked troubled. Naomi saw it. "You've gone quiet again. Why don't you just say it."

"Okay," Larson agreed without looking to Naomi. "I can't go back in there. I don't know why. I don't know what to say. The last time we were together, I ran away. I feel like running now."

"There's the cliché," Naomi said, laying a hand on Larson's leg. "You can run but—"

Larson cut her short. "I'm not running. There's a time to talk it just doesn't feel right tonight."

"I don't think it's our words that are important," Naomi suggested.

"Mr. and Mrs. Larson," Josh Logan called from behind the Larsons as he held the screen door open. Tammy appeared. "Your daughter would like to join you."

Tammy crossed the porch. Surprised, Larson and Naomi pushed to their feet. Tammy moved between them. She kissed her mother on the cheek, then her dad. The screen closed as Logan withdrew. Tammy sat down on the steps. Her parents followed her lead. Naomi took her daughter's hand in hers.

"You working tonight, Dad? Tammy questioned with a look at Larson.

"Yeah, we've got a major VIP in house and Lady Luck's got a show tonight."

"You think you could get me in to see her some night?"

"Maybe," Larson said. Reaching, he ran a hand through Tammy's hair. "Maybe the three of us."

"I'd like that."

———

GUEST RELATIONS HAD DONE their job. The Plush bus, as valet tagged it, was waiting at the front entrance. A smiling Jamal, holding Rosie Martinez's hand along with his three imports and Shirl Conners, climbed aboard.

The bartender on the bus mixed drinks for all as they moved slowly with the flow of traffic on the Strip. The towering Strat Tower stood waiting in the distance, basking in the afternoon sunlight. Jamal and Rosie sat shoulder to shoulder on a comfortable couch at the rear of the Plush bus. Rosie seemingly had a thousand questions for Jamal. Where was home, did he have family, what did they do, did he have a car, what was the weather like in the Arctic? Jamal corrected her geography with a smile.

Rosie kept Jamal busy with questions to minimize any from him. She had a cover story ready, she would claim she'd only been in Vegas for three months. Actually, it had been three years. Transferred in to work in the spa at the new Westin. Not really, but she had worked in a spa until caught on camera giving a guest a hand job, but Jamal seemed much more interested in Rosie's breasts than what she did to earn money. Money wasn't associated with work in Jamal's world. Money was bait, and Jamal was fishing.

As the Plush bus traveled north on the Strip toward Fremont Street, Rosie spotted something on the sidewalk. She pointed with excitement and shouted, "Look! Newlyweds."

Jamal turned to look. A flashing neon sign read, *Best West Weddings*. Coming out the open door of the makeshift chapel, a middle-aged bride and groom, dressed in their best, were greeted by a waiting couple who cheered and threw confetti in the air.

"Oh," Rosie pleaded. "Could we stop? I've never seen inside one of those. Could we please?"

"Driver," Jamal called, gesturing toward the curb.

A smaller sign on the doorway of the chapel read, *Divorce-20 Minutes / Wedding-15 minutes. Video included—Free Estimate.*

Rosie, taking Jamal by the hand, led him to the open

door of the chapel as a shiny black limo pulled to the curb to pick up the newlyweds.

"Wanna get a free estimate?" Rosie asked Jamal after signing a guest book just inside the door.

She led Jamal down the center aisle of the small chapel. A man sat sleeping in one row. Another man in a dark suit and tie stood behind a podium at the head of the aisle. Seeing the approach of Jamal and Rosie, he pushed a remote button, and a loud instrumental version of *Here Comes the Bride* began playing. Jamal waved a hand at the man, and the music stopped abruptly. The man smiled and lifted a Bible in his hands. "Whom God has brought together, let no man tear apart."

"Thank you," Rosie said, pulling Jamal closer. "We're just looking."

"The path to a happy marriage often begins with just a look."

"This is Jamal," Rosie said with a broad smile, "and I'm Rosie Martinez. We were on our way to dinner."

"Your arrival is timely," the suit and tie assured. "Our no-holds ceremony includes dinner for two at the Yard Bird."

Jamal raised a hand. "Thank you, but we have plans."

"We can do better than fifteen minutes," the suit suggested. "The knot we tie never comes loose, and we'll forward a video and a copy of your Nevada marriage certificate."

"Perhaps tomorrow," Jamal said, pulling Rosie away from the podium.

"Or maybe after your dinner," the suit suggested as Jamal led Rosie toward the open door.

———

At the Silver Palace Luke Mitchel and Candice were attending the PM Security Watch briefing. Anakoni Stone, the uniformed watch commander, sat in the front with Candice as Luke walked up and down the center aisle between the rows of uniformed officers.

"As I speak, engineering is up in the Eagles Nest putting bolts in the patio door," Luke said to the collection of officers. "No one will be going out on the balcony tonight."

"Jamal's MO," Luke continued as he returned to the head of the room. "Has been play and party. He did it yesterday and more than likely, he'll do it today. He left after Twenty-One. He got on the Plush bus with five others. We can expect him back in three to four hours with a lot more than that."

Luke looked to the watch commander, Anakoni Stone. "I want two officers at the top of the elevator and another two at the bottom. No whores, no cheats on the elevator. Surveillance will help us with anyone recognized. The only people going up to the Nest tonight will be those Jamal invites."

The cell phone beneath Luke's jacket vibrated. He paused and pulled it from his belt. The caller ID showed it was Jackie Fallon, the GM's executive assistant. "Jackie, it's Luke."

"Boss is here. Can you come up?"

"Be right there," Luke answered, pointing a finger at Candice. His attention went back to the uniforms. "We've got a full house. Lady Luck's sold out. It's going to be a busy night, but more importantly, you're going to make sure it's a safe night."

Luke headed up the center aisle toward the door at the rear of the briefing room. Candice followed. Anakoni Stone, the watch commander, wearing a uniform shirt that announced he was a combo of fit and fat, moved to the podium. "Okay, boys and girls, here's who's doing what tonight. Jacobs and Grisson, you've got guest parking. Hummel and Wilson, cash cage."

———

JACKIE WAS at her desk in the GM's outer office when Luke and Candice arrived.

"You ever get a day off?" Luke questioned.

"Had one in June," Jackie answered, gesturing to the open door of the GM's office. Luke and Candice moved for it. Greg Larson, jacket off, tie loose, was pushed back in the chair behind his desk. Tom Roberts, the *I'm-too-young-for-this-looking card room manager,* sat beside Jack Lester, the Table Games floor manager in two chairs in front of Larson's desk.

"Couple chairs over there," Larson said to Luke. "Grab them, please."

Luke gathered and moved the chairs. He and Candice sat down beside Roberts and Lester.

"We were just going over wins and losses," Larson explained. "So far, Tom tells me Jamal has kicked our butts. That's because everyone kicks our butts at Twenty-One. We need to get Jamal back in the men's club. I'm talking high stakes. We got a dealer that he won't ignore, but before we get his money, we need to get his attention. Tom, no more pussy games. He comes into the card room you give him the bum rush but get him into high stakes. Luke, where is Jamal?"

"I talked to valet," Luke explained, "when the Plush bus pulled away, so did a valet in one of our Mercedes. He's running a loose tail. I'm told the bus stopped at the Strat, they took a ride on the sky cars, walked Fremont and then came back to the Steak House at Bellagio. Jamal is hanging onto a Hispanic skirt. So far we've got no dirt."

"When he comes back, what happens? Larson questioned.

"Last night," Luke added, "Jamal went to see Luck, then up to the Nest telling everyone in sight it was party time. A couple hours later, someone tossed the potted plant over the rail."

"Seventy-three floors. Holy shit," Larson said aloud.

"Surveillance is still looking," Luke continued. "In the interim, we had engineering bolt down every potted plant west of the Mississippi and secure the doors to the balcony."

"So, we're looking at another party tonight?" Larson questioned.

"Bet on it," Luke answered.

Larson pushed out of his chair and walked to the floor-to-ceiling window with its nighttime panoramic view of the Strip. "The odds of winning in our casino is 47.37 percent," he said with a glance back at the others. Luke wondered if Larson was talking to them or thinking out loud. "Every game has its own odds," Larson continued. "Keno, poker, Blackjack, Craps, roulette, and even slots have different payouts and odds. Of course, we can't forget Sports Book."

Larson returned to his chair as he continued, "There's the timeless cliché that echoes, Vegas was built by losers. Resorts World cost four point three billion dollars to build. The recently opened Fontaine Bleau cost three-point-seven billion dollars, and the Silver Palace, well, I won't comment officially, but our construction cost is at five billion dollars."

"Where does all this money come from? Look at what

big dog Vegas Casinos earn. The MGM Grand's gross for the twelve months was $7.35 billion, an 18.03 percent increase year-over-year."

Larson made a note on his desk pad before looking to the waiting faces. "Those are earnings. Who lost money? Who gave the MGM Grand seven point thirty-five billion? Was it a cashier's check? No, some of it came from the couple from Dayton, Ohio, in Vegas to celebrate their twentieth, or maybe it was the two guys from Trenton who had a system for winning at Twenty-One. Then there was the just-married couple, from Orlando who lost it all on roulette. They called Mom for tickets home on Southwest."

He raised his pen and pointed it at Candice. "If the majority of those coming to Vegas lose money, why do they come back? Which most do! Why? Because the next time...they may win. The next time, their luck will change."

———

THE PLUSH BUS arrived from the Bellagio. It was now crowded with thirty-eight people. They departed the Silver Palace with six passengers. Among the crowd coming off the bus were five young men wearing red hats with MAGA insignias. Jamal, with a smiling Rosie Martinez holding onto him, staggered as he led the parade through the card room to the private elevator reserved for the Eagle's Nest. There, security officers asked for identification, "Driver's license, passport."

"Fuck you! You're not getting my ID," one of the MAGA hats complained.

"Kiss my ass," another suggested. "We don't have to show you shit. This is America."

Jamal, on his way to being drunk, heard the complaints. He intervened. "He's right, Cop. I invited him, piss off."

"Cop! He ain't no fucking cop. No license, no training, no guts."

A round of laughter followed.

Luke watched the encounter on a screen in his office. Candice stood at his shoulder. Luke picked up a radio and keyed it. "Gate Keeper Ten to Davis and Goss, at the elevator. Cancel the ID checks. Let them in."

One of the MAGA hats overheard the radio message. "Fucking A," he shouted, raising a fist to the waiting crowd. Shouts and cheers erupted. The officers stepped aside. The crowd surged onto the elevator. Jamal and Rosie, all smiles, were among them.

Although the Eagles Nest had a well-stocked bar, as soon as the crowd pushed in, there were immediate calls for more. In the director of security's office, Luke and Candice watched as the private elevator made trip after trip until the crowd was gone. The GM sent up a DJ and six cases of cold beer. He charged it to Jamal's account. As the hours passed, the noise grew louder.

Luke knew his decision to fold on the ID requests was going to become a morale issue, although folding was better than fighting. The once-upon-a-time cop left in Luke from his days with the LAPD wanted to kick some MAGA ass, but he knew he worked in an environment where the satisfaction and comfort of guests was premier. Luke planned on attending Securities' three daily briefings, there, hopefully, he could explain the logic. If there was any.

It was after one when Shirl Conners and the three girls Jamal brought from Dubai marched out of the room carrying their bags. Luke and Candice watched, but all they could do was guess. That was until the concierge from the front desk called surveillance to alert them the three girls were flying to the UK on a United flight in the morning and Shirl Conners was going home for what she claimed was badly needed rest.

"So," Candice speculated, "doesn't leave Jamal with much in the way of choices."

"I get the feeling he may be smelling roses tonight," Luke suggested.

The idea that Luke would work a twelve-hour shift and then Candice would follow on another, suffered the same fate as letting guests slide with their graphic insults to a security officer. They sat in the director's office and switched scenes on their monitors. Drunks came out of the penthouse. One tried urinating in the corner of the hallway. Another unzipped in the elevator in front of two women. Both were introduced to the street behind the Silver Palace. Luke and Candice could see the intoxication when guests came out. What they couldn't see was the cause. Was it drugs, liquor, or both?

The DJ packed up and left after two a.m. It was a sign the party was over. Others followed until it could only be speculated as to who remained. Rosie Martinez finally came out, staggering, holding onto walls to eventually make her way to the front entrance. There, she climbed into an SUV cab and disappeared into the night.

"Let's go to bed," Luke suggested, pushing to his feet from behind his desk. KC King was now the on-duty watch commander. Luke had confidence in KC.

"I was beginning to think you'd never ask." Candice smiled from where she sat on her side of the office.

"Maybe tomorrow." Luke yawned on his way to the door. "Don't forget to turn the lights out."

———

THE SILVER PALACE had a good night. Lady Luck was a sell-out. The card room drop raised eyebrows and the mess in the kitchen proved F&B got it right. Tom Roberts considered calling the GM with the good news, but he'd heard Larson had left the property. Roberts knew why. Larson was shacking up with Charlotte Johnson, the Black Fox, who was once the HR director at the Palace. Tom was tired too. He decided a limo was the best choice since daylight was still a couple hours away.

———

GREG LARSON WAS LOOKING FORWARD to climbing into bed with a naked woman, although the woman wasn't Black, and she had the same name as his. Larson was late. Sparky barked when he parked near the garage, but the Rottweiler's tail wagging assured Larson he was recognized. The dog followed him into the dim master bedroom.

Naomie's voice startled him. "I was beginning to wonder," she said in the darkness.

Larson pulled off his pants to lay them over the back of a chair. "Thought you were going to have Josh Logan call me. Remember the dinner payback thing?"

"Didn't work out," Naomi said, sitting up in the bed. "Josh had some early morning thing with the American Legion. He asked Tammy's counselor, Clark Nelson, to bring me home. Clark's girlfriend came along."

"So now we owe them a dinner?" Larson sat down and pulled his socks off. He wished he could see Naomi. Was she naked? All he could see of her was a silhouette. He decided the risk was worthwhile. It was late, he was tired. He expected she was, too. Having her warm flesh against him was a pleasant thought. He pushed his boxer shorts to the rug.

"Clark gave me real insight into Tammy."

"Tell me about it," Larson said, crossing to the bed.

"He said Tammy's choices, her arrest for prostitution, the meth ODs, were events she knew would get attention. We were divorcing. Forcing her to make a choice. Do I stay with Mom or go with Dad? She couldn't decide. Meth stepped in and helped."

Larson pulled the sheet and covers back and climbed into bed. He reached and ran his fingers down Naomi's arm and found the swell of a breast. She was naked. He reached and pulled Naomi against his nudeness. She was soft, warm, and sensual.

"Enough talk," Larson whispered, tracing a path from Naomi's neck to her mouth with light kisses. Suddenly, out of the darkness the big Rottweiler jumped onto the bed, pushing between them.

"Down, boy," Naomi snapped.

"You talking to me or the dog?" Larson smiled.

―――――

A FULL HOUSE meant the six thousand eight hundred and fifty-two rooms of the Silver Palace housed thirteen thousand guests. As a result, days off were canceled for housekeeping, room service, F&B staff, card room and security. Three thousand plus employees spread over three shifts climbed over the Palace like an army of busy ants. Among them was the housekeeping team of Thelma Rollins and Ida Perez. The two women had sixteen years of service and experience. They could make any room, anywhere, look inviting. Thus, the director of housekeeping, assigned the dynamic duo the task of not only cleaning but putting the Eagle's Nest back together again.

Clean sheets, room spray, toilet paper and a vacuum were among the things the duo carried to the ornate wooden doors of the Eagle's Nest. They rang the door-bell and waited. There was no response. They rang the bell a second time. Again, there was no response. Ida knocked hard on the double doors.

"Housekeeping," she called.

They chatted in Spanish, checked their fingernails and waited. VIPs were nothing but a pain in the ass. Finally, the two exchanged a look and slid a black vinyl universal key through the heavy ornate lock on the door. Thelma pushed the door inward.

"Housekeeping," she called again.

The expansive living room was a mess. Paper cups, glasses, silver ware and dirty dishes were everywhere mixed with pillows on the floor, a single high-heeled shoe, a man's shirt, tickets from Lady Luck's show, twisted chairs, dirty ashtrays, cigarette papers, marijuana residue on a glass tabletop and a bra hanging on the shade of a table lamp.

The housekeeping duo knew they would be there awhile. Ida parked her vacuum, left Thelma to pick up trash, and went to look at the master bathroom. A routine had developed. Ida cleaned bathrooms, liquor bars and dishware. She had been in the Nest many times. She wasn't prepared for what she found in the master bath tube.

Ida's loud scream frightened Thelma. She dropped her dust mop and ran to Ida. Ida stood holding the door frame of the master bath. In the oversized tube, which was filled with soapy water, was the body of a naked man. The man's head was beneath the water. His open eyes stared up through the murky water. His tongue was swollen and pushing out. His cheeks were swollen. His expression showed a look of fear. His head and shoulders were beneath the water, but his arms were extended with his hands holding a death grip on the sides of the tube. His knees and bare feet stuck out of the water with his feet resting on the wide edge of the tube. His stomach was swollen. The head of his penis stood straight, breaking the surface of the water. Thelma reached Ida, looked at the naked man in the tub, and joined in her frightened scream.

KC King was the first security officer to arrive on scene in response to reports of two women screaming in the Eagle's Nest. The two housekeepers had seen enough. KC found them in the expanse of the living room where Ida had collapsed in a chair with a hand gripping her heart, gasping for breath. Thelma stood nearby leaning on a bar top, head lowered.

"What's wrong?" KC demanded as another officer arrived. It was Dianna Jackson, a young Black officer. She was out of breath. Thelma raised her head and pointed at the hallway. KC and Officer Jackson moved down the hall into the master bedroom. The bed was unmade. Male clothing, cigarette papers, liquor bottles and scraps of food were scattered everywhere. KC looked and saw the tablets on the glass surface of a bedside table. He moved cautiously to the open door to the en suite master bath.

"Holy shit." KC grimaced when he saw the naked body lying face up in the bathtub. The man's head and shoulders were beneath the water.

"My god," Dianna gasped behind him.

KC moved quickly to the body in the tub. He pushed

an arm beneath the man's neck and lifted. Dianna was quickly to KC's side. She grabbed a wet arm and pulled. Both ignored the splashing which soaked their uniforms. The man's stiff body fell with a thud to the tiled floor surrounding the tub. Water ran from his mouth and nose. His eyes were open and staring at the ceiling. KC kneeled beside the body and pressed a hand to the man's neck in search of a pulse. He found nothing.

KC looked to Dianna. "He's dead."

FOURTEEN
AFTER SHOCKS

Luke's cell phone lying on top of a bedside table in his sixth-floor room began to vibrate and dance in a circle. In his dream, Luke let go of the log he was riding in a raging current and reached for the annoying cell. "Hello."

"Boss, it's KC. I'm in the Eagles Nest. We've got a dead man up here."

"What! A dead man."

"Drowned in the master tub." KC sounded out of breath.

"Who found him?"

"Housekeepers. I don't know their names."

Luke swung his feet to the floor and switched on a bedside light. "Okay, keep them there. No one else in or out. Is it Jamal?"

"He's all swollen and shit. I think it's him."

"Start taking pictures. I'll be up."

Luke tossed his cell phone and grabbed his pants from the back of a chair.

KC was taking pictures with his cell phone in the master bathroom when Luke arrived. Dianna Jackson was with the two housekeepers in the living room. They looked shaken, frightened. Dianna worked at blotting water out of her uniform shirt with a towel.

"KC is in there," Dianna said, gesturing toward the master suite.

Luke offered a nod and moved toward the hallway. KC paused from taking pictures as Luke entered. He exchanged a look with KC and moved to the naked body which laid awkwardly, arms stretched, eyes staring at the ceiling. Luke looked at the lifeless form. It was Jamal, the kid he'd brought to Vegas from Dubai, the kid he'd talked to on the airplane, the kid with a big heart, the kid with all the money, the kid who gave to others, the kid who lay dead at his feet.

"It's Jamal," Luke said, looking to KC. His voice was strained, tense. He hoped KC didn't hear it.

"There's a couple tabs on the table beside the bed. You don't have to be a rocket scientist to connect the dots," KC suggested.

"You found him?"

"Housekeepers were first."

Luke drew in a deep breath and turned away from Jamal's body." Start a log. I'll call nine-one-one. Looks accidental, but with a loss of life, it belongs to Metro PD. I'll reach out to them and the GM."

KC was punching data into his cell phone.

Greg Larson was sound asleep with his body pressed against his estranged wife's nudity. They were in the Master Bedroom of the Larson home in the gated Valley of the Fire near Red Rock Canyon. Sparky, the big Rottweiler lay curled at the foot of the bed. Larson's cell phone, forgotten in a jacket pocket, somewhere in the dark room began an electronic chirrup. Naomi pushed on her husband's shoulder, "Greg, it's your cell."

Naomi pushed away from her husband as the cell continued to rattle in the darkness. She lifted an arm from her neck and swung her feet to the floor.

Pushing to her feet, Naomi searched in the darkness. She guessed right and found Larson's jacket on a recliner. She dug in a pocket and found the cell.

"Hello."

Luke was surprised by the feminine voice. He stood with his cell to an ear in the master bedroom of the Eagle's Nest. He was certain he knew who's voice it was. He was hesitant, but the call was important.

"Naomi," Luke questioned cautiously.

"Luke," Naomi answered awkwardly. "Yes, he's here. Just a minute."

The nude Naomi, cell phone in hand, moved to the foot of the bed. She reached over the dog and shook her husband's foot. "Greg, it's Luke Mitchel."

Larson sat up in the bed. Naomi pushed the cell phone into his hands. Luke's exchange with Naomi explained a lot. Larson had not only returned to his estranged wife, he was sleeping with her. The reality of it made Luke smile. Nothing wrong with a husband and wife sleeping together. Considering their friendship, why Larson hadn't told Luke puzzled him, but where you slept, or who you slept with, was private, kinda, but not anymore.

"This is Larson."

"Boss, Jamal is dead. Housekeeping found him. Drowned in his bathtub."

"Holy shit!"

"Paramedics are on their way. Metro PD is coming too."

"All right, I'll be in," Larson said, looking at his wife's breasts. She stood in the shadows at the foot of the bed.

Luke had the two housekeepers escorted to security's interview room. They were relieved to get out of the Eagle's Nest.

He called surveillance to have them put together the images and timeline of those in and out of the Eagle's Nest in the past twelve hours. Luke's next call was to the cash cage. He told the supervisor any and all cash assets on deposit for Jamal Hassan were to be considered frozen. Luke was asked to hold while the supervisor looked at the account on her computer.

"He has thirty-eight million, two hundred and seventy-six dollars on deposit."

"Freeze it," Luke ordered.

Luke's next call was a wake-up.

"This is Candice."

"Candice, it's Luke. I need your help. I'll fill in the blanks when you find me. Reach out to Gayle, too," Luke suggested. "Have her come in early. I want a CD of everything that's happened at the Nest last night. Who went in, who came out. Drunks, drugs. She'll know what we're looking for."

"Done," Candice assured.

Two uniformed metro PD police officers were escorted to the Eagles Nest by day watch commander Mario Lopez, who had been called in early by KC King. The officers surveyed the scene in the master bath, looked at the body, lying naked and awkward beside the tub, and reviewed the Cause of Death declaration left by the EMTs, which read, *Death by Drowning. No Evidence of foul play.* The metro officers called for detectives to assume responsibility for the investigation. KC King assigned an officer to stand by at the base of the private elevator and another at the top. They were told only police officers were allowed access.

Luke, glad to leave the body and the investigation in the hands of the metro police, went to the employee dining room. Death and hunger. He couldn't explain it. There, he collected a coffee and several pieces of toast. He was enjoying the toast when Candice found him. She had her own coffee.

"Maybe next time I'll get to see the body before the Police get here."

Luke crunched a piece of toast. "You feel cheated because you didn't get to see a naked guy."

"This is Vegas. Naked isn't hard to find," Candice said, reaching to take a piece of Luke's toast. "What happened? Jamal drown. Why?" Candice questioned.

"Couple tablets on a dresser beside the bed," Luke speculated. "Figure he took some and got in the tub."

"Not likely he knew what they were."

"Fentanyl," Luke suggested. "Autopsy will tell us. Remember the Hispanic girl? Good-looking. Looked like she was last out."

"Yes, we watched her. She took a cab."

"We need to find her. See if the cab kept a record of the pick-up. We've got cameras out there."

"Surveillance Ten to Gatekeeper Twenty." It was Gayle Turner's voice on the compact radios both Candice and Luke carried.

Candice pulled her radio from beneath her jacket. "Twenty here. Go surveillance."

"Twenty," the radio answered. *"GM is on property."*

Candice clicked her radio twice. It was the code for *message received*. She looked to Luke. "Got her working on the CD you asked for."

Luke took a final drink of his coffee. "Let's go talk to the boss."

Luke and Candice were surprised to find Jackie

Fallon at her desk outside the GM's office when they arrived. The door to the GM's office was closed.

"Don't you usually come in after sunrise," Candice said to Jackie.

"He called. Said pack my lunch, it was going to be a long day. Is it true, Jamal Hassan is dead?" Jackie questioned as the intercom on her desk buzzed. She punched a key. "Yes, sir."

"They here yet?" It was the GM's voice.

"Yes, sir."

"Send them in."

Luke and Candice were surprised to find Greg Larson was not alone in his office. A younger man, in need of a haircut, dressed in a hoodie, jeans and sneakers sat in front of Larson's desk. Seeing Candice, the young man pushed to his feet.

"Grab a chair, Luke," Larson suggested. Luke pulled a chair as Larson continued, "Luke, Candice, this is James Collins. He's our bad ass corporate attorney. I picked him up on my way in. Jim, this is Luke Mitchel, our director of security and his assistant, Candice Somebody."

Candice and Luke accepted the hand Collins offered and then sat down as Larson continued, "Jim and I just got off the phone with the State Department. They're not happy about this but they'll handle notification to Jamal's father. So, get ready to pay more at the pump."

Jim Collins looked to Luke and Candice. "Mr. Mitchel, I understand the police are still on property."

"My name is Luke, Mr. Collins," Luke answered, resenting the age tag. "Yeah, metro police are still here. Four of them. Two uniforms and two detectives."

"Did Jamal have any cash in his room?"

"We had no probable cause for a search, but Jamal has

thirty-eight million plus change on deposit in our cash cage. I placed a freeze on it."

Collins looked to Larson. "Does he have the authority to do that?"

"Yes, he does," Larson answered.

"And it was you," Collins asked, returning his attention to Luke, "who called the police?"

"Yes."

"My purpose in being here this morning," Collins explained, "is the possibility, no, the probability of the Silver Palace's liability."

"Which is the same reason I called the police," Luke answered.

Collins nodded agreement before adding," You were among the few on the scene of this young man's death. Can you share your observation?"

"He appeared to have drowned in the bath tub," Luke answered. "He was pulled from the water by two of my officers. They found no sign of life."

"Have either of these officers ever dealt with the death of a guest before?"

"I want to be certain. Allow me to check on that."

"Of course. The reason I ask is the probability of his father questioning any delay in having his son examined by qualified emergency first responders."

"I'm the one who called nine-one-one."

"And in your opinion, Director, how much time passed from the time the man was discovered in the tub until you made that call?"

The room went silent as Luke decided James Collins was a prick. After an awkward delay he answered, "I can provide the time the man was discovered, and I can get you the time I made the call for the EMTs."

"You're not on the witness stand, Director. Give us a ballpark number."

Silence returned to the room. Luke looked to Larson. He could see the GM thought the question was fair. Luke knew the answer he was considering was not good news.

"My AM watch commander called me. I have a guest room here. He told me two housekeepers had found a man drowned in the Eagle's Nest tub. I dressed and went up to the scene. I recognized the dead man as Jamal Hassan. His body was lying on the tile floor next to the tub. Two of my officers had pulled him from the tub. I had no doubt the man was dead. I'm a combat veteran. In Afghanistan, I saw dead men. After my service I joined the LAPD. In my police experience I saw many dead men. One of them was my police partner."

"Impressive," Collins said, "but the question, Director, was how long after he was found were the paramedics called?"

"Thirty to forty minutes," Luke answered soberly. "We were in no hurry. The man was dead."

Collins looked to the GM. "If I were this dead man's father and I learned of a thirty-to-forty-minute delay before qualified EMTs were called, I would sue. You're going to hear from them."

Larson's fingers drummed the top of his desk before he spoke. "Jim, I'd like you and the lady to step out. Allow me a moment with my director."

"Of course," Collins answered. Candice was already on her feet. She deliberately touched Luke's shoulder and then led Collins to the door where they stepped out. Candice closed the door quietly. Larson leaned into his desk, looking at Luke. "All right, now it's just you and me. What the hell happened to Jamal."

"Autopsy will tell us," Luke answered. "We found two

tablets on a bedside table. We're guessing Pentitol. I'm sure Metro will seize them as evidence."

"Pentitol. Somebody gave it to him. He went through customs. He didn't bring anything but money."

"We've got a lead on who was last out. Young Hispanic. Good-looking."

"We're hanging out, Luke. You gotta find this girl. Right now, the compass is pointing at us. You go find her. I'll take care of Collins."

"We will," Luke said, pushing to his feet. As he moved toward the office door, he paused and glanced back at Larson. "Tell Naomi I said hi."

"Fuck you too," Larson said as Luke opened the door.

———

GAYLE TURNER WAS PROVING her value as the surveillance supervisor. She had a video ready for review when Luke and Candice arrived. "Frick and Fratt found it," Gayle explained. She punched a button on her keyboard and the screen on her desk lit up with a nighttime image of the front of the Silver Palace. The auto doors parted, and the image of a young, attractive Hispanic girl walked out with an unsteady gait. She balanced a purse in one hand and extended an arm on the other. A valet appeared. He offered the girl a hand which she accepted. He waved at a waiting cab. A green SUV pulled into view. The valet opened the back door of the cab and helped the girl in.

"Freeze it," Candice barked as the back door of the cab closed.

"Tighten it, please."

Gayle went back to her keyboard. The image of the cab's rear door stood frozen as Gayle zoomed in, revealing *Strip Tease Trans.*

"Find them," Luke ordered.

―――――

NAOMI LARSON SURRENDERED to her motherly instincts and drove the thirty-plus miles to Out of The Shadows Rehab Ranch near Boulder. She didn't know what was wrong. She just knew the last time she saw her daughter, something wasn't right. They had sat on the porch steps for a while. Their talk was about Tammy's friend who also ran away. Except her friend was only gone hours before she returned, while Tammy was gone overnight.

Tammy confessed to using a drug. A giveaway, a try-and-buy scam. Tammy thought it was crystal meth. The man lied. Shocking, but there was more. Naomi wasn't sure what the more was, but it was time for show and tell. She was showing and Tammy was going to tell. Her story was too short. It wasn't that Tammy lied, she just didn't finish. There was more and it had become a haunting, worried compulsion. Naomi wondered if Greg could help. No, this was between mother and daughter.

The main house was empty and quiet. Naomi looked for staff. She found patients but not many. They told her it was a DWYW day. Do What You Want. Josh and several counselors were away meeting with someone, somewhere. Naomi decided to wait in Tammy's room. She was shocked when she found Tammy lying on her bed. Tammy was quickly up and wiping away tears. Pushing into her mother's arms, she sobbed heavily." Mom, I lied."

Naomi stroked Tammy's hair as she held her. "You don't have to tell me anything. I just wanted to see you, make sure you were okay."

Tammy let go of her mother and sat on the unmade

bed. Naomi sat beside her. "I'm told it's a DWYW day," Naomi said, taking her daughter's hand in hers. "So here I am. What would you like to do?"

Tammy took a deep breath, trying to control her emotions. She squeezed her mother's hand and looked to her eyes. "Mom, he raped me."

Naomi nodded and ran a hand along Tammy's jawline." You're safe now."

"What if I'm pregnant?" Tammy bowed her head.

"You'll do whatever is best. When's your next period?"

"Two weeks. Sooner."

"Time is on your side. Have you told anyone else?"

"No, I didn't mean to lie. I was ashamed. Now I'm frightened."

"Do you feel safe here?"

"Yes, I love the garden."

"Then enjoy it. You won't know anything for two weeks. I can keep a secret. Can you?"

"Yes," Tammy confessed. "Thank you for caring. Thank you for coming. I thought one of those test kits."

"You don't have to decide today. I could find a kit if you want," Naomi suggested.

Tammy reached and pulled herself into her mother's arms. "So, my mother, buy me a pregnancy test." Tammy straightened herself and searched Naomi's face. "Mom, something's different about Dad. He's acting strange."

"He's not acting. Something is different."

Tammy pushed away. "Is he okay? He's not dying."

"He's fine," Naomi smiled. "I don't want you worrying so I'm going to tell you."

"The divorce is final?"

"No, the divorce is over. Your dad came home. I mean

home to stay. I invited him. He accepted. You're going to have to put up with both of us all over again."

Tammy raised her mother's hand and kissed it. "That's why you drove out here isn't it? You wanted to tell me."

Tears welled in Naomi's eyes as she thought about what her daughter suggested. A tear spilled and traced down her cheek. Tammy reached and brushed it away.

"It's okay, Mom. I'm happy for you."

FIFTEEN

KISS AND TELL

LUKE KNEW a badge would get more than a telephone call. He opted to drive to the headquarters of *Strip Tease Trans*. Gayle, with a help from Google, found the address on Paradise Road. Candice rode with him.

"Can you believe this Jim Collins guy represents the Silver Palace? Luke questioned as he navigated streets leaving the busy Strip. They were driving one of the Silver Palace's big Mercedes.

"I thought he was cute," Candice suggested. "You know, instead of a suit and tie with a notebook, he wore a hoody and jeans."

"Cute?" Luke argued. "He was three notches below our dress code."

"We dress like we're from the nineties," Candice countered.

Luke found the address they were looking for on Paradise Road. It was an older three-story building with *For Lease* signs in most of the first-story windows. Luke parked the Mercedes on the side of the building behind a green SUV with *Strip Tease Trans* stenciled on it. He hoped they would find a directory inside the building. There was none. Candice followed as he searched for an occupied room. He finally found an office with a *Help Wanted* sign hanging on its open door. Luke stepped into the room to find it was full of aging computers. They were stacked everywhere. Candice dared a look inside. An older balding man wearing headphones and latex gloves sat working with his back to them as he worked on circuitry inside an open computer.

"Sir," Luke called but got no response. He tried louder. "Hey!"

The man turned, looked at the two and then pulled his headphones away. "Sorry, you here for the interview?"

"No," Luke answered. "We're looking for Strip Tease Trans."

The man pulled his latex gloves off. "You have to be careful with these older transistors. Get a little sweat on them and puff. So, you want to be a driver, right?"

"No," Luke answered, "we're looking for Strip Tease Trans."

"Well, you found us. This isn't about that insurance thing, is it? We can't be responsible for lost cell phones. No matter what was paid for them."

Luke knew it was time for the badge. He pulled his gold and silver director's badge from his belt and held it up momentarily then quickly clipped it back in place. "One of your cars made a pick-up at the Silver Palace early this morning. Young Hispanic girl. Twenty-five. Do you keep records? We need to know where she was dropped."

"Records, huh," the man said, digging at an ear. "Computer I'm working on will get me into the cloud so

I can save everything." He shrugged his shoulders. "Until then."

"I hope you don't need the cloud to tell me who was driving last night. Who made the pick-up at the Silver Palace?"

"Oh, the Silver Palace. Yup, I remember it."

"And who was driving?"

"That would have been me." The man smiled. "Just trying to make a buck until I find someone willing to work overnight."

Candice saw Luke was losing his patience. She pushed by to speak to the man. "Hispanic girl. Mid-twenties. We need to know where you dropped her."

"Got it," the man nodded. "East Sahara. Under the freeway. There's a Smart and Final right across the street. I dropped her at the condo's on the right. She tried to pay me with a Citi bank card. We don't take credit cards. If we did we'd have to roll a receipt, have the payee sign it, then when we get back we have seventy-two hours to file a claim, make a hard copy for our file, then print one which I email to, lets see, Master Card is in Phoenix, Citi Bank, I think is, in New York, maybe New Jersey."

"The condo where you dropped the girl is on East Sahara, right across from Smart and Final?" Candie questioned.

"Right. Straight across. I remember because Gloria buys our coffee there. You know they carry seven assorted brands. All of them cheaper than Walmart. We live just a couple blocks from Walmart. I got an oil change there last Thursday."

"Did you see the girl go into the condos?"

"Yeah, it was gated. You know one of those nice iron see-through gates. Good for keeping prowlers out. She used a key to get in. Used to have one of those at my sister's place."

"You said you don't accept credit cards, but she presented one?" Luke asked.

"She was nice about it." The man nodded. "Put the card away and went for the money. Fare was twenty-two dollars. She gave me a twenty and a ten. Said keep the change. You know I don't like carrying folding money or coins at night. Although my sister collects coins. I always look at them. You know for the date and condition."

"Did she say anything about where she was coming from?" Candice added. "What she was doing out at that hour?"

"No, she talked on her cell all the way over there."

"Never a mention of her name or anybody's?" Luke questioned.

"No."

"Just talking to that phone. You know how kids are about their cells. I have this nephew that—"

"Thank you," Luke said, cutting the man short.

"Where did you get all these computers? Candice asked with a glance around the room at the stacks of computers and monitors.

"Ritz Carlton out at the lakes. At least it used to be. They had a casino of sorts. When they shut down I made a bid on them. They cut a lot of the circuit wiring. I'm putting Humpty Dumpty back together. I'll keep a couple. You interested. I'm not asking much."

"You've been helpful. Thanks," Candice said. Luke had already turned for the door.

They were walking to their car when Luke's cell chirruped. He pulled it from his belt. "This is Luke."

"Luke, I got two attorneys from some fucking law firm in Beverly Hills, sitting outside with Jackie," Larson growled in his ear. "They flew out here in their own fucking jet. Guess what? Akeen Hassan hired them. They're here for Jamal's money and more. Get your ass up here."

"Going to take a couple minutes, boss. I'm over on Paradise. We're looking for that Hispanic skirt."

"I'm in a world of shit and you're in Paradise. Get the fuck back here, Luke." Larson hung up.

Luke looked to Candice. "Can you guess who that was?"

———

THERE WERE two men sitting in Jackie's outer office when Candice and Luke reached the GM's office. The older of the two well-dressed men wore a turban. They were smiling at Jackie's recounting of her recent vacation in Saudi.

"I especially loved the menus. I couldn't read them, so every meal was an adventure."

The two men, Starbucks in hand, were entertained.

"It is much the same in Beverly Hills. The menus should be in Arabic."

Luke and Candice offered smiles to the two men but turned their attention to Jackie. "The boss wanted to see us."

Jackie nodded, keyed her intercom. "Sir, Luke and his assistant are here."

"Send them all in," Larson's voice answered.

The four joined Larson and Jim Collins, still wearing his hoody, in the GM's office. Chairs had been arranged in a comfortable arch in front of Larson's large flat-screen TV.

"Gentlemen," Larson said, directing all to the chairs.

"This is Luther Mitchel, my director of security and his assistant, Candice Webber." Candice gave Larson a look but accepted her new last name. "Luke, Candice, this is..." Larson gave up and looked to Collins. "Jim, save me from ruining their names."

Collins pushed out of his chair. "Of course. My Pleasure. Luke, Candice, this is Amin Bashir and Abdul Dawould. They're representing Akeen Hassan, the father of Jamal Hassan."

Looks of acknowledgment were exchanged, but no one stood or offered hands.

"So, tell us why you're here, gentlemen," Collins said, choosing a chair.

The Turban spoke, "We have been hired to represent the estate and properties of Jamal Hassan by his father Akeen Hassan. We share his shock and grief at the untimely and unnatural death of his son. In the Arab world there is a fine line defining possessions. What is owned by one family member is also the property of others. It is our understanding Jamal has considerable funds on deposit here in your casino. We want immediate possession of those monies as well as any and all personal properties. Cooperation is appreciated, although I must say, cooperation is no shield against responsibility."

Larson looked to Jim Collins, who in turn looked to the Arab attorney's. "We are saddened by the death of any guest, but when the death of a concerned guest may be the result of his own reckless conduct we must decline any release of monies or properties until there is a complete an accurate accounting of any related costs. As said, gentlemen, cooperation is no shield against responsibility."

The Turban smiled and spoke again," In lieu of your

cooperation our next step will be the filing of a wrongful death action with the Clark County Superior Court asking for an order to release. There is little doubt it will be granted."

"Abdul." Collins smiled. "Allow me to remind you this is not Beverly Hills. This is Las Vegas, we have no secrets. What happens here is quickly known around the world. The filing of a wrongful death lawsuit could lead to open discloser of pictures, images and conduct that will shock not only Las Vegas, but the world." Collins paused and looked to Luke. "Mr. Director, I understand we have some images these gentlemen may find informative."

"Yes, we do," Luke said, stepping to a CD player setting beneath the flat-screen TV. He lifted a CD from a jacket pocket and pushed it into the machine. Immediately, the screen lit up with colorful images of Jamal stepping off the Silver Bullet at Harry Reid International, followed by his arrival at the casino. Climbing from a limo at the Casino with his three young, scantily clad imports, Jamal is greeted by the GM, the card room manager and a line of attractive servers. Then, the image switches to a Twenty-One table where Jamal is the single player at the table.

Jamal is served drink after drink by an attractive server who he pats on the butt repeatedly as he plays, wins, drinks more, then orders drinks for a crowd of spectators growing around. More drinks are delivered to the crowd. Jamal raises his glass and encourages all to join him in drinking, which they do. Jamal slides from his chair at the Twenty-One table, holding a bundle of money. He tosses a hand full of currency at the dealer. Bills flutter to the floor to be gathered by eager spectators. Drink in hand, Jamal is assisted in his walk by his three young assistants. He staggers to the elevator. Obviously intoxicated, Jamal waves at guests to follow. The image switches to the private elevator showing it packed with smiling guests, where Jamal downs his drink, passes his empty glass to one of the girls and turns to unzip his pants. One of the girls grabs his hands and shakes her head. Jamal shrugs his cooperation. On the penthouse level the excited crowd comes off the elevator to follow Jamal to the double doors of the Eagle's Nest. There, he tries to unlock the double doors with his vinyl electronic key. He tries repeatedly. Finally, one of the girls takes the key and quickly opens the door. The crowd surges inside.

The images switch to a variety of shots depicting server after server repeatedly coming off the elevator with carts loaded with bottles of liquor, cases of beer, and food.

The two Arab attorneys watch the images in sober silence.

On the flat-screen a guest staggers out of the Nest's double doors, holding the wall as he makes his way to a nearby corner where he unzips and urinates on the carpeted floor. Then, inside the private elevator, crowded with guests, another young man unzips his pants and urinates. Guests push away from him.

Jamal is depicted as he waves and climbs aboard the plush bus with a crowd of guests pushing and shoving to join him. Jamal, holding a young Hispanic's hand, follows her inside. The Plush bus returns to the Silver Place, where an intoxicated Jamal is helped off by the young Hispanic. He staggers and has difficulty walking but he waves and invites more to follow him to the elevator. Deliveries by carts filled with bottles of liquor and cases of beer follow.

The next scene shows night shots of the front of the Silver Palace and the Strip's sidewalk, with a metro police car, an ambulance, five uniformed officers, and a bloodied man lying on the sidewalk with a hysterical woman at his side. The police inspect damaged cars. The man on the sidewalk is loaded into an ambulance which pulls away as the screen goes dark.

Collins pushed to his feet and looks to the attorneys. Larson watched them, trying to read their reactions. They were giving none.

"Gentlemen, I think you must agree that showing this collection of candid images depicts Jamal Hassan as a drunken, reckless young party animal. Compounding the hosting of drunken parties is the fact, allow me to say that again, the fact, that during one of these hosted parties, someone, a male, urinated on a potted plant on the balcony of Jamal's suite and then tossed the pot over the railing. It fell seventy-three floors, injuring two young newlyweds who just happened to be walking by. The explosion of the pot also resulted in damage to passing automobiles. There is clearly a criminal link between the perpetrator and Jamal who invited, and in all probability, provided him alcohol and drugs, or both. There is also the fact the metropolitan police collected marijuana and a variety of drugs, yet to be identified, in Jamal's room subsequent to his death."

Collins continued as if talking to a jury. "If a lawsuit is filed, we will contest it which will result in a court hearing. A hearing open to the public. A hearing at which these images will be shown. That decision, gentlemen, is yours."

The two attorneys exchanged a look, and the Turan pushed to his feet. "Are you willing to provide us a copy of this CD?"

Larson answered for Collins. "Yes, we'll give you a copy."

The Turban looked to Larson. "There is still the matter of the recovery of a large sum of money on deposit in Jamal's name."

"Jamal Hassan did not check out," Larson answered. "He died in his room. There is the matter of accounting costs. A hold has been placed on the monies. After our expenses are recovered, we'll release the hold."

"May we have a moment?" the Turban questioned.

"Of course," Collins answered, gesturing to the door. Together, the two men walked to the door and stepped out. Once they were gone Luke returned to the chair beside Candice.

"When we went to see the guy at Strip Tease Transport," Candice whispered, "I didn't take my bag."

"Did you really need it."

"I thought we'd be coming right back. Instead, we ended up here."

"Your point is?" Luke questioned quietly.

"I don't have any lipstick. The piece of toast you gave me wiped it away."

"I didn't give. You took, and who's going to notice your lipstick."

"Maybe you haven't noticed but I'm the only woman here."

"I don't carry lipstick," Luke answered.

A rap sounded on the door as the two attorneys opened it. Larson motioned them in. Neither sat down.

The Turban spoke," It would seem cooperation is best for all the parties involved in this unfortunate incident. If we could have a copy of the CD just shown we'll consult with our client and get back to you."

Larson nodded, pushed to his feet. "Agreed," he said,

looking to Luke and Candice. "Can you provide these gentlemen with a copy?"

"In minutes," Luke assured.

"While waiting," the Turban added, "we noticed a Sports Book on our way in. We'd like to see what the odds are between the Rams and the Raiders. Would you mind calling my cell when the CD is ready?"

"Not at all," Larson assured, pushing to his feet. "Please, make yourselves at home. I'll call as soon as the CD is ready." He walked with the two men to the door. When they were gone he returned, closed the door and made a fist-pumping motion, "Hooray! Did we kick ass or what."

Luke joined in the smiles as he led Candice to the door. "We'll get a copy made and get it over here." Collins was busy looking at Candice, exchanging looks and smiles as he worked at putting chairs back where they belonged.

"And thank surveillance for a nice piece of work," Larson suggested, moving to the chair behind his desk. "One remaining piece of business, Luke."

Luke and Candice paused at the door. Both looked to the GM.

"Someone's to blame," Larson said, sinking into his chair." Akeen Hassan is going to want to find who killed his son. He's got the money. I want you to find them first."

"We've got some ideas," Luke assured.

"Well, turn your ideas into reality," Larson ordered in a firm tone. "I don't want Akeen pointing a finger at us. You find them and we'll let the Metro and Akeen decide what to do with them. Just get it done."

"We're on it," Luke assured after exchanging a look with Candice. He knew Larson's order was serious.

The late-day rush was building for the Silver Palace. Walking to a back-of-the-house elevator Luke and Candice could see it and feel it. Servers pushing carts covered with white linen, housekeepers with their arms loaded with towels and shampoo, and dealers tucking in their white shirts and snapping on cuff links.

"I heard the GM," Candice said as they reached the elevators. "How do we make it happen?"

Luke looked at her. "You know you're not wearing any lipstick."

Luke met with Gayle Turner in surveillance to get a copy of the CD made and delivered to the general manager while Candice went to their office to get her bag. Returning, she met Luke near the elevators. "Where are we going?"

"Engineering," Luke answered. "They've got a van that looks like they bought it used. We're going to borrow it and find the young Mexican that lives in a condo across from Smart and Final."

"A stake out. Count me in."

Luke looked at her as the elevator arrived. "I see you found your lipstick."

Engineering was not thrilled over the request to borrow the van, but after it was passed up the line to their director who was in Pittsburg on business, it was approved.

"Gonna take us a while," the duty engineer told them. "She's full of glass for the new pool on tower B. We'll get that out and fill her with gas. Give us an hour or so."

As Luke and Candice walked away from the engineering complex near the rear entrance, Candice glanced at Luke. "We have two towers, right?"

"Right," Luke agreed. "A and B. You heard him."

"How do they tell them apart?" Candice questioned. "Isn't there a chance they could get A and B mixed up?"

"Promise me you won't ask them that while we're together."

The day had been long with only toast and coffee as fuel and looking at an hour wait, they decided on employee dining. The room was crowded. Day shift was winding down, and the evening shift was suiting up. The result meant five thousand employees were in transition. Most hungry. Candice and Luke joined the crowd and moved down the buffet line after Luke was asked for ID. Candice was all smiles.

They filled their trays and chose a table in the middle of the room where a dealer, looking much like a male model, sat alone with an empty tray, reading a newspaper.

"Anybody sitting with you?" Candice asked.

The dealer lowered his open paper, looked at the two and folded it closed. He pushed out of his chair and gathered his tray. "It's all yours," he announced and moved away. Candice and Luke sat down.

"Maybe it was the color of your lipstick," Luke suggested.

"I'm not the one they asked for ID," Candice defended from across from Luke.

"How could they not know who I am?" Luke said, tasting a french fry.

"You're not in uniform and we have what, ten thousand plus employees."

Gayle Turner arrived at their table holding a tray. "Not interfering with some confidential discussion, am I?"

"No, please," Candice answered. "We were just talking

about downsizing the surveillance staff now that AI can fill in the blanks."

"AI," Gail said, "helped me find Strip Tease Trans for you."

"Gayle," Candice questioned, "Do you know the difference between tower A and tower B?"

"Yeah," Gayle answered. "Tower A's is in front of Tower B."

"Wouldn't that depend where you were standing," Candice suggested.

Gayle ignored Candice's comment and looked to Luke. "Got the CD to the GM. Did he like it?"

"The GM liked it," Luke answered. "He sends his thanks, which I'm going to put on paper and send it to your troops. By the way, I like your lipstick."

"Thanks, it's new. Supposed to last all day."

"You hear that, Candice."

They sat and talked. The buzz in the house was the death of Jamal Hassan. Luke gave Gayle the details she needed without ruining their dinners. The two women then moved the talk to painting. Gayle was planning to paint the interior of her condo then sell it and buy her first house. Luke and Candice, both condo owners, offered their choices and opinions. Neither saw owning a house as a choice worth pursuing. Minutes quickly multiplied to an hour. Candice shared their plan to use engineering's van to stake out the Hispanic girl as a suspect in supplying Jamal with the drug, leading to his death in the bathtub.

"Wish I could help," Gayle told the two.

"You have," Luke assured. "Without you, we wouldn't have a place to start."

Luke and Candice returned to engineering. Numan, the duty engineer, gave them the keys. "She simmers a little about fifty. We got her all cleaned up. She's in space nineteen."

The once-white van was easy to find. It was the only van in employee parking. "Me first," Luke declared, climbing in behind the wheel. Not only were they the only van in employee parking they were the only van moving with the evening traffic on the Strip. There were limos, cabs of all colors, buses, SUVs and every model of car manufactured in the past ten years, and then there was Luke and Candice in the dented, scratched, once-white van, borrowed from engineering.

"We should have used my car," Candice said as they did the stop-and-go routine of the busy Strip.

"You drive a two-door Mazda?" Luke questioned.

"Yes."

"That's why we didn't use it."

———

TRAFFIC on the Strip finally yielded to Sahara Boulevard. Luke turned left, drove under the busy interstate and found the parking lot for Smart and Final, just like the balding computer guy said. Across from the parking lot stood a three-story condominium. The front was protected by an ornate iron gate. The Smart and Final store was still open for business, but their parking lot was spacious and uncrowded. Luke picked a spot two rows back from East Sahara Boulevard facing the condos. He put the van in park and set the brake.

"Stakeout," Luke said, slouching in his seat." It's been a while."

"I saw one on the show Cops once," Candice said and then asked, "how do we know she's in there?"

"We don't," Luke confessed. "That's why we're on a stakeout."

"Did you notice there's a gated drive that goes underneath the building?"

"Yeah, but if she had a car, wouldn't she have used it last night."

"You ever park out front at the Palace. Valet isn't a cheap date."

"You have a better plan? I'm listening."

Luke played with the radio on the dash. Country, rap, and then talk. A host on KXNT News Radio was taking calls about how visitors to Las Vegas had changed their attire and the city. Luke listened as he watched the distant gate on the condo and passing traffic. News came on at the top of the hour. Most of the cars in the parking lot disappeared. Eventually, the lights faded in the store behind them. Luke could smell Candice's scent. It was pleasant. He worked on gathering nerve for his comment. "I like the perfume you're wearing."

"That a compliment? I'm not wearing any."

"Then they have an engineer that does," Luke suggested.

"Wanna play moment of truth? I ask a question, you answer truthfully. Then it's your turn."

"Kinda girly, but go for it."

"Are you dating?"

"No," Luke answered after giving the question thought. "After Barb's death, it seemed, you know, inappropriate somehow."

"Your turn."

"How's being my assistant."

"Good one. It's challenging. I like the title. I worry I'm not being much help."

"Today would have been tough without you," Luke

said, twisting in his seat to look at Candice. "You're good with people. Smooth."

"Why did you hire me?" Candice questioned.

Luke studied her. "Truth, huh. Okay, why did I hire you? I liked what I saw. You know the job. You worked uniform and surveillance. GM likes you"—he hesitated a moment then smiled at her—"and we once kissed."

"Have you kissed anyone else since then?"

"It's my turn," Luke said, looking at her.

"Sorry."

"Have you kissed anyone else since then," Luke questioned.

"That was my question," Candice protested.

"*Was*," Luke said, offering a smile as he looked at her.

"No, I haven't kissed anyone since you."

Luke twisted more in his seat. "What are you waiting on?"

Candice studied him for a moment in the shadows, then reached, taking Luke's face in her hands, she pulled him to her and kissed him.

At first, it was Candice kissing Luke, but passion swelled, and the kiss continued into heavy breathing. Luke's hands, like Candice's went to her face, then her neck and shoulders, exploring, touching, feeling. Luke pulled her against his chest in the space between the two seats. Candice responded and pushed into him, moaning under their kiss.

Luke kissed her ears, her throat and then the base of her neck, pushing the top of her blouse aside, he kissed lower and lower. Candice raised her neck in encouragement. One of Luke's hands went from her neck to her waist. He massaged the warmth beneath her blouse. Their kiss continued as his hand moved up to pause at the base of a breast. She moaned and his hand moved up, cupping the breast. He felt the smoothness, the warmth. A hand moved to unbutton the front of her blouse. Breathing hard, Candice pushed a hand along Luke's belt, then the warmth of his body. Luke pushed into her as her hand moved to his erection. She squeezed. He moaned and kissed down her chest, then pushing away her bra, he covered a nipple with his mouth. His tongue teased at it. Candice moved her hand from his erection in search of a zipper. She found the top of the zipper and pulled.

Her hand pushed into Luke's open fly. She searched and found an opening in his shorts. She took his erection in her hand. It was warm and hard. Candice massaged the erection as Luke's hand pulled the top of her slacks open. His hand pushed deep between her legs. Candice moaned and parted her legs. She raised her head as passion swept over her. Suddenly, headlamps sweep over them, erasing the shadows.

"Luke," Candice said, pushing away from him. Confused, Luke sat up. He saw the headlamps. Red lights began flashing.

"Oh, shit!" Luke gasped. He tried pushing his erection into his pants as Candice pulled on her twisted bra, trying to get it over her exposed breasts.

A uniformed officer rapped on the window and shined a flashlight through the glass. "Open your window."

"Oh, my god," Candice mouthed. Luke looked at her, waiting, as she tried straightening her blouse.

"I said open your window," the officer repeated.

Luke nodded and reached to roll the window down. The light from the officer's bright flashlight blinded them.

"I'd ask what you were doing but it's obvious," a voice

behind the bright light said, sweeping it slowly over Candice and then Luke. "Stores closed. You have no business here. This is Vegas. Get a room."

As suddenly as the flashlight appeared, it was gone. A car door slammed. The red lights blinked off. The head-lamps swept away and as the police car pulled away, Luke reached and awkwardly pulled his zipper up. Candice untangled her bra, positioned it, and buttoned her blouse. They did not look at one another.

SIXTEEN
PLAYING WITH FIRE

THE DRIVE back to the Silver Palace seemed much longer than the one to the parking lot on East Sahara. Luke knew the streets and shortcuts but even those were proving challenging. Candice tried to lose herself in the allure and glitter of nighttime Vegas but her thoughts were filled with regret and worry. She had lit the fire. She kissed him, baited him, wanted him. None of it brought her any comfort. Leaning on an armrest, Candice stared at the passing cars, SUVs, and cabs. All seemed filled with smiling couples. She had few options, and all were painful. She knew she had to resign. She started the fire.

Luke wasn't sure what to say, so he said nothing. Their relationship had been filled with smiles and humor. They enjoyed seeing one another, working together, just being together. All of that vanished when the officer rapped on the window of the van. Luke wanted to tell Candice he would fix it, he wanted to reach out and touch her, he wanted to tell her she was beautiful, that none of it was her fault. He knew this would happen and hoped it would happen when he hired her, but the driveway into employee parking stole his opportunity. A security officer at the gate to the parking structure offered a wave. Luke nodded in return.

The silence continued after they parked the van and marched toward the employee entrance. Candice was first through the doors where KC King, the AM watch commander, stood talking with the two officers posted there.

"So, how was the movie?" KC smiled at a sober Candice who walked a few steps ahead of Luke. She offered no acknowledgment and continued on toward the back of the house.

Luke paused with KC and the other two.

"How'd the stakeout go?" KC questioned.

"Not good," Luke answered.

Luke had learned police work was like ice skating. You fell down a lot, but you had to keep getting up. He was getting up after the close encounter in the parking lot. Plus, he needed a diversion, something other than a guest room on the sixth floor. The room was comfortable, but he didn't want to be the only one there. The stakeout was a strike out. He'd run into walls before. He was no longer a cop who had the power to demand answers out in the world, but he was the boss of a talented, diverse team. He needed help and he had an idea where he might find it. He guessed Candice had gone to her room. A truck had ran over their relationship. He had no idea how to cope with it. His attraction to Candice was proving to be hazardous. For now, she had to wait, or was it a case of him running away from her? Whatever, he needed time.

A back-of-the-house elevator took Luke to the surveillance unit on the third floor. Lorie Taylor, the unit's new AM supervisor replacing Candice, was at Gayle's desk when he arrived. Taylor was an attractive Vegas-looking brunette in her thirties.

"Evening, Chief," Lorie said, offering Luke a smile. "We watched you and Candice come home in the van. Any luck?"

"Nothing," Luke answered.

"I had instructions from Gayle to call you when you came in," Lorie advised. "She said the valet you had follow the Plush bus with Jamal and gang, finally brought up the video he shot. Gayle reviewed it, did some editing. Would you like to see it?"

"Yes, show me." Luke was excited.

Lorie invited Luke to sit down beside her desk as she pulled up a video on one of the monitors on the desk. "Here we go."

Luke watched as the Plush bus moving in the heavy traffic on the nighttime Strip traffic, flashed its brake lights and pulled to the curb in front of the Ever Lasting Love Wedding Chapel. A door opened on the side of the bus, and an attractive, dark-haired young Hispanic pulled Jamal out the door and across the sidewalk to where they disappeared into the chapel. Luke watched intently. A few minutes passed and Jamal reappeared with his arm around the neck of the girl. They conversed animatedly as they returned to the bus and climbed in.

The images stopped. Lorier looked to Luke. "Is it helpful?"

Luke's eyes moved from the monitor to Lorie. "That was more than a quickie. One of them was planting seeds."

"I think you can credit this stop to the girl."

"Glad valet got it. Frick and Fratt here tonight?" Luke questioned.

"It's a full moon," Taylor answered. "They're here."

The Chinese Duo Luke was referring to as Frick and Fratt were Lee Kang and Jay Roberts. Both in their twenties and both engineering students at UNLV. Gayle Turner hired them as consultants after meeting them at an electronics show in Vegas. Luke and everyone else preferred the Frick and Fratt nicknames they were tagged with better than their true names.

"They're in their closet," Luke questioned.

Lorie Taylor nodded. "Want me to get them? They're working on a camera to provide images of the front, sidewalk, and up to the glass-walled pool on the edge of our roof. You know, the one we're all calling the pot cam."

Luke nodded as Lorie pushed out of her chair.

Waiting, Luke looked through the heavy glass floor-to-ceiling wall that separated the supervisor from the maze of large screens and images on the other side. Six agents, two women and four men sat inside, watching and manipulating the ever-changing images.

Taylor returned with Frick and Fratt, the two young Chinese consultants. "Would you like privacy?" Taylor questioned, pausing at the door in the wall.

"Evening, guys," Luke said, looking to Frick and Fratt. "We'll need a couple more chairs." Chairs were gathered. Lorie resumed her seat at the supervisor's desk, monitoring three screens. Frick and Fratt sat facing Luke behind Taylor.

"You two ever work in daylight?" Luke asked.

"School," the two men answered in unison.

"I've got an address where I know a young dark-haired, attractive Hispanic in her mid-twenties lives," Luke began. "We tried a stake out with no luck. I'll give you the address. It's a three-story condominium. I don't even know how many units. Finding anything about her is important. We can show you what she looks like. Lorie's got a video for you. I know that's not much."

"The address is?" Frick questioned, holding a pen over a notepad.

"One-three-nine-eight-two East Sahara," Luke answered.

"We'll work on it," Fratt assured.

"Anything else?" Frick questioned.

"That's it, sorry."

The two men nodded, pushed from their chairs and moved to exit through the glass door in the surveillance wall. Luke looked to Lorie Taylor as she turned to him. "I don't think they ever say no."

Luke pushed to his feet. "I hope this won't be their first time."

———

NIC WILSON, the thirty-two-year-old pimp, who bought an insider's tip that Jamal Hassan, the billionaire son of the richest man in the world, was arriving at the Silver Palace, was in shock. He had just paid three grand to a young server at the Silver Palace to learn Jamal Hassan was fucking dead! Drowned in his bathtub. A filthy rich Arab who lived in the desert drowned in a bathtub. Nic's plan was shattered, his monies lost. He walked the halls of his five-bedroom mansion on Terrace View just off Sunset, cursing and swearing. The three whores in the house hid from him. His Doberman didn't understand the profanities, but he knew the tone and anger. The dog bolted through a doggie door to hide in the darkness of the garage.

The plan had gone so well. Nic paid almost two

grand for twenty-six-year-old Rosie Martinez's makeover, the little bitch, and that wasn't counting the hours of personal coaching before he put the candle on the cake. Jamal went after the bait like a hungry fish. Now the rich sonofabitch was dead, and worse than that, Rosie Martinez killed him. The plan was simple, get next to him, get something with Jamal's signature on it. Nic knew forgers. A forger would copy the signature onto a marriage license and a marriage certificate. Nevada law would then be on their side, showing Rosie Martinez as Jamal Hassan's legal wife. She would have a legal right to half of Jamal's monies and property. Not with him dead, Nic reasoned, as the thought took hold. Maybe they could have had it all. Rosie, as planned, succeeded in getting Jamal into a wedding chapel. Nic was there minutes later to buy the video. He had proof!

All that remained was giving Jamal a drug to ensure his cooperation in signing something, anything, but the cunt Jamal hired from the Silver Palace to become his cultural adviser was always in the way, counting money, advising, signing for everything. Nic bought Rosie what his drug dealer said was the best. One tab, quick to dissolve in a drink, guaranteed, but the little bitch Rosie, instead of putting the tab in Jamal's drink, put it in his hand. It didn't take the drug long.

Dazed, Jamal decided on a bath. Rosie pleaded with him, but she was pushed aside. Not wanting to be caught with drugs, she left the other tabs on a bedside table. Now, instead of a signature, they had a body, but Nic realized he still had a chance. Chance, shit, he was about to retire.

———

AT THE SILVER PALACE, Candice Harmon lay in her guest room bed wondering what the day would bring. Candice envisioned being called into Luke Mitchel's office where he would ask her to resign. All it needed was her signature. She knew Luke's reputation for doing what was right, and resignation was right. HR would be finding a litany of reasons for her dismissal. She had lured a director into a sexual relationship, which interfered with achieving a department goal. Candice considered writing an apology and leaving it on Luke's desk. Next came the thought of pushing it under his guest room door, which allowed her to dream of knocking on his door, throwing herself into his arms, push him onto the bed and finish what they had started. What was there to lose? She was going to be fired. A solid knock on her guest room door startled her. Candice pushed off the bed, slipped on a robe and went to the door to look through the viewer. Her heart stopped. Luke Mitchel was outside her door.

Candice ran a hand through her hair, wet her lips and opened the door.

"Can we talk?" Luke asked.

Candice stepped aside. Luke entered and chose a chair next to the bed, ignoring the bra hanging on its back. Candice closed the door and leaned on the side of the bed facing him. Her heart pounded in her ears.

"I probably won't get this right, I'm not sure I know what's right," Luke began nervously. "But I know we can't have what happened tonight, happen again. If we were reported we'd both be fired. I like my job. I think you like yours. So, from now on, on-duty, we play it straight. Off-duty, away from the Silver Palace, out of sight, never a word to anyone, we do what we want. What I need tonight, Candice, is a yes, or a no?"

A tear traced down her cheek. Candice nodded, "Yes."

Luke pushed to his feet. He reached and took Candice by the shoulders. "Then one last time." He kissed her lightly on the cheek and moved for the door. "See you at the office."

His ride on the Silver Bullet had been through enough time zones to make Luke wonder what day it was, followed by Jamal Hassan's throwing money at the world, a potted plant acting like a falling star and a passionate stake out, all left him exhausted. He slept dreamless for three hours before his cell phone did its humming and dancing on a bedside table.

"Hello," Luke managed after a strenuous reach to find the noisy device.

"Luke, it's Gayle," the familiar voice of the surveillance supervisor said in his ear.

"Gayle," Luke whispered into his cell phone. "Unless there's six people dead in the casino, I'm going to…"

"Don't say it," Gayle cautioned. "I'm calling because you set this in motion."

"I hope it's not another truck."

"It's not a truck. It's Frick and Fratt. They've found something. They don't have a class until later this morning. They want to know if you want to meet before they leave."

Luke pushed the sheets aside, swung his feet to the floor and turned on a bedside lamp. "What did they find?"

"Luke, I just got here."

"Okay, okay, I'll be down. Call Candice, have her meet me in our office. I'll reach out when we get there. Tell Frick and Fratt I'll make it fast."

Luke dressed, passed on shaving, brushed his teeth, combed his hair, strapped on his gun and headed for an elevator. He was still turning things on in his office when a rap sounded on the door.

"It's open," he called.

Candice opened the door. Behind his desk, Luke paused and looked at her. Her hair was perfect, eyes bright, fresh wardrobe, no wrinkles. He couldn't help but smile. "You know as assistant director, you don't have to knock, and you look great this morning."

"Thanks," Candice answered. "Wanna tell me what's going on?"

"After our kinda sorta, strike out, stake out, I got the idea of putting Frick and Fratt to work finding our Hispanic beauty. Valet, tracking the Plush bus for us, recorded them stopping at a wedding chapel on the Strip. Jamal and the girl did a quick in and out. I made sure Frick and Fratt got a copy. I told them to fill in the blanks."

"They've found something?"

"Let's hope," Luke answered, picking up the phone on his desk. He dialed. "Gayle, it's Luke. Gangs all here. Send them up."

Candice went to her desk and called room service to order coffee for four along with a variety of pastries. Hanging up, she looked to Luke and said, "What they don't eat, we will."

They waited. Candice at her desk while Luke arranged two chairs in front of his. "You get any sleep?" Luke questioned.

"I worried about my fish. They're spoiled. They think they should be fed every day."

"Big fish, little fish," Luke questioned.

"Tropical, big and little," Candice answered. "You'll have to come meet them."

A knock on the door delayed Luke's answer. Candice,

closer to the door, pushed out of her chair and opened it, revealing Frick and Fratt. They both offered smiles to Candice.

"Congratulations, madam director," Fratt said. "Director's gain, surveillance's loss."

"I'm sure the director will enjoy having you close," Frick added.

Candice looked to Luke and smiled. "You know these two speak the truth."

Luke pushed to his feet. "We're told you may have something. Appreciate you staying overnight."

Candice closed the door as the two men sat in front of Luke's desk. Both carried electronic notebooks. Candice rolled her office chair to the side of the two men.

"When you're ready," Luke urged.

The two men opened their notebooks. Frick spoke first. "Some of what we've done is best kept under the cover of darkness. We've found truth often hides there. Many times, it does not like being discovered, but we've found some things that you may find helpful."

Candice deliberately avoided looking at Luke, she concentrated on the two men.

"You gave us an address where you suspected your unidentified female suspect might live," Frick continued. "We went to the net and looked for titled ownership of the building. It is owned by Nevada Investments. They hold titles to six condominiums in the city. They are insured by Welker Insurance. Insurance companies demand a list of named occupants."

"We discovered among the occupants of the condo on East Sahara there is a twenty-six-year-old single Hispanic female by the name of Rossette Martinez. She resides in unit fourteen."

Frick looked to Fratt, who continued, "Again on the internet we found Miss Martinez has a Facebook account. She has eighteen friends. All with Hispanic surnames. She also has a valid Nevada driver's license, a birth certificate showing birth in Austin, Texas. We found no record of that. She also claimed a widowed mother living in Parker, Arizona. Again, this could not be verified."

A knock sounded on the office door. Fratt paused as Candice opened the door. A young male server stood waiting with a cart. He smiled, pushed the cart into the office, and pulled away a white cover to reveal a pot of coffee, four cups and a variety of pastries. "Coffee for four and fresh pastries."

"Thank you," Luke said as the server withdrew and closed the door.

Candice poured coffee. "Gentlemen, coffee as you choose, with pastries. Please, help yourselves."

Candice knew how Luke liked his. She prepared it and set it in front of Luke along with a pastry. He thanked her with a smile. Frick prepared a cup for himself and one for Fratt.

Fratt sampled his, looked to his digital notes and continued, "Under personal information, Rossette listed a cell number. We found the number coded to the Freedom Phone network. Freedom Phone maintains a file of personal information on those who use their service. Not only does Rossette use them, she pays extra text service fees. Her monthly billing revealed multiple texts to a particular number. We were able to find a file on the written texts because they are electronically timed and kept for billing." Fratt paused and looked to Frick. "Give a text example."

Frick looked at his notebook and read, "Nic, Jamal

refused to drink, said he didn't feel well. Gave him the pill. He got in the tub, passed out. He wouldn't wake up. I left."

Frick paused as Luke and Candice exchanged a look. Luke returned his attention to Frick. "What else."?

"Next is a text from this individual to Rossette," Frick said, looking to his notes. "Go to the Silver Palace. Move on Jamal. Get invited to the penthouse."

"Who is this person?" Luke questioned.

Frick glanced at Fratt, who answered. "His cell revealed his identity. Nicholes Wilson, age thirty-two. He lives near Sunset. We couldn't get his criminal history, but we found public records showing six arrests for pimping and pandering."

"He's Rossette Martinez's pimp," Luke concluded. "Anything else?" he pressed.

"We couldn't find any history of employment for either, although Rossette's monthly condo rent is Twenty-One hundred dollars and Wilson's mortgage payment is twenty-eight hundred."

"And we've got the names and addresses on both."

"We do," Fratt assured, taking a final bit of a pastry.

"Gentlemen," Luke said, leaning into his desk. "As always you've found us what we needed. We thank you."

Fratt pushed to his feet. Frick followed. "We have a class starting in forty minutes."

Candice pushed to her feet. "Thanks, guys." Luke followed her lead and stood.

"May we?" Fratt questioned, looking at the remaining pastries.

"Of course," Candice answered. "Would you get us a copy of this?"

"Sent it before we came up," Frick said, following Fratt to the door. Both carried pastries.

Candice closed the door behind the two and started gathering cups and napkins. Luke sank into his chair. Candice moved around his desk, took his face in her hands and kissed him. Luke stiffened at first but then yielded to it. When the kiss ended, they looked at each other.

"That's a thank you for last night," Candice said, "and wipe the lipstick off your mouth." She gathered his cup and moved away.

Luke wiped his mouth. "We have to be careful, girl."

"Kinda like what they told us," Candice suggested. "We have to be careful what we tell and careful not to tell where we got it."

The telephone on Luke's desk rang. He gathered the receiver as Candice pushed the room service cart into the hallway. "This is Luke."

"Luke, it's Gayle. You sitting down?"

"I live on the edge, Gayle. What is it?" Luke was on the edge. Frick and Fratt had given them invaluable insight into Jamal's death, but Luke was uncertain what to do with it. The irony was it was different but yet the same as he and Candice. Knowing was great, but along with knowing, came uncertainty.

"Nic Wilson and Rossette Martinez just came through the front door. Lorie spotted them and alerted me. I got them on the monitor on my desk. They went straight to the concierge desk where they demanded to see the GM."

"Holy crap," Luke said into the phone. Candice saw his reaction as she closed the office door. "What is it?"

Jackie Fallon was at her desk outside the general manager's office when she got the call from Luke. "There's two of them. They're demanding to see the GM about Jamal's death. Candice is bringing them up. Make it happen."

Jackie heard the urgency in Luke's voice. She knew he was serious. "He's in a meeting right now with Jim Collins. They're doing Facetime with the State Department. It just started. They may have to wait."

"That helps. Thanks."

Luke arrived a few minutes later. Candice was sitting, waiting with Nic who held a briefcase in his lap. Rossette was at his side. Both were dressed in their best and neither knew who Candice or Luke were. The reception area was comfortable. Luke sat across from Candice, who, playing a role as casino escort, toyed with her cell phone. Nic and Rosie whispered quietly to one another while Jackie Fallon worked on her computer, ignoring it all. Minutes drug by until the door of the GM's office finally opened, and Jim Collins came out. He glanced at all but smiled and paused near Candice.

"Miss Webber," Collins said, "I believe that's what the GM said your name was, but I found your true name is different. Would you like to tell me what your real title is?"

Candice forced a smile at Collins. "I wear a lot of different hats, I have a lot of titles. Today, I'm an escort for visitors."

Collins glanced at Nic and Rosie sitting beside Candice, then back to her. He connected the dots. "Well, nice seeing you, Candice. Remember, you're buying when we do drinks at the Eye of the Tiger."

"I haven't forgotten."

Collins moved on, passing Luke he glanced, but didn't speak. A buzzer sounded on Jackie's desk. She picked up the receiver, listened, and then looked to

Candice and the couple with her. "You may go in. The GM knows it is urgent."

Greg Larson pushed to his feet as Candice led Nic, briefcase in hand, and Rosie into his office. She gestured to the chairs in front of the GM's desk as Luke stepped in behind them, closing the office door. Nic held his briefcase to his chest and looked to Luke.

"I don't like what I'm seeing," Nic said anguishly, looking at the faces. "Come on, Rosie, we're outta here." He moved for the door, but Luke stepped in front of it.

"Get outta my way," Nic warned, reaching for Luke. Luke grabbed Nic by the wrist, spun him with a hard shoulder push while shoving his arm high into the middle of his back to slam Nic against the wall. Rosie filled the room with a sharp scream. The office door bust open and Mario Lopez, the day watch commander and a second uniformed officer burst into the room. Lopez was quick to pull out handcuffs and with effort, shackled Nic's wrists. "You pricks, you'll regret this," Nic growled from against the wall.

Candice took the hysterical Rosie by the shoulders and sat her down in one of the chairs in front of the GM's desk. "Shut up!" Candice ordered.

"What the hell's going on?" the stunned Larson said, looking at the crowd in front of his desk. Jackie escorted two men into the office. Luke looked at the two and then the GM. Lopez and his partner held Nic against the wall.

"Boss," Luke said to Larson. "This is Detective Hanson and Mattingly, metro police. I think they're going to like what is in Nic's briefcase. Larson stared as Luke picked up the briefcase, opened it, and pulled out two documents. "Listen to this." Luke read from the paper, "The Commissioner of Clark County, Nevada, hereby grants Rossette Martinez and Jamal Hassan the license and the right to enter into the lawful and legal state of marriage, signed by Rossette Martinez and Jamal Hansson."

"He made me do it," Rosie cried. "He made me sign it. I didn't want to come here."

"And a second document reads," Luke continued, ignoring the girl. "Jamal Hassan and Rossette Martinez having appeared before me, with God as their witness, are hereby declared husband and wife, again signed by Jamal Hassan and Rossette Martinez."

"Fuck you," the handcuffed Nic protested from the wall. "You got no right to go in my briefcase."

"I'm not a cop," Luke said, offering the two documents to the detectives, "but these guys are."

Jackie returned to the crowded office and went to Luke. "As often said, shit happens. The front desk called. There's a woman waiting, saying she's not going to move until she sees you."

Luke looked to the two detectives. "Gentlemen, could my watch commander take these two down to our interview room? Candice, my second in command, will brief you. I'll be right back."

"How about me, Luke?" Larson said from behind his desk. "You wanna put me in the loop or do you have more surprises coming."

Luke looked at the general manager and then Candice. "Candice will fill you in."

Candice granted a nod. Luke moved for the door.

The back-of-the-house rlevator was empty. Luke breathed a sigh of relief as he listened to Henry Manchin's "Moon River" play as the elevator vibrated and then stopped on the main floor. Luke cut across the busy card room, wondering who was demanding his presence at the front desk. The last time this happened, it was an unhappy guest who had lost her cell phone. Luke studied the figure at the front desk as he approached. There was something familiar about her and then as she turned to him the years fell away. Luke recognized her. It was his ex-wife. She was older, but not much. Luke could tell from the look on her face that she recognized him.

"Karen?" Luke questioned, stopping a few feet from the woman. She turned, taking the shoulders of a thirteen-year-old girl nearly hidden behind her. She moved the girl to face Luke.

"Jill," the woman whispered to the young blonde. "This is your father."

Luke and the thirteen-year-old stared at one another.

ABOUT THE AUTHOR

Dallas Barnes, a former Director of Security & Surveillance in Las Vegas as well as a Los Angeles Police Homicide Detective, is the author of twelve novels. *Vegas Odds* is the third novel in the *Vegas Trilogy* series based on his experiences while serving as a Director of Security & Surveillance in Resort & Casino environments.

MGM Grand Signature—Las Vegas, NV
Hyatt Regency Resort & Casino—Lake Las Vegas, NV
Fantasy Springs Resort & Casino—Cabazon, CA
Agua Caliente Casino & Resort—Palm Springs, CA
Augustine Casino—Coachella, CA
Morongo Resort & Casino—Cabazon, CA
Blue Water Resort & Casino—Parker, AZ
LAPD SWD/DIV Homicide—Los Angeles, CA

It is safe to say Dallas Barnes knows what he writes about.

ABOUT THE AUTHOR